The Secret Son

Jenny Ackland is a writer and teacher who lives in Melbourne. *The Secret Son* is her first novel.

The Secret Son

JENNY ACKLAND

ALLEN&UNWIN
SYDNEY • MELBOURNE • AUCKLAND • LONDON

First published in 2015

Allen & Unwin
83 Alexander Street
Crows Nest NSW 2065
Australia
Phone: (61 2) 8425 0100
Email: info@allenandunwin.com
Web: www.allenandunwin.com

Cataloguing-in-Publication details are available from the National Library of Australia www.trove.nla.gov.au

ISBN 978 1 92526 616 0

Internal design by Christabella Designs
Set in 12/19 pt STIXGeneral by Midland Typesetters, Australia
Printed and bound in Australia by Griffin Press

10 9 8 7 6 5 4 3 2 1

The paper in this book is FSC® certified. FSC® promotes environmentally responsible, socially beneficial and economically viable management of the world's forests.

To Anthony, thank you for the time and the space.

I am the master of my fate,
I am the captain of my soul.

WILLIAM ERNEST HENLEY, *Invictus*

That the effort failed is not against it; much that is most splendid in military history failed, many great things and noble men have failed.

JOHN MASEFIELD on the Dardanelles Campaign

There is no difference between the Johnnies and Mehmets to us where they lie side by side here in this country of ours . . .

ATATÜRK

It was April 1990 and two men drove east in a '53 Eldorado Cadillac. There was a taxi sign on the roof and the chrome was perfect, the trim intact. The car was flanked with long fins, shaped like a woman's thigh.

Istanbul was behind and a package of cheese and parsley pastries lay between them on the bench seat. Cem Keloğlu didn't know much about Harry Forest other than he was a retired historian from Australia and travelling to the same village as he was. They'd met on the plane from Melbourne.

Nothing had been said for the last two hours other than 'Do you want the last piece of pastry?' (Cem) and 'No thank you, you have it' (Harry). Then, a minute later: 'What do you think Saddam's doing?' (Harry), followed by 'I don't know' (Cem).

'It'll be something about oil, I suppose,' Harry said, but Cem didn't respond.

They'd left Miriam in Izmir hours before and the sun was setting behind them as they crawled the final few kilometres up a steep mountain road, a road that had narrowed to a small, rocky, barely-sealed stretch. In the near distance Cem could see a village, a random scattering of buildings, blue-doored white-washed houses. The place seemed deserted, but there was a central square with a lit-up hall that glowed dull in the dusk.

Harry asked Cem to pull over.

'I have to tell you what brings me here,' the older man said.

In the paddock nearby were some small dirty sheep, and down the road towards them loped a dog, haunches higher than shoulders, its glassy eyes fixed on the car. It drew closer, a spiked iron collar around its neck. Both ears were cropped.

There was snow on the ground and the heater didn't work and their breaths showed in the air. Cem was tired and cold and, at first, when Harry leaned in, he thought the other man was going to kiss him and he pulled back, but instead Harry started whispering, the words tumbling from his mouth.

Cem listened and tried not to smile. He reached out a fingertip and touched the blue glass charm that hung from the rear-vision mirror. It was there for luck, to protect against harm while travelling. The dog sat on the road, watching.

'That's crazy,' Cem said when Harry stopped talking. 'I mean, no offence, but you know what it sounds like you're saying?' He reached for a cigarette. A new smoker, he was trying to persist with the Maltepes, but they were rough. He lit the end and tipped his eyes back out of the smoke. Across the road was a forest with closely-packed trees, dense and black. The dog got up and moved nearer, walking sideways as if it had an itch in its rear.

'It sounds like you're saying Ned Kelly fought at Gallipoli and stayed behind in Turkey.'

Harry shook his head emphatically. 'You're not listening.'

'Yeah, 'cause what you just said is impossible,' Cem said.

'Not *Ned*.' Harry inched closer on the seat. There was a manic energy about him. 'Ned would have been too old, and besides, he died in the gaol like everyone thinks. No, I'm talking about his son. I believe Ned Kelly had a son who fought at Gallipoli and settled in a small village in central Anatolia—the village we are about to drive into.'

Even Cem Keloğlu, son of Turks who had migrated to Melbourne, a boy who grew up in an environment severely lacking in Aussie traditions and stories, knew that Ned Kelly had died childless. They sat as the chilled air wrapped around them.

'But Ned Kelly didn't have a kid,' Cem said.

'Ah, but are you sure about that?' Harry Forest replied.

Cem stopped smiling and his heart drilled inside his chest. The dog got up and shifted towards the car and from up the hill a whistle sounded. The dog lifted its head.

I

The lies we tell ourselves are far larger than any others can say to us. You may not believe but there is truth in all of it.

AUNT BERNA

Chapter 1

I

In the mid-1880s, the Victorian town of Beechworth was mostly flat with some undulations of broad, green hills, and enormous boulders that lay about as if scattered. James lived there with his mother, Madela, and when he was little she told him stories about giants throwing the huge slabs of rock.

'They go crash,' the small boy said.

'Yes.' His mother went to the stove, wondering whether they needed more wood. They did, so she went behind the sturdy house to the pile and carried in a few armfuls.

'I'll help you when I'm bigger,' James said, trotting beside her.

He often went to stand in the bull paddock, to find a spot and stay there, wiping his shoes through the grass, looking back to the house. Sometimes, his mother came running from that direction, waving her arms and shouting. When his mother came running at him like that, he said he was searching for a four-leaf clover.

'Looking for you, Mama. For luck.'

Sometimes it rained and sometimes the sun was shining, but often, several times a week, whatever the weather, his mother would find him in the paddock and come running at him across the grass to gather him in her arms and take him inside. At night, after she kissed him and before she snuffed the lantern, James asked again about his father, even though he knew she didn't like this question.

'Who was my dada? Was he a very big man?'

'The biggest.'

His mother took his hand in hers and told him it was time to go to sleep. She kissed him again.

'Was he very, very big?'

'As big as a tree.'

'And a bull of a man. That's what you said.'

'Is that why you go in the paddock, love?'

'I think the bull can tell me.'

'Tell you what?' His mother sat down on the edge of the bed again.

'Where my father is.'

He looked at his mother and knew there were secrets there. She didn't like to talk about the man who had been his father, about what his name was or where he might be now. He asked and she was patient with him but never said much. It wasn't fair. All the boys at school had fathers and sometimes, when he and his mother went into town with their horse and cart, he saw other boys carried up high on men's shoulders, being taken into the sweetshop. It made him sad, but his mother didn't tell him much and the bull hadn't told him anything at all.

'He had my freckles, didn't he?' A skinny arm crept out from under the rough blankets. Two dark spots on his arm above the wrist.

'No, my love, you have his freckles.'

'But they're mine.'

'They belong to both of you.'

'Just one more story?'

James never wanted his mother's stories to finish. The Thousand Stories he called them, about the angry man with a beard who wanted to cut off his wife's head and the clever girl who kept telling him stories until the sun came up. James would like to listen to those stories all night, until the sun did come up.

'One more?'

His mother said no and he breathed her in, smelled the smoke that caught in her dark hair, the scent of lard. Sometimes he could see flour on her nose but not tonight. Baking day was not today. He turned in his bed and went still. Madela looked at her son and saw the softness of his white scalp shining through his cropped hair. He always went to sleep quickly. She felt tender and scared for him as she blew out the flame.

II

James and his mother were known for the bees. They lived on a property out of town a way, on land that was edged along three sides with forest, with enough trees to lay out an extensive run of hives.

The bees were his friends. As his mother said, they were easy to hold if you loved them. James grew older and wandered between the boxes, reaching out a hand here and there to touch the wood. He felt the thrumming hearts within, the centre where the queen sat fat and glossy. He never got stung and his mother said he was lucky that way. When he handled the queen, the bees flocked to his fingers, but no matter how much he sniffed his hand afterwards, he couldn't tell what it was that drew the others. He stood at the edge of the forest, trailing his finger-tips along the trunks of the eucalypts, inhaling their greyish green, closing his eyes as he wandered, breathing in the smells. He noticed the drops of water beading along the fence, and the way the grasses lay either this way or that. He heard the sweet ringing of the birds and the drip of rain. The patterns of nature were all around him but especially in the bees.

If he wasn't with the bees he went to the bull, and his mother kept finding him in the paddock.

'Come out of there,' she called. 'It's dangerous.'

He stood, facing the animal. It watched him from the furthest corner. He turned his back and counted as high as he could go. He thought about stomping hooves, round, flaring nostrils and long sharp horns, but the bull never came near.

'I'm not scared,' he told his mother as she climbed through the fence and ran across to grab him and march him to safety. 'I'm lucky.'

'Why do you keep going there when you know it's dangerous? I've told you to stay out.'

Back in the kitchen James reached for the jar of honey and ladled it onto his bread, golden strings lacing the wooden table. He ran his finger through them and put it in his mouth.

‘But, Ma, I told you—I’m not scared.’

One day, the bull charged. It was at the moment that James found a four-leaf clover. He bent over to pluck it and the bull hit. His mother, at the copper, heard the yelp and went running to the crumpled boy in the middle of the paddock. The bull was standing over him. She pushed the bull’s snout away as she got her son up. It pawed the ground and she tweaked its ear and it turned and ambled back to the corner. James tried to tell his mother about the clover, but she said she didn’t care about it, no matter the number of leaves.

‘You could have been killed.’

‘But I got it,’ James said, opening his hand.

His mother told him it had been a silly thing to do.

‘Would my father come if I died?’

‘Listen to me, love: he can’t come. He’s dead himself.’

A buzzing started in his ears and it seemed it would never stop.

When his mother did the baking, he went to the bees. He made sure the water drums were full because bees got thirsty, especially in summer. In winter, the insects were slow and invisible, turning in their hives, forming their special bee circles to keep the boxes warm. He peered into the tops of the hives and learned about the patterns. He watched them, and by the time he was eleven, he knew them all.

‘The bees are dancing,’ he told his mother. ‘They’re dancing in circles together.’

III

One morning before school they sat at the table. James was almost his adult height, already one inch taller than his dead father. He had taught himself to walk on his hands and he could juggle five matchboxes, but still to the other children, he was an outsider.

'Do you think I'm queer?' he said to his mother.

'Who said that?'

'No one. The other children say it's strange that I don't get stung and also that I fall asleep in class all the time.'

'Not queer at all, love. Bees know what's in your heart. People who get stung have a shadow that the bees can see and it frightens them. But don't sleep in class. You sleep too much and one day you'll miss something important.'

'I'm not sleeping; I'm meditating on my blessed heritage.'

She frowned at him.

'Just kidding, Ma.' He chewed his bread. 'At school they say your name is funny. They say it's not even Irish. Do we come from another country?'

His mother explained that there was no special reason why she was not a simple Mary or Beth; Madela was just a name her parents liked.

'Your family is not from abroad?' He was disappointed. He liked to imagine her ancestors had come from Egypt or Spain, somewhere far like in his *Cole's Funny Picture Books*, but she said that wasn't the case. She was proud of being different, she said. There were lots of Marys in the area, lots of Beths, but only one Madela.

'Just as there is only one you. Remember, it's not wrong to be different.' She kissed his cheek. 'Now go and check the chooks for me.'

He went out to the hen yard and collected the eggs from the laying bins. He fingered the birds that hadn't laid and went back to the house cradling the eggs in his arms. He thought about what his mother had said and supposed that she was right. It was not wrong to be different but it wasn't quite right either. If they had to be at all exotic, like the *Apis mellifera*, why couldn't they be from more exciting stock, originating from a travelling circus perhaps, or with famous explorers as forebears, such as Mr Burke or Mr Wills, brave men who'd struck out and crossed tricky terrain. It didn't matter that they'd perished; they had tried something that required risk and determination. He wondered if his father had been a courageous man. Not knowing much about his father meant he had more room to fill his imagination with the kinds of possibilities that were tantalising to a fourteen-year-old boy.

IV

Each spring they moved the hives. His mother used an old wheelbarrow, but since James had been small, he'd helped carry them from place to place. At first it had been one wooden box, but now it was two or three stacked in his arms.

'You can't move them together like that, you'll get stung,' his mother said each time as she trundled the wheelbarrow along beside him, pausing now and then to press at her forehead through the bee veil with the back of a gloved hand.

'But I always do it like this, Ma.' His arms jerked the boxes against his stomach in a rattle. Mountain Greys were mild-tempered and slow to rouse. 'You know I never get stung.'

One spring, he found a .31 calibre pocket Colt revolver wrapped in leather strapping shoved into the cavity behind the stove. James had no interest in guns and he put it back in the hole, next to some one-pound notes that smelled of earth. He was more interested in the newspapers in the shed, old *Ovens and Murray Advertiser*s dating to the late 1870s. His mother had wrapped old pots in them. He thought about those papers for a long time.

'Are we related to Ned Kelly?' he asked his mother the night he found the newspapers.

Madela kept her face angled to the lantern. She was patching and the light was dim.

'Who, love?'

'Mr Kelly, the bushranger.' He looked at her, unsure whether he wanted it to be so. His ruminations on potential fathers had included prime minister, policeman, gold prospector, football player, king, explorer. He wasn't certain about adding bushranger to the list but it was the first time his surname had matched that of someone significant.

His mother said there might be some distant family connection.

'Did someone say something to you at school?'

'No, Ma. I don't think they know nothing at that school.'

'Anything, Jim. They don't know anything. You keep away from the other children; people like to make trouble.'

Each Sunday, James and his mother sat in the chapel, side by side. He struggled to keep awake during mass, barely listening, until one day the priest leaned forwards and stared right into his centre.

'What do you know absolutely?' The man in the pulpit locked eyes with James, pointing at him, then he talked about truth and he talked about proof, how the first did not rely on the second. When he talked about faith, James listened carefully. The question echoed in the back of his mind as they walked home.

'I've found my father.'

'What?' Madela's hand went to her mouth.

James held up the Bible. 'God is my father.'

'Oh, don't do that, Jim. Please. You'll stop my heart one day. And try not to fall asleep in church, love.'

'That wasn't sleep, Ma. That was deep, blessed prayer. I was meditating on everything the minister was saying.'

Madela hugged him. 'And don't be cheeky.'

They were not people who talked much about things other than the seasons, the bees and the land. Sometimes stories filtered through from the outside world, carried into their house in the very occasional newspaper or gossip from the woman who ran the store, a person who seemed not to notice Madela's reserve.

The woman would chatter in a loose way that made James uncomfortable. He preferred to wait outside the shop, where he'd lean against the pole or stand next to their horse's head, holding its cheek with one hand and waving the flies away from its face with the other.

In 1898, the year before James went to work at the local tannery, a letter arrived. Letters of any kind were an occasion, but this was something so extraordinary it made Madela pull off her gloves and bat away her netted hat so that it flew off and rolled across the floor to the skirting board. Nothing ever made James's mother take off her bee outfit once she had it all in place. It was just after breakfast, and they'd been about to go to the bees.

'It's your aunt. She's died.'

'Was she old?' He moved to the bread box. Another slice with honey and butter might be a fair idea.

'You eat too much honey,' his mother said, sitting down. 'You'll turn into a bee.'

'I know. Buzz.'

'She was thirty-five. Is that old? I suppose it might be to you. At seventeen everyone adult seems old.'

He stayed near the bread bin. Maybe he was addicted to it in the way that people talked about liquor.

'Was she your older sister or younger?'

'She was your father's sister, not mine, but she was like one to me for a short time.' She held up the piece of paper. 'It says here milk fever; that she went mad and drowned herself. Sometimes women with a new baby can change and become dark, but I don't think it was the milk for poor Katie.'

She blew her nose and went into her bedroom.

'I'll only be a minute,' she called.

When she came out, she asked him if he'd had his extra slice. She picked up her hat and gloves and spun to the door, energy spiking out of her. James knew his mother as languid and soft, as slow as honey pouring onto bread, but now she was walking fast towards the forest.

'Come on, Jim,' she called over her shoulder. 'We have work to do.'

Later, in the evening, he found her in her room, sitting on the bed with a box open next to her. She told him to come in. Her voice was different.

'Sit down. I want to show you something.' She gave him a man's pocket watch which had the initials MK inscribed on it. 'Your father gave this to me; he found it amusing that it already had my initials on it. Look, it's got my hair and his as well, there on the other side. And a photograph of him. You should have these now.'

He held the heavy chain between his fingers. He didn't want the hair of a dead man. He studied the tiny photograph. The man had eyebrows that were as black and horizontal as his own.

'This is him. And this.' Madela passed him a proper photograph. In it, the man was standing, his pants strapped for riding and wearing a dotted shirt.

His mother opened a handkerchief to show him a gold nugget. 'This was properly found, down on the river. Your father was camping and he tripped over the hardenbergia on the bend and there it was. He called this one his "chook botty bullet".'

James picked up the nugget. It was smooth and round.

'He found it?'

'Yes. And this one too, smaller but still valuable.'

The second nugget was rough and about as long as a finger. His father had been a gold prospector. What was so secret about that? He looked again at the face of the man in the picture. This was his father, but it was the face of a stranger. He was disappointed. His father had been an ordinary man.

'What happened to him?'

'He had enemies, Jim, and they killed him.'

'Was it a fight?' Involving liquor, James supposed. He didn't want to ask if his father had been a drunkard. Suddenly, he knew the truth of it. His father was an ordinary man, a man who drank and fought other men. An immoral man who camped by the river and didn't wash.

'I suppose it was,' she said. 'One that went for years.'

'I'm never going to fight.'

His mother said she was glad to hear it, that he would keep safer that way. 'You keep these things safe too, love.' She pushed at her hair. 'If anything happens to me, you should think about going away, even to London. You can sell the gold and go. Sometimes it's important to stay put and sometimes a person needs to go, but you mustn't run. It's like the bull—if you run, you'll be chased.'

James didn't understand what his mother was saying. He hadn't run in the paddock, the bull hadn't chased him. And she was different. Her voice was never jagged like this. He realised she was afraid.

'Maybe you should go now,' she said. 'Go to the city.' She was patting at her eyes. He had never seen his mother cry.

He stood up and tapped his boot heel against the edge of the door. 'I'm not leaving you, Ma, don't be silly.'

The picture and watch stayed on the shelf at the top of his

wardrobe. The gold nuggets were put back in a hole in the floor-boards with the dresser pulled across it. They stayed in place as the seasons turned, as the bees did their work, and James didn't look at them again until his mother died.

That unexpected day had started as any other. Who would have known that there was a corner in that particular morning, and that around the corner lurked something surprising and terrible? It happened immediately after breakfast, when she fell over and hit her temple. It made a shocking sound, that cracking of her skull on the edge of the verandah.

Once the house was quiet and empty, James allowed himself to weep. It had taken time for the people to leave. The neighbour, Mr Lester, had lingered longest on the porch and finally walked away without speaking. James lay on the bed a while with his arms behind his head. He didn't think he needed to make a plan. It all could continue as normal. He got the things from his wardrobe and lay back on his bed. He held the picture of his father up to the oil lantern and the shadows moved across the face of the man in the photo.

'Tinker, tailor, soldier, sailor. Rich man, poor man, beggar man, thief.'

Maybe not a prospector as such; maybe a dabbler who'd been lucky—the type of man who didn't work too hard at anything for long. A man who wore a hat like that and had that look in his eye was not a man mighty in spirit; not brave and just and deserving of his mother. This was an ordinary man who had been taken from him before he was born, a man who had left his mother alone. Now she was gone too and he supposed this made him an orphan. It was 1904 and James was twenty-three years old.

Over the next weeks James tended the bees. He talked to the hens and the horse, called out to the sheep that lined the fences on his way to the tannery.

He went to work and hauled the skins and at night stayed quiet and read the family Bible or the old, battered Walter Scott novel, or sometimes the copy of *Bleak House* that he'd got from Ingram's. Occasionally, he pulled out the first *Cole's Funny Picture Book* he'd had since he was a child.

Go to the top of a mountain, the introduction read, *so that you can see 50 miles in all directions; you then observe a space 100 miles in diameter. Now the world contains 25,000 such areas as that.*

He tried to imagine such a vast space but couldn't. There were no real mountains where he lived, but it was no loss. He'd never cared for mountains because he liked to be able to see the land around him. He'd never really considered travel or other ways of life, and his narrow world suited him but sometimes he felt lonely. He was used to feminine company and missed his mother. He'd had some small thoughts that he might get married, maybe to Betsy Lester, the daughter of the farmer on the adjoining property. Betsy was kind and her father was a nice man who shook your hand with a firm grip, and held your shoulder in a way James imagined a father might. Betsy had three brothers and this appealed to James as well, and if they got married he would leave the tannery and get a job at the *Ovens and Murray.* While newspapermen weren't his type—they talked politics and religion, and he preferred simple conversation—a wife wouldn't want a husband who came home stinking of fire and death. He wondered how he would garner his courage—and it was a matter of courage, he realised; perhaps the most extreme type of bravery for a man like him to make an approach and open himself to love. He would be a gentle husband; surely no woman could object to such a man.

He went to the front window and looked out at the flat land. His foot was itchy and he pulled off his boot and sock and smelled the ripeness of the wool. He was a single man tending to his own hygienic requirements, but once he got married, he would make sure to keep a cleaner person, and he wouldn't get so odorous at the newspaper. He went to the back porch and stood looking out across the paddock to the grey nubbled trees and dotted hives. Everything that he needed was here. He would go and talk to Betsy's father after church on Sunday.

V

In the paddock, he stood with his back to the new bull. It barely moved, occasionally waddling to the dam then back to its corner, balls jutting and redundant. When he closed his eyes he could smell his mother. The bees were calling him from the forest.

'Hello out there!'

It was Bert Lester from next door. James had intended to talk to him about Betsy the following day and here he was now. James stood in the other man's bull paddock. He walked to the fence and held out his hand.

'It's never done you, has it?'

'Not this one, but the other had a go when I was little.'

They shook hands and James asked Bert if he wanted a cup of tea.

'Ah, listen, son, we have some business to discuss. Tea would be fine, I suppose, but you'll need to hear what I have to say. I've given it a few weeks but now's the time, I'm thinking.'

'Of course, Mr Lester. Let's walk across.'

They went to the house, James chatting about various pollen miscellanies. Possibly Mr Lester wanted to buy some of the land. If he offered a good price, James would consider selling. He and Betsy would be able to manage easily on a smaller block, but he'd retain the treed land for the bees.

James handed Bert Lester a mug of tea. He pushed the honey jar forwards and when the neighbour waved it away spooned two into his own mug.

'Son, I'll get it out. Your mother was only staying here. She didn't own any of it. I was sorry for her and you both so I let her stay for as long as she wanted.'

James stirred his tea.

'She didn't have much support in the beginning, not that she would ever take much. The family tried, but she didn't want to see them. As it turned out, she stayed a fair while. I used to know her, when we were young. We were connected, I suppose you could say.' Lester blushed. 'But I need the place back now. I feel bad, because it's no fault of yours, but my daughter Elisabeth is getting married and I've offered it to her and my future son-in-law. Things have been hard with the drought, the depression.'

'Not at all,' said James after a moment's thought. He drummed his fingers on the table. 'I was thinking I'd probably take off for Melbourne and you've made my decision for me. It's a grand thing, truly it is.' He rubbed his hands through his hair. 'Yes, it's a terrific opportunity,' he went on. 'I probably would have stayed here rotting with my bees if you hadn't come with your offer.'

Bert Lester squinted at him. 'Offer?'

'Yes. Opportunity is a gift. Would you like another?' James got up and went to the stove and put his hand directly on the kettle handle. He stood holding the top of the hot kettle but Lester said no thank you to more tea, he had to go.

Later, James lay on his bed with his boots on. His hand throbbed. He'd put honey onto his palm and wrapped it in a water-soaked cloth.

'Honey fixes all pain and all sadness,' he said into the room.

The sun sank out of the sky and the lanterns stayed unlit. He lay on the mattress he'd slept on since he was a pipsqueak and waited for the sun to rise. In the morning, he went and urinated out the back and breathed the sharp eucalyptus aromas and they helped to steady him. Back in his room, he took off his boots and climbed under the blankets properly. He watched the sun light the window-sill, and then the walls around the bed, its rays sneaking in past the pushed-back curtains. Outside, he could see the trees and a fly that kept hitting the glass. It was going to be a hot day and the honey would be flowing.

He walked to the forest, where he sat with the bees for the rest of the day. Then he rode to Bert Lester's and told him he'd be gone by the end of the week. He gave a short formal speech to express the gratitude he felt for Mr Lester's kindness and generosity. He said he knew that his mother would feel the same if she wasn't dead.

He packed the house but had nowhere to send the contents so he left things in piles along the skirting boards. He supposed Betsy and her husband could decide what to do with it all. He planned to take the first *Cole's Funny Picture Book*, the photograph of his parents plus another of his mother, the pocket watch, the Bible and a bouquet of carefully selected bird feathers—magpie, cockatoo and hen—pressed between the pages of the Bible. He would wrap the gold nuggets in a length of green fabric that he'd found in his mother's drawer and tie them around his middle under his shirt. He also took the revolver from its hiding place, and put it at the bottom of his bag.

On his last night in the house he dreamed like he had when he was a boy: fresh and free and ecstatic. The next morning he woke up early and got ready to leave. He left the tannery and the cows, he left the sheep and the horses. He left the bees, left all of it behind, and took the train to Melbourne.

Chapter 2

I

James found a job at *The Argus*, in the printing shop, preferring not to work in the office where the copy men were too talkative, too rowdy. He had few friends and little chance of keeping bees. The small lodging house where he lived, next door to the newspaper offices on the east end of Collins Street, had no garden—not that he expected the landlady would consider the idea of bee boxes even if there was space. Even so, he strolled and listened for bees, studying the plants in the area. The Fitzroy and Royal Botanic gardens had suitable flowering plants and trees, and he often walked through the parks, writing down types of flora in a notebook, alert to the sound of humming.

'You need to meet someone but you're too shy,' his friend Charlie said. Charlie worked at the paper too, in classifieds. He was brash and had big ears, pale hair and a vast appetite for beer and crude jokes. He'd latched on to James who, like most reserved men, had been unable to shake off the unsolicited companionship.

'I can only be how I am,' James said.

He broke his working life with swims at the newly-opened baths in winter and the open-water swimming club at South Melbourne in summer. He found that doing laps helped with his wrists and shoulders which were stiff, a legacy from his time at the tannery. He'd found a bookshop, EW Cole's Book Arcade, the same man responsible for the *Funny Picture Books.* It was a place with many titles and restful nooks where a man could sit and read without pressure to buy. He'd made his way through some of Dickens (particularly the orphan stories) but not the English playwrights, nor was poetry to his taste as he found it a bit floral. He had discovered a fondness for Austen but kept that quiet from Charlie. Next he might look at the Americans, or maybe the Russians.

He worked hard at the newspaper in the manner of a man who does his job without fuss. He had no thoughts of love or travel, none that were much to do with ambition or achievement. He went to work and went home, sometimes having lunch with Charlie but usually finding an empty corner in which to eat his meal. Nature and paddocks had been replaced by machines and industry. The smell of printers ink and hot metal, the enormous rolls of paper, the thud of the press became part of his daily life. When the machines were at full roar, the building shook, and even at night, from his room in the boarding house next door, he could hear the thunder of the rotary press, the cylinders spinning in their frames. It was ironic that, as a man who sought the quieter places, he'd found work in such a loud environment, but the clamour made conversation difficult, so that even amid the chaos, James had found a kind of stillness.

II

He'd been in the city two years and the book arcade now stretched across three blocks. James was changing accommodations, but as he walked down Collins Street, carrying a small suitcase, he decided to take a detour. He went to the second-hand department on the first floor, past the painted rainbows that arched above the doorways, and sat down on a cane chair in a quiet corner. He wouldn't nap, he told himself, but he dozed off after reading a few pages of *Madame Bovary*. He woke with a jolt when the band started and saw there was now an elderly gentleman in a top hat seated next to him. James had seen the man about the shop before. A regular customer it seemed. On the man's lap was a copy of *Bleak House*.

'That's an excellent book,' James said. 'You must buy it.'

'You think so?'

'*Bleak House* is my favourite of Mr Dickens's novels.'

'You've read all of them?'

'Well, some. But that particular title is the highest in my affections so far.'

'You feel emotion for novels, how wonderful.'

'Yes, sir—well, that one to be sure,' said James. 'And the Bible, which isn't a fiction but the truth. But it's the *Cole's Funny Picture Books* that complete my holy trinity.'

The other man's white eyebrows went up. 'My word,' he said. 'Bit old for that aren't you?'

James smiled. 'I might be. I'm twenty-five and I first flicked through one when I was about six, and I've read them over and over ever since. I can recite more of the *Funny Picture Books* than the Bible and they've served me well in hardship. Perhaps more than the holy book—but don't tell anyone I said that.'

'I won't say a word. Well, a reader at any age is a blessing.' He held out a hand. 'I'm Edward Cole,' the man said. 'It's my *Funny Picture Book* you speak so highly of.' A tiny furry face peeled back the man's lapel like a bedspread and chittered at James. 'And this'—Cole held up a finger and the marmoset climbed on—'is Alphonse.' He waved his other hand. 'My store.'

James introduced himself.

'And the suitcase. What does it mean?'

'I'm moving rooms. Too many drunks at the other.' He didn't say they were mostly workers from the newspaper.

'What a sad cliché,' said Cole. 'Perhaps I can help. Do you need a job?'

James said he had a job, thank you, but when pressed admitted it wasn't what he'd hoped. He tried to decline a dinner invitation, but Cole was firm.

'What about your father, Jim—if I can call you that?' Cole said. 'Is he around?'

'No, sir. I never knew him. Both my parents are dead.'

Cole went to the shelf nearby and searched for a moment until he located a book and pulled it down. He gave it to James. 'Here, read this: Kipling's *Kim*.' He explained that while Kim mightn't be as fine a character as Jarndyce from *Bleak House*, James should read it anyway because it would take him places he had never considered going.

'I think you might find it important,' Cole said. 'Have you read the Americans? I'd suggest them next. Not the Russians or French. Not yet, anyway.'

The man bent to pick up the case.

'I have a daughter about your age.' He handed the case to James. 'My wife is away with her sister in the country—she's an invalid, you know; the sister not my wife—and consequently the house is too damned quiet.'

When they arrived at the large house in Essendon, James used the bathroom. In the mirror he saw his stubbly chin and that his hair needed a cut. He wondered if he had any odour about him; sometimes it seemed he could still smell the cow hides on himself and if it wasn't that, it was ink. He was going to say thank you and leave. He didn't want to meet the daughter looking like a crazed swagman. He went to the back porch where Cole was, prepared to say goodbye, but from the porch he saw the garden and vivid levels of colour, banks of flowers atop flowers, with shrubs and trees around the edges. He could hear bees; they hadn't yet gone to bed in the warm summer evening.

'Yes, this house is too quiet.' Cole was smoking a cigar and pointed at the cold meat and salad laid out on the table. 'Needs children it does, running about. If only I could sleep at the arcade, near the monkey room, I would go to bed listening to them.' He held out his hand and the marmoset climbed up. Cole gestured to James to take a seat. 'I'd enjoy that. Or I'd like to sleep out here.' He pointed at the house. 'My daughter is too damned modern. Always off somewhere and getting herself about on the trains, riding a funny old bicycle. Now she's haranguing me about something called a motor buggy. She wants a motorcycle. Can you imagine it? She'd need to wear pants!'

'I can hear you, Dad.' A young woman stepped out onto the porch and extended her hand. 'I'm Linda. How do you do?' She sat down, shaking her head at her father, who was holding up a plate of ham and another of chicken. 'I want to sit a while and listen to the garden,' she said, pulling out a cigarette.

'She smokes as well.' Cole passed the plate to James.

'I'm right here, Dad.'

'So, my boy, help yourself. There's some nice horseradish cream. What are your plans for tomorrow? Work?'

James nodded.

'Where do you work?' Linda said.

'At *The Argus*.'

'They're a bunch of rabid conservatives down there, aren't they, Dad? All smart city blokes.' She looked at James. 'You don't look like a conservative.'

'I work with the presses. We don't see much of the copy men—or reporters, as they call themselves.'

He surreptitiously studied the way his index finger rested on his fork to make sure it was clear of the tines, like his mother had shown him.

'She doesn't hold back, does she?' Cole said. 'Tells me that my hat is silly—but if a man can't wear a top hat in his own shop, then where can he, I ask? Do you like your work? Are you passionate about it? That's the main thing. And what's your position on Deakin? Or, if you prefer an easier question, what are your thoughts about divine versus human origins of religion?' Cole laughed as he speared some chicken with his fork.

James tried to think. He started with the easier question.

'Well, I've always believed in God.'

'Yes, but which came first is what I'm saying.'

'God, of course,' said James.

Cole leaned forwards, intent. 'And politics?'

'Humans need systems and management. We are weak, flawed. We need direction. Much like bees.'

'Bees?' Linda said.

'We kept them in Beechworth. Bees are organised and simple, they don't have much range of existence, but humans have the best and worst of all that can be found in humanity. A bird can't walk where it wants, it can only fly and tweet, but at the least a bird is able to exist independently. A bee can't do much on its own, but as part of a community it makes honey, conveys directions to its peers. A man, while he can't fly, can reach all the corners of what it means to be human. Sometimes with choice and sometimes without. I'm not explaining myself very well.'

Cole was looking at James thoughtfully. ' "Humanity," you say.'

'Bees communicate?' Linda took a piece of chicken.

'Yes, with circles.' James blushed.

'There's so much beauty in humanity,' Cole said. 'And nature is extraordinary too. We are lucky to live in these times.' He poked at the cold sliced potato. '"All the corners of what it means to be human." I like that. Some say these times are not like the old days, but I say they are only getting better.'

'You say man can't fly,' said Linda, stubbing out her cigarette. 'But he will, Dad says, and I say women will too. They're called aeroplanes. Here, take another piece of chicken. Or ham. There's plenty. Mustard?'

'Ah, the flying machines. They seem like folly now, but maybe it will happen. She's mad about the idea.' Cole started to eat. 'You're from Beechworth, you said, Mr Kelly?'

'Yes.'

'Not related to Edward Kelly, are you? He was from up that way.' Cole was looking at him, a piece of ham on his fork halfway to his mouth.

'No,' said James. 'My mother thought there might have been some distant connection. You're not the first to have asked. You should hear some of the nicknames I get at work. I suppose it's an understandable error.'

Cole's ham continued its journey.

'I think my father was a prospector,' James said. 'Gold.'

Cole nodded as he chewed.

'How long have you been in Melbourne?' Linda asked.

'Since my mother died two years ago.'

Linda had a speck of cream on her lip. James wanted to say something about it but forced his attention back to his plate, to his fork and how it rested in his hand. He heard the bees in the garden and he listened to his hosts conversing easily. How was it possible to have known her only fifteen minutes yet for her face to be so familiar?

Her hair was cut in a blunt line across the top of her eyebrows. He didn't know what the style might be called but, like her, it was straight and serious. He hadn't noticed hair like that on other women. Usually they had it gathered all together at the back in a puffy fashion, fixed with pins, he thought. His mother had used hairpins, small metal things that she dropped in a pile on the table beside her bed at night. But Linda didn't seem to have anything like that in her hair, not that he could see. He wanted to point to her lip and suggest there was something there. Another man, like Charlie, would reach out a finger to wipe it away, but of course such a thing was impossible for him. She was laughing at her father now, her eyes sharp, shifting between her father and him and back again, and all he could do was look from her hair to her lips and back again. He realised her hair was the exact shade of a Caucasian bee's furry thorax and looked as if it would feel extraordinary under a man's fingers.

'Do you think you might be interested in a little bookish business?' Cole was saying, wiping his mouth with a napkin. 'I'm always on the hunt for good people.'

'Sir?'

'Yes, come and work for me.' Cole was smiling. 'You've been at *The Argus* long enough. Come and help me and Linda—we need you.'

James cleared his throat; there seemed to be something stuck there, perhaps a piece of chicken or ham, tomato, bread even. He felt entirely caught off guard, as if these people were somehow invading his privacy, albeit in a warm and friendly manner. He had to admit, though, that in the case of the daughter, of Linda, invasion wasn't an altogether unpleasant notion. Whether he could work near her was another issue.

'I've been hopeful of a promotion.' He coughed properly, embarrassed by the coughing, embarrassed at his own emotions.

'How long have you been so?' Linda said, smiling. 'Hopeful, that is.'

He had to look at her; to do anything else would be rude. She still had the cream on her lip, but just as he tried to find a response, her small pointed tongue snuck out to lick the white smear away. She seemed to be laughing at him. Not so serious after all. He cut his piece of tomato into a smaller piece.

'Or you can help me with my skulls, if you like,' Cole offered. 'They require cataloguing.'

'Morbid and grotesque your skulls are, Dad.'

'It's called phrenology. A new science.' Cole winked at James.

'I worked at a tannery, but I would prefer books to skulls, even so,' said James.

'Alright then. It's settled. You have a place to stay tonight?'

'Yes, but it might be too late by the time I get back.'

Cole looked at his daughter. 'Alright with you, girl?'

'Fine with me. He seems harmless.' She smiled at her plate.

They finished their meal and Cole went inside to get his hat after suggesting a turn around the garden.

'It's rude to stare, you know,' Linda said once her father was gone.

James apologised.

'But it's good you're not a conservative,' she added. It wasn't a question. 'I can see you're one of those men who feels many things and never imposes a thought or action on another person. You forget about yourself and what you want, if you ever really know it in the first place.'

They sat in silence until Cole rejoined them.

'So!' Cole said. 'You'll stay with us tonight. You can sleep out here and realise my ambition for camping. Tomorrow, I promise I will release you to your lodgings. Shall we look at the garden?'

Later, they had a final cup of tea on the verandah. Linda kissed her father's cheek, said goodnight to James and went inside.

'I'm off to bed too,' Cole announced after ten minutes more. 'I hope the mosquitoes aren't too bad out here. We'll never attain world peace and harmony while they're about. Goodnight.'

James thought about world peace and harmony as he lay on the verandah waiting for sleep. He was in a narrow canvas camp bed with a frame that creaked in the quiet night. Positioned under the window leading into the sunroom of the house, with a mosquito coil burning on the ledge, James lay still, trying not to move. Usually he fell asleep quickly but not tonight. What was it his mother always used to say? That he might miss something important if he slept too much, but he was certain that he wouldn't miss anything more tonight. He didn't notice any mosquitoes but instead listened to the soft noises of the people inside the house, his ears especially tuned to the murmurings of the young woman, Linda.

He remembered the daughter at the boarding house he'd left, how he'd been summoning the courage to ask her out. He had circled the idea for weeks, egged on by Charlie, but nothing had happened, and now her name had been wiped from his mind and her face was gone too.

He lay with arms under his head. The garden had been lovely and the bees plentiful. In the morning, he thought, he might take another stroll around to see how things looked in the strong sunlight. See what the bees were up to. After he'd made this decision, he turned over carefully and went to sleep.

III

James had always supposed it nonsense, the notion of a love that came barrelling at a man in an instant. As he grew to know the Coles, he learned more about Linda and found that all of it embellished and none of it detracted from those feelings he'd had immediately upon meeting her. The feeling was always with him, whether he was saying goodnight to her after work, standing outside the shop on Collins Street or walking with her in the garden in Essendon after occasional dinners. His emotions seemed to swell with happiness and he noticed how Linda's eyes glowed silver in the dark, how in the day they were golden, a perfect complement to her hair. She had the habit of sliding a pencil on top of her ear so she always had something to write with. She wrote up cash slips at the shop, made inventories and sometimes she forgot she already had a pencil in her hair and would slide another into the other side. She would walk the shop floor insect-like with her antennae reaching forward, leading the way as she moved briskly from shelf to counter and back again.

The effect of it made her less formidable, but any time he came face to face with her he was overwhelmed by the force of her personality.

It wasn't surprising that she was guarded against any intimation of romance. He discovered this through his observation of her with others, not through his own personal experience. He had never approached anything of that nature with her; he was a man who was comfortable in his passivity. The world had enough pushy blokes, men who went after things and got them no matter what. If he had to put a label to himself he knew what it would be. He was a drone.

His life was trams and trains, street noise and markets. Seasons rolled through the city; wet streets and howling southerly winds followed by hot summers and blustery northerners, winds that might peel the skin from a man's body. Regardless of the weather, the season or the state of the country, his feelings about her remained constant.

IV

A glimpse of dark nylon at the top of the ladder, an ankle he wanted to encircle lightly with his fingers. Sensible, laced round-toed shoes with low wedge heels. White collar and dark tie simultaneously conveying intent and restraint. Hair now cut even shorter at the back to reveal her pale neck, another place he wanted to press his lips. These were the things he wanted. The only consolation—and it wasn't a small one, James managed to convince himself—was that she refused all other admirers equally.

He occasionally went for dinner at the house with Cole and his good-natured wife. Linda was sometimes there, sometimes not, and when she wasn't, James was bereft. Charlie got engaged and married, and had four children, and he was invited to their place for Sunday lunches. As he sat amid the chaos of a young family, with Charlie's jolly red-faced wife bringing plates from the kitchen, children hanging off her legs, he felt the pain of not having the same for himself. When he was there he missed being in Essendon, but when he was in Essendon, with the kindly Cole and the sometime Linda, smoking and talking about where she wanted to go in the world in her aeroplane and who she wanted to meet, the emirs and tsars, the camel drivers and scarab sellers, those were the times he found most painful of all.

Charlie started to make suggestions of another type.

'It's not that,' James told him. 'There's a woman at work, but she's not interested.'

'Is *she* that way?' Charlie was grinning, picking at his teeth.

'No. She's independent and wants to travel. She wants to fly.'

'What on earth do you mean, "she wants to fly"?'

'She wants to learn to fly aeroplanes. She doesn't want an ordinary life.'

Charlie pulled his plate towards himself and started eating. 'Well, that's all she'd get with you, mate. An ordinary life. Gravy coming, love?' he called to his wife. 'You know,' he said to James, dropping his voice, 'just find a nice girl. A man can't be too fussy.'

James shook his head. 'I'd never marry without love.'

Charlie kept his eyes on the doorway. 'We don't all meet a grand passion,' he said, his voice still low. There was a moment where his face slid to glumness before it brightened and he straightened, turning to his wife as she came in bearing the gravy jug.

'Here it is, you,' she said, glancing at her husband with love. James watched them and saw the simple comfort there. But he knew himself. He'd never kill a man nor would he marry without love.

James was either at Charlie's place for Christmas and New Year, or with the Coles. There were picnics and films, trips to Luna Park and the public gardens, and walks along the beach or the river. The two families welcomed him, but for a man who'd never been truly lonely before, it seemed it was all he could feel now.

V

She was not a standard woman so James decided he would try to be other than a standard man. Somehow, he managed to banish a little of his shyness and replace it with something riskier, and so it was Cole surprised him one day in the shop as he was hunched over a card on the bench.

He flipped the card over, keeping it out of view.

'You know I adore my rainbows,' Cole said carefully. 'I like what they symbolise. She's a rainbow, but not because she's colourful. She shifts when you move towards her, is only visible at a distance, even for me. She's always been that way.' He paused and waited for James to look up. 'Still, you chaps have to try, I suppose.'

Cole went to talk to one of the assistants and James, embarrassed, turned the card over again and wrote:

> The Rose is red, the Violet is blue,
> the Honey is Sweet and So are You!

It was desperate and entirely wet, but it was the best he could do for now. All the books in the world couldn't make him a man who could say the words he wanted to and do the things he ought.

Over the next few years he gave her a card on the same date in February, cards she politely accepted but which never seemed to make any difference. After they'd been displayed on the mantelpiece of the house in Essendon for a number of days, they disappeared to who knew where.

VI

He always knew where she was in the shop. He knew when she arrived and when she left each day. He was aware of what she was doing, whether attending to customers or wrapping books, talking to one or other of the shop attendants, giving instructions, taking inventory. She'd be over at the symphonium, or in the monkey room, always in sight as he assigned himself tasks he could do while keeping her in his peripheral vision.

Some things had changed in seven years. Lighting and transportation, and the city growing around them; the Melbourne Cricket Ground, the new station at Flinders Street. What hadn't changed in all that time was the way he felt about Linda, and her firm lack of encouragement. In the seven years Linda had learned to drive a car and still talked about aeroplanes while he seemed to stay the same.

Then the war was on. After all the dinners and lunches, trips to the beach, tram rides and armfuls of books, James felt something change in him too. Perhaps it was the war that made him bold. It was as if a fever was upon the whole city.

'Look,' she said to him at the end of that first week in winter when everybody was talking about what the war might mean. 'What are you doing?'

'What do you mean?'

'Every time I turn around, you're right there.'

He apologised and picked up a pile of books.

'I'm not the one for you, Jim, and I am truly sorry about it.' She gave him a smile and he would have liked to think there was regret in it, but there wasn't. He told himself she wasn't being cruel, that the equation was simple: as much as he couldn't help loving her so she couldn't help not loving him. It was the rudimentary mathematics of attraction and desire, but it was no comfort.

'I don't want to be hurtful, especially not to you, Jim. But all I want to do is learn to fly.' She turned back to the shelves. 'A husband would stop me flying,' she said over her shoulder.

He wanted to assure her he wouldn't stop her doing anything, that he'd happily climb into the back of some villainous contraption and be taken up into the sky if it would only make her say yes. But he didn't say it. All he did was say that he understood and carry the books to the shelves to put them in their correct places.

VII

In the end, everything happened in the month of February in 1915. Linda announced she was going for a flight two days before St Valentine's Day. She'd found someone who would take her up, she said, and she walked around the floor briskly, her cheeks pink. She was friendly at work, warm even, treating James like a friend; sure now, James suspected, that she had him at a comfortable distance after their conversation.

'I'm going for a flight next Friday, aren't I, Dad?'

Cole turned slowly at the counter. He had aged badly over the years.

'Apparently you are, my dear. James, you should come and watch. Give an old man some moral support.'

'You know you're as excited as I am,' Linda called as she went to the shelves. She was humming.

Hobson's Bay was clear. The pilot, a toothy man named Hawker, was energetic and handsome in his camel-coloured breeches, with a thin moustache that caterpillared across his top lip. Hawker flashed his big white teeth at Linda and she smiled politely at him, but it was the shining white Sopwith biplane that she had in her sights. She leaned against the fuselage and rubbed her fingers across it, tenderly hooking a pinky around one of the lift wires.

They took off from the beach and everyone looked into the sun to follow their progress, hands shading brows as the plane roared across the sky overhead, banking towards St Kilda. Cole kept hold of James's arm.

'I don't think much of him,' was all he said.

James strained to see Linda's face as they landed. She jumped from the plane's wing and Hawker called over his shoulder to the crowd, jerking a thumb at her.

'She's a chatterbox this one.' He grinned, his teeth filling his mouth. 'Didn't stop talking the whole way. What's that lever, what's that gauge? Are you planning a trip to Sydney? Can I come?' He made his voice girlish.

Linda had red spots high on her cheeks. 'I'm going to Europe to learn how to fly.' Her voice was hoarse from shouting over the engine. 'I don't need to go to Sydney, so it doesn't matter that you won't take me.' She came over and took her father's arm, and James was on her other side so she took his too and they walked to the car, Linda talking. She had money saved, she said, and didn't need a man to help her. Cole commented that he wasn't sure Europe was the place to be at the moment.

'What do you think about this war?' he said, turning to James. 'Are you for countries enacting violence upon each other?'

'I don't believe in it. I don't think men should do the dirty work of politicians. Lives destroyed, families ruined. It's too awful.'

'A pacifist then?' Cole peered at him.

'I suppose so. It's a better word than others I've heard.' James had never thought properly about any of these things. 'I would fight if the country truly needed me, but I'd not kill a man. Someone's loved one, a father or a son. I'd not be able to forgive myself that, even in battle. Luckily, I'm getting a bit old. I don't think they'd want me.'

'They're thinking about raising the age limit,' Cole said.

'Jack at the shop was talking about enlisting to impress a girl,' Linda said, laughing. 'How foolish is that?' She was filled with energy as they walked, her head swivelling from side to side to look at her father, then at James, and back again.

When they reached the car, James decided the card he gave her the next day would be the last one.

VIII

On Monday, James arrived for dinner at the house in Essendon. Earlier, he'd been to the pub with Charlie and Barry, who was also from the paper. James had planned to have two beers, but the others insisted he have not only beer but a whisky as well, to celebrate, and he found himself complying out of despair as much as anything. The whisky had slowed the blood in his veins and made him stupid. Drinking it was the second stupid thing he'd done that day.

He stood in front of the row of Valentines on the mantelpiece. There was an extraordinary, elaborate job comprising a neatly-decorated box with a satin cushion. It was perfumed and decorated with flowers and coloured shells, and a tiny blue taxidermied hummingbird. James picked it up, looked at the back of it. He checked inside and saw the name. Someone called Francis. He swore under his breath. It was bloody impressive. He found his modest card, sitting towards the back of the group, startling in its ordinariness. He swore again.

'Probably a soldier gave her that card,' Charlie would say later, when James told him about it.

He caught her in the hallway, between the dining room and the kitchen.

Linda smiled and stepped towards him and said hello but he moved her backwards to the wall and kissed her on the mouth. Later he told himself that it hadn't been aggressive, that it had been soft and sweet and lovely, but all that came later, once he was back in his room and seeing how things had truly been. At dinner, Cole remained the same towards him, warm and fatherly and effusive, but Linda was furious.

James told them his news.

'Do you think they'll teach you to fly?' Linda's voice was loud and it made him look up from his potatoes.

'I told you that's all she can think about,' Cole said.

'I'm a fair rider,' James said. 'I'm thinking to try for the light horse brigade. There are no planes at the front anyway.'

'You're too sweet and gentle for it,' Linda said through her teeth.

'I'm not; not really.'

'Oh, you very much are.'

The unwanted kiss had done nothing. Even in failure there were no benefits, no gain in tainting his reputation. She saw him as a nice man, a boring man. Someone who didn't make his passions known. A man who worked in a bookshop, an ex-tanner and beekeeper, yes, a juggler, and also athletic, but still a man who delivered unimpressive Valentine cards. A man who would have been content to live on some land with bees, alone. She had the full measure of him.

'War is where men are made,' James said, miserable. At the enlistment that morning, he'd stood with the form in his hand, watching the ink dry. As soon as he'd handed it over he knew it was a mistake. He'd gone home and shaved off his beard, thinking that if she saw his bottom lip he'd be revealed as a lover.

'But how will you kill men?' Cole asked. 'When it comes down to it, as they say?'

'I'm too good a shot. I'll make sure I miss.'

'But it's war,' said Linda. 'That's what they expect. How can it not come to death in war? They'll hang you as a traitor.'

'I know it's war,' James said. 'But I won't kill any man.' He was a fool, as Charlie had said, and this was further proof.

Cole cleared his throat and folded his napkin.

'You can try, I suppose, my boy. Keep that head down. And you've shaved, I see. Linda, our Jim's beard is gone.'

Linda regarded him with cool eyes. 'I hadn't noticed,' she said.

James had enlisted and shaved and none of it changed anything, but it was too late now. He'd declared his intentions and a chap must follow through.

IX

Cole was at Port Melbourne to see him off. The steamer waited, patient and vast. When he'd left the shop, James had looked Linda in the nose and shaken her hand when he said goodbye. She told him she didn't like goodbyes, that hellos were much better. She gave him a stiff hug, told him to look after himself, and ran up another ladder. James picked up his bag and left.

On the dock, James reached into his pack to pull out the bouquet of feathers.

'Can you give this to Linda for me?'

'You do know, don't you, that unless you grow a pair of wings there's no hope?'

James said that he knew.

'Do you have any photographs to take? Of your mother, at least?'

James pulled out his two photographs and showed them to Cole.

'That's my father. This is my ma.'

Cole looked for a long while at the photograph of the man with dark hair and dismayed demeanour.

There was hustle on the dock, men moving around pushing barrows of kit bags, soldiers calling out to each other, women crying with no sound, children running up and down. James looked around at the spectacle of it all.

'You'll keep them safe, won't you?' Cole said finally. 'They'd want to go with you, you know. Especially your mother.'

James put the photographs back into his pocket and patted his chest.

'Can you keep this for me?' James gave Cole the Colt revolver, wrapped in a piece of pudding cloth. Cole held it up.

'I'd better not let my daughter see this, she'll want to learn to shoot, no doubt. To go with her planes.'

There was a call to board and James put his hand out to Cole, but the older man grabbed him and pulled him in for a rough hug. They separated and Cole wiped at his eyes, his nose and cheeks red. He said something about being a sentimental old fool. People started to throw streamers from the dock.

'I believe we are all men together. All men as one. It would be extremely hard to shoot at another man regardless of his nation or politics, and religion is the worst reason of all to kill someone. Even if someone was trying to kill me, if it was their job, I still don't know that I could do it.'

'I know,' said James.

'Blast. I didn't bring any streamers,' Cole said, blowing his nose. 'Who thinks of such a thing?'

'It doesn't matter,' said James. 'Thank you for coming to say goodbye. I'll write to you.'

'I want to give you something to take with you. Here, take Alphonse.'

'No, I couldn't.'

Cole insisted. 'He'll help you with the sirens! He can plug your ears if he has to, or tie you to the mast. At the least he'll keep you company.'

James accepted the marmoset and walked up the plank onto the *Ulysses.* Alphonse, confused and nervous, burrowed into the space between James's neck and uniform collar. From the observation deck James searched for Cole in the crowd, found him, and lifted his hand.

James waved at Cole until he couldn't tell him apart from the other faces in the crowd. The ship passed through the heads and out to sea. What was he thinking, going abroad to war with a marmoset clutching his ear?

He was a man who could aim better than anyone, a man with callused hands and stiff shoulders, a man over thirty now. How to know when to stick at something and when to give up? This was a question he didn't have an answer to, other than that it had simply been time for him to be elsewhere. If there was nothing for him in one place, there might be something in another, even if that place was certain to be filled with death and despair.

Chapter 3

I

It was early September of the second year of the war and quieter than James expected. There'd been weeks on the boat, with the press and smell of men's bodies all around him, followed by time spent in Egypt for training. Cairo had been a strange place, filled with heat and noise and its own pungent odours that drifted in the air, so to now be in the Dardanelles was at times almost peaceful. Sometimes, everything outside of him stopped and he could hear his blood move, and then a lazy shell would burr overhead and lodge in the ground or ping off a spade at the edge of the trench. There'd be a flurry to the sides, men moving and crouching and swearing, calling it *non-bon mate*, and then the whole world would fall to silence once more.

The landscape was scarred by ridges and gullies, naturally formed through the weathering forces of erosion, and the beach was littered with supplies and piles of sandbags and rolls of barbed wire and behind it all, the cliffs rising in stark relief against a cloudless sky.

It was a kind of shock that seeped into him, and it took a while to become accustomed to passing through the pits of bodies, pushed as they were to the sides of the trenches, the smell of oily fat flesh and the daily sight of swollen dead faces, grimacing in the heat. Dead hands brushed against his leg as he passed, and one in particular emerged gruesomely, one which the men shook as they went by, their boots unsteady on the bottom because of stepping on all the poor chaps underneath.

On the boat from Lemnos, James had made two acquaintances. Ernest Peas and William Gravy, larrikins from Deniliquin, were quick-witted and kept their Enfields loaded as they lolled about in the trenches, their hand-rolled cigarettes dangling from dry bottom lips.

'We're waiting to meet a Lamb, you know,' said Ernest.

'I knew a Roger Lamb once,' said James. He remembered the boy at school, sitting up the back with small ears that curled over at the top.

'Well, that's that then,' said Ernest. 'We're not gunna find one for ourselves. What are the chances now?'

Ernest was the more talkative of the two. On the boat, he'd come out with a string of jokes about dysentery and the thought of all that shit had made James feel light-headed on the hot rolling deck. He told them that bees could develop dysentery.

'If they're unable to void, is what I mean. You know, they need to do their cleaning, go on flights. Like walking a dog.'

'You're pulling me leg,' said Peas. 'Bees crap?'

'Who woulda thought,' said Ernest, lighting a cigarette and flicking the match into the water. 'Who woulda bloody thought?'

II

The first man James almost killed was not much more than a boy. He'd dared stick his head up to peek over at the enemy dugouts and across the way, not far at all, was a soldier, empty-handed, balancing on the edge of a parapet. When he saw James, the boy lifted his pointy cloche hat and bowed, and he could see the Turk's smile, as white and clean as bones in the sun. James lowered his rifle and released his finger from the trigger. He'd been squeezing it. He sat down in the trench, breathing fast, surprised by how close he'd come, how his nerves had taken over without thought.

III

In August, more men arrived, their faces fresh and plump, a mix of old and young. They didn't think of their wounded comrades being offloaded in distant ports, but those faraway men, injured and retired, often recalled the foreign land they'd left behind. Farmers' sons thought of all the blood and bone, which would usually make a barren land fertile; and smithies' sons thought of the lead that had impregnated the earth, all the dead bullets that would lie forever in a place that would never bloom.

James was almost paternal with them, and he amused the young ones with his jokes and tricks, rubbing their spirits with humour and kindness. He listened to their yearnings for food and mother-love, clean sheets and a cup of tea without flies in it. He listened as they talked about their families and didn't even remember that he had none. Out in the world, in another land far from home, he felt new and enriched with possibility.

He found it hard to sleep, but once he managed, his nights were filled with bees. He could smell them in his dreams, and they brought comfort. In his sleep he wandered the hives and lay on grass so soft, so delicious, that a hungry man could turn his head to the side to take a sweet bite of green and listen to the buzzing that pressed around him until he woke.

At night, before closing his gritty eyes, after touching his middle to check the gold, placing a finger to his left breast to find his pocket watch, making sure Alphonse was settled, he sat wedged into the earth with his small Bible and took his mind back to the bees. He told himself to remember them as if in the act of remembering he could ensure continuance of self and escape from the chance of death. He thought of the bees so that they would come to him in his sleep. They would know him again because in the months since leaving home, his beard had grown back, and his bottom lip returned to mystery.

IV

The days of September were idyllic and long, and the sun stretched to push the afternoons into languid evenings that were thyme-scented and expansive. An informal pause in shooting to bury the dead led to a get-together, with the two sides swapping buttons from their filthy uniforms, small groups of men standing together exchanging a few words, lighting one another's cigarettes, miming and trying to make each other laugh. Those days, radiant sunsets appeared with their pastel pinks and purples, oranges and greens that washed the sky and created a beautiful lid for the tired horror below. At four o'clock each afternoon, white clouds rolled across the sky as the sun went down, creating glorious vistas that made even the most exhausted and sick soldiers look up and let their mouths fall into soft smiles.

There were times spent swimming in the cove, the colourful waters shifting in hue. James loved to float in the warm bath of the sea. Ducking under, once he'd spotted an old man turtle, ponderous and slow among the rays of sunlight. There were porpoises that rarely came near, preferring instead to hover and watch the swimmers from the deeper blue, their eyes keen and human-like.

Alphonse didn't like the water and preferred to stay in his billy up in the trench, but in the cove, James floated on his back, naked and open for long minutes of pleasure watching a hawk circling above. He dried off on the beach and the breeze blew a page of the *Ballarat Courier* against his legs. He picked it off himself and read the headline: DEATH IN THE DARDANELLES. He folded the page and tucked it under someone's boot, scanned the beach and inhaled the aroma of herb-fresh mixed with tobacco. He was alive and death seemed impossible. He would remain on this earth a while longer.

One moonless night a few of them snuck down to the beach.

'Come and see,' a young farmer from Shepparton said. 'There's sparks in the water.'

The phosphorescence surrounded them, silver flecks of light that surged and streamed and made James and the others boyish in the night. They lost themselves in the fire-lit water, floating and dipping and splashing, holding up hands to watch the light slip off their blackened fingertips. As long as James lived he would never forget the night the sea became silvered with sparks. Then a bullet slapped the water and they crept back to the trenches. Before he tried to sleep in his earth-bed, James saw a shooting star and formalised the wish he'd carried with him from home: to stay alive and kill no man.

V

Ernest was complaining about the biscuits. They were all tired of the biscuits, tired of the moaning, but then a shell hit one of the soldiers sitting nearby. It took off the top half of his head and he fell over neatly in front of them.

'Cripes,' said Ernest, 'it's bloody Longers.'

Jack Lonergan, best torpedo kick in Cairo, dead in a trench at the Nek.

James lifted his rifle, found the sight, found the man and flinched, dropping his barrel. He couldn't do it. He stepped towards Lonergan and then caught one himself in the chest.

He sensed brightness and woke up. The walls were blinding canvas, the sounds around him muted and soft. He lifted his left arm and there was some pain. He raised his other hand to feel around his waist and then checked the small pocket. The watch was still there, in position, over a place which hurt when pressed.

People moved about the tent. Two men brought in a new person on a stretcher and tipped him onto a camp bed across the way, ribbing him, the soldier wisecracking and saying it was nothing, just a scratch.

'Bandage me up and let me back at 'em,' he said.

'You need a nice cuppa first,' said a medico. He planted a palm on the man's forehead and pushed him onto his back.

It was the Red Cross tent, a place filled with men in pyjamas reclining on pillows, drinking tea and reading *Punch.* James stretched his arm and his knuckles hit something hard. There were boxes stacked there, lined three deep.

'Socks,' the man in the next bed said. 'And jam. They ran out of sandbags. If there's one thing we ain't short of, it's supplies, mate. Supplies and flies.' The man laughed. 'Supplies, flies and lies.' He laughed until he coughed up bloody spittle into a kidney dish. A medical officer brought mugs of black tea and, while they cooled, James lay back. In the calm, white place, men murmured. He dozed. He heard someone say he'd been hit by a bullet in the chest but that his armour had saved him. He opened his eyes and there was a ring of grinning medical staff ranged around the end of his bed.

'We left it there so you could see it for yourself.'

He moved his hand to the place once more and felt a tear in the fabric, below the button. He took the watch out and there was a dent in the case but he flicked the latch and the lid opened easily.

'What are the chances?' said one doctor. 'They were calling you bloody Ned, while you were out. Tiniest armour in the world, we thought. We laughed our fucken arses off.'

More people stopped by his bed to commiserate on his impending death and to ask whether there was anything anybody could do for him in these, his last hours. Did he want them to take care of his wife, the monkey? Did he want them to inform his parents, the baboons at the Taronga Zoo? Knuckles prodded his upper right arm in schoolboy bockas and they called him Tick-Tock, and while it was all amusing, James remembered Lonergan and how he had looked when he fell over, surprise laid out across his face. How he'd had the Turkish soldier in his sights but had been unable to loose a bullet at him.

Across the way, a young boy with a blindfold lay in one of the beds. Beside him were a neatly-folded uniform and a Turkish cloche. The staff was busy, chatting and tending to patients with legs propped up, bandaged heads, broken bodies.

James looked back at the Turkish boy. He was flat on his back, arms beside him, his hawkish nose angled to the roof of the tent. As James watched, the boy brought a hand up to his face, scratched around his chin, rubbed his nose then, with a single sly digit, lifted the blindfold. A dark eye caught James's. The boy smiled and the blindfold was moved back into place. Was he thief or spy or both? What acting had he done to be allowed to stay put in this tent or to get here in the first place? With its ration boxes lining the perimeter, all those socks and tins of jam, guns propped against a makeshift wall, boots parked under beds, the place was filled with valuables. The Turkish boy's blindfold was still in place but his lips moved as if he were singing. The man on the other side of him explained how the young soldier came to be there. He'd been carried in while James was still unconscious.

'One of our lot was out in the middle, had been there for hours, yelling about his legs, calling for his mother. He'd go quiet and we'd think he was gone, but then he'd start up again. We was hoping he'd cark it, but he kept at it; I wanted to shoot him myself. Then, out of nowhere, up pops this bloody bloke.' The man gestured at the boy in the bed. 'Holds his hands in the air, walks over to our man, picks him up and carries him over to us. I reckon the noise was driving them stir as well. Anyway, he lowers him down, and he fucken falls into our dugout. Abdul! He's fainted. I can see he's almost starving, clothes swingin' off of him, and he's got this nasty wound on his hand, with pus on it and going green. He wakes up, I point at his hand and wave for him to come with me and he does. "Mayte" he says, and "yes", and that's about it. So I'm thinking we blindfold him and bring him here—and then there's a few pops and my mate next to me, his sight gets shattered. Some goes in my face. So here

I am and there he is.' The soldier exhaled in a low whistle and there was admiration in the sound.

James watched the Turkish boy. His lips were still moving and he was smiling and tapping his fingers on top of the sheets.

VI

James returned one of the *Bulletin*s to an officer and thanked him. As he was leaving, one of the staff tried to put a bucket on his head and they all laughed. James laughed too. It was a funny joke. As he walked past the end of the Turkish boy's bed, the soldier lifted his blindfold and winked at him.

Back in his dugout, Alphonse nestled behind James's ear, grasping it like a handle with his soft monkey fingers. James told the others about the Turkish soldier, even before he told them about the tent, the boxes, the food and the smorgasbord of reading material. Ernest sighed and stretched and leaned against the side of the trench. He rolled a smoke and lit it.

'I've heard them say they sometimes treat one of those blokes and let them go back,' said William. 'The blindfold's for security purposes.'

'That so?' said Ernest. 'I'd shoot 'em.'

'This boy helped one of our men,' James said.

'Even so,' said Ernest, 'I'da shot him.' He sat down.

Alphonse travelled across James's shoulder to Ernest's then climbed down into his lap and into his cupped hands.

'You're a funny blighter, aren't you?' Ernest said to the animal. He had become morose over the last fortnight and Alphonse was drawn to him, touching parts of his face, looking into his eyes. Ernest pulled out a forty-niner from his pocket and gave it to Alphonse, who sniffed at it and pushed it away.

'Even Alphy don't want none of them biscuits. Good taste, that monkey,' said William. 'Discerning.'

'He's a marmoset,' said Ernest. 'A marmoset with a sophisticated palate is what he is.'

'Do you think he really was a spy?' James said.

'Who cares?' said Ernest.

Alphonse skipped back across to James, lifted his pocket flap and climbed in. A shell exploded nearby.

'He knows when they're comin'.' Ernest held up the biscuit, now covered with dirt. 'An improvement, I might suggest.' He blew on it and started to gnaw one of the corners. 'Whose turn is it to make the tea?'

VII

The second time James came close to killing a man was in November. The enemy sniping calmed and the men repaired parapets and sent out teams to get water and firewood. James was on cookhouse fatigue. He left Alphonse curled in his hanky inside the billy. The days had become cold and he was tired and stiff from his chilled earth-bed. He was still having trouble sleeping.

He walked away from the encampment, thinking about honey and bees, and was almost at the clutch of trees under which he'd been told he'd find some good wood. He stopped when he saw a Turkish soldier urinating against a grassed incline. The boy paused and turned and looked at his gun which was propped nearby. He looked back at James, lifted a hand and called out something. It was the boy he'd seen in the hospital tent. Unnerved, James lowered his own gun; he hadn't known it was at his shoulder, but his finger wasn't yet on the trigger. He waved back and dipped his head. He said sorry and walked away with a bad shake in his legs.

VIII

Towards the end of November a blizzard hit, then pelting rain and storms that lasted three days. The seas churned and the roaring sky spat out forked lightning. They huddled in the trenches, almost driven mad by the continuing southerly gales. The gunfire had ceased and around them the world dripped. As the men became more miserable, some became delirious and talked about walking home. Others tried to be funny, but their jokes were limp. December was worse and sleep was still elusive. All James could manage were patches of dozing, and he would sit hunched through the night, listening to his own breath for hours. Their battalion took over the frontage occupied by the thirteenth and they were told all fire was to match the enemy's. Rumours travelled the trenches like happy rats, informing the soldiers one day that the evacuation would be brisk and wild, while the next they heard it would be enacted in careful waves of total silence. No one knew what to believe, but they all sat tight and tried to stop their minds turning to the sweeter thoughts of home.

William complained about the cold and James gave him his blanket during the day, which the other man wore draped across his shoulders like a cloak. They called him The General but the laughs were thin and bitter air seeped into the middle of the men, reducing their syllable count. One night, as they all huddled despondent, someone suggested they might have to surrender.

'Surrender?' a cracked voice retorted. 'Don't be bloody silly. We're gettin' outa HEYAH.' Someone started singing the Geelong Football Club song, a lone reedy voice. A rattle of gunfire from the Turkish side stopped the singer.

'See? Even those fellas over there don't like your fucken team,' someone said.

IX

James had been scratching calculations into his small pocket book, recording patterns in the rifle fire. He'd seen the changes in the bees' behaviour back in Beechworth; how they danced in summer, telling each other where to find flowers. How they'd vibrated around the queen, shivering, in winter, their movements keeping her warm.

He had realised that there were patterns in the gunfire as well, patterns that came as waves of shots from both sides. There was a natural regularity in the firings and it made sense. Humans shooting guns would fall into their own regular sequences.

The evacuation was on and, to prepare, small crews destroyed equipment. They buried bully beef and pulled apart sandbags. They burned the catapult and destroyed the rubbers and, one night, ammunition and grenades were dumped in the latrines. Over days, in staggered groups, men with boots wrapped in blankets began creeping out, some giggling hysterically at their mates who theatrically minced along tiptoe, other men shushing with shoulders tense, waiting for the crack of Turkish gunfire. Gradually, the Allied forces bled out of the trenches and away to the waiting boats.

James sat and waited. They would tell him what to do. Alphonse nestled into his neck, squeaky and tense. Someone tapped James on the shoulder.

'You the one who's picked the patterns?' The soldier's eyes were bloodshot. 'Come with me. The captain wants to see you.'

He was taken to the command where the captain, a man called Crowder, spoke to him about setting up automated rifles to help disguise the retreat.

'If these guns can be set to go off intermittently, the bloody Turks won't even realise what's happening. But they're not like the Hun; these blokes aren't stupid. It won't be easy to trick them.'

Captain Crowder paced in the small area.

'Jesus-fuck, what the hell is that?' He blinked at Alphonse, who had crawled out of James's pocket.

'It's Alphonse, sir. Sorry, sir.'

'You had that here all the time?'

'Yes, sir. Sorry, sir. I got him instead of a streamer, sir.'

Captain Crowder reached forwards and Alphonse jumped across.

'Well, I'll be damned. He's gorgeous.'

James looked at the captain. 'That's what people say, sir.'

'Simply charming, aren't you?' Crowder crooned to Alphonse, holding him and telling him what a good boy he was. He held his hand out to James, who took the marmoset back. 'We'll want six rifles. Get rid of the safeties and magazines. We've got a list of where to put them.' The captain nodded to the red-eyed man standing nearby. 'This is Franklin. He'll help you. You got the string? Did they give you the goddamned string?'

'Yes, sir. We've found some manila rope, sir. I tried that, it's good.'

'Good work, Franklin. We've got a bit of drizzle on tonight, gentlemen. It could be tricky.' Crowder cocked his head at the pounding rain. 'Listen to that. That's the sound of home, isn't it? Rain on a roof.' He chuckled. 'Used to keep me awake as a boy. Tin roof, hated it when I was small. The things we miss now.' The laughter faded from his voice. 'So, I think that's about it. Have a man near each rifle ready to light at oh-two-forty. You'll be one of them, Kelly, and we'll find someone else to stay with you. We do this right, they won't know we've gone. We'll be back on Lemnos for Chrissy and I believe there will be a very large mail to greet us.' The captain looked wistfully at Alphonse.

James and a private named Pollard were to be among the last parties out. In pairs, they would creep out right at the end, on 20 December. James said goodbye to Ernest and William, telling them he'd catch them on the boats or Lemnos, and to save some Christmas pudding for him. They offered to take Alphonse and James handed him over, but the marmoset jumped back onto his shoulder.

'Wants to be the last man out, I suppose,' James said.

He had four blankets and they kept him dry and warm. Pollard slept around the corner of the angled sap, out of sight but not far away. When the skies opened again through the night, the moon misted over with clouds. When James lit the fuses between two and three am, the rope burned well. And when he curled into his blanket tent, warm and comfortable and mostly dry in his dugout, he went to sleep.

X

The final groups of men moved out. No one ran, smoked or talked. There'd been nothing from the other side in response to the rifles. On the beach, the men waited another ten minutes to make sure no one had been left behind. Just as they were about to leave, a man came stumbling down to the beach. A notoriously deep sleeper, Pollard had jolted awake, clambered out of the trench and run in silent panic down to the last group, where he was quietly gathered into the solemn clump of men. Once they were away, they ribbed him on the boat.

'Lucky we didn't leave you there, you dickhead.'

Pollard rubbed his neck, smiling, his eyes locked on the spit of land growing faint in the distance behind them.

XI

James woke and it was dawn. For the first time in months he'd slept deeply. He kept checking the sky, aching but warm in his hole. He sat for about half an hour, thinking. The sun was starting to appear. He couldn't deny it; he had been left behind.

They would come soon, he supposed. He made sure he had all his things packed; the items from the shrine he'd made in the little niche in the side of the dugout. He checked the photos of his parents, his favourite *Cole's Funny Picture Book* that he'd carefully carried from home, and patted his waist for the nuggets. If he was taken, even if they killed him, he didn't want to leave any of it behind. He held out his hand to Alphonse, who had begun to chitter with agitation. If he walked to the cove, he'd see the boats gone. If he walked to the cove, he'd see the enemy and they'd see him. He supposed that he might die, once they found him, but it was not such a bad place to do it, quiet as it was with the sun beginning to creep over the edge of the cliffs. He picked up a rosemary sprig from the shrine and stuck it under his nose. He breathed it in and thoughts of roast lamb from Sunday lunch at Charlie's snuck into his head before he could push them away. His ears started buzzing with fear.

The light increased and still he sat there. The sun's rays lengthened over the top of the trench and it was full morning. He had to do something, but just as he gathered his muscles there was movement at the top of the trench. A rifle first, a shadow and a face angling down at him. The face was a familiar one. It was the boy from the Red Cross tent, the one he'd seen near the tree when he'd gone out to collect wood. The boy's mouth was moving, but James couldn't hear anything above the buzzing in his ears. He lifted his hands and waited for the moment where he got shot, but a hand extended and James reached for it and let himself be pulled out. He stood with his hands above his head.

At that moment, Alphonse popped out of his pocket and the young Turk's eyes widened in surprise. The boy stepped back and tripped over his feet. He lay on his back laughing, gun dropped to his side and his feet splayed wide in the mud. On his feet were two left boots.

'Hello.' The boy was laughing. 'Yes,' the boy said. 'Hello. I Ferhat.'

The Turkish boy Ferhat walked James to a clearing where there were piles of stores, and some donkeys tethered to a small tree. James saw soldiers in the distance, kicking at uniforms and packing cases, holding up tins of food. He expected them to come over with raised voices, but Ferhat took his arm and led him to a place behind the Turkish frontline which seemed to house a temporary cooking area. There was a small iron barbecue with coals in the bottom and vegetables grilling on top. Nearby, a young girl used a thin wooden rod to roll and turn a large pancake-type bread circle on top of a dome-shaped cooking apparatus. James looked around. People were about, near and far, and all seemed busy. The atmosphere of the place seemed to be like that of a picnic.

Ferhat gestured for James to sit down on a thin flat-woven carpet which was spread on the ground, then went to the barbecue. He came back and passed James a folded-up pancake with vegetables on top. James looked around for a plate but there was none. Ferhat went back and got himself some food, then kicked off his too-large boots at the edge of the blanket, sat down cross-legged and started to eat. James ate too. The soft vegetables were delicious; he recognised green pepper, onion, but there was one he'd never seen before, it had seeds with a greyish flesh and purple-black skin.

'Good?' the boy said to him. '*Bon*?' Ferhat was also eating a whole onion, biting into it like an apple.

James said yes, it was *bon*. There was a stretching in his pocket. Alphonse climbed out, nose twitching.

'*Allah-h'allah*. Monkey. Come.' Ferhat tore off a small piece of the flat bread and held it out to the marmoset, who ran and nestled at his neck. As he fed Alphonse, Ferhat pointed to the girls nearby with his chin and said something. He grabbed a rifle and held to his shoulder and peered through the sight, pointing it at a tree.

'No,' James said. 'Not possible.'

'Yes. *Oui*, *si*.' The boy finished eating his pancake.

Snipers? The girls were about sixteen.

'Your prens,' said Ferhat. 'No come English.'

James couldn't understand. The buzzing in his ears was a little better but it didn't matter. He supposed he was a dead man but, strangely, the next morning he was still alive.

XII

Ferhat seemed to be getting ready to leave. He handed James a rifle and the reins of a mare and James rubbed a bent index finger against the softest part of her nose. He barely allowed himself to hope as they collected three donkeys from a ravine, roping them easily as they stood drinking at the small stream that flowed there. Loaded with their supplies, the guns, ammunition, food and canvas, the donkeys were nimble-footed and comical as they waited on the shale slopes. Ferhat worked like a demon and all that morning no one came and asked who James was or what he was doing there. No one came at all.

'Where's your captain?' James tried to ask. 'Your boss?'

Each time Ferhat shook his head to the side as if to say 'no', always smiling, showing those clean white teeth.

At the top of the cliff they stopped to look down onto the beach where an orderly line of dead horses stretched on the sand. To the rear were whole cities of tents, vast piles of clothing, bully beef. Hills of timber. They stood looking out; James in his regulation uniform, dirty and damp, and the young Turkish soldier wearing a strange ensemble comprising an Australian hat, puttees wound around his midriff, breeches cut from canvas and on each foot a left British trench boot.

XIII

They rode for twenty-two days. Ferhat pointed to things and said the Turkish word, and James gave him the English word in return. Outside villages, Ferhat made small camps and left James with the horses and donkeys while he went to ask for bread and onions.

Once, he brought back olives. The first one James tried he found extraordinary, loving the salt and the bite of the flesh between his teeth. For breakfast they ate eggs and black bread. They got water from fountains at the side of the road and Ferhat made a different gesture each time he tasted; pinched fingers and palm up or a showy spit to the ground, but to James all were sweet and cold.

One night, James showed Ferhat the pocket watch that had stopped the bullet. The boy turned it over and over in his hands. He understood immediately what had happened.

'It was here,' said James, touching his breast. 'In my pocket.'

'*Allah-h'allah*,' said Ferhat.

Often at night, before they slept, Ferhat talked. James didn't understand and his thoughts drifted towards the land back home in Beechworth and what Betsy Lester might be doing right then. He thought of what it had been like to swim in the dappled water of the river in summer, to sit before a roaring wood fire in a stone hut with snow on the hills in the distance. He thought about his mother and about the man in the photograph who was his father. He thought about Linda and the bookseller Cole. He even thought about Hawker, the big-toothed pilot who'd made Linda so angry. The only thing he didn't think about was the Australian Imperial Force.

His ears were still buzzing, but he found the tinnitus a comfort. It was as if he had bees with him. Sometimes, though, as Ferhat slept, James would stare at the sky and wonder what in God's name he was doing there.

They passed around a small mountain, the end of the Sultan range, where they had to cut through to the other side. Ferhat rode with his revolver resting on top of the pommel and James's hands were red and iced tight onto the reins. The wind had become cruel and his neck was locked as he swivelled, seeing men in the shadows. Ferhat had stopped talking, had stopped his whistles too. James swayed in the saddle with fatigue. How would it be to swim in a summer ocean without fear of bullets? The water would hold him, let him float free, and afterwards he could lie in the sand and feel the sun on his skin. A game of cricket. He shut his eyes and his shoulders rocked to the side and he hit the ground hard. Ferhat came to him and pulled him upright.

'Mayte. *Bon?*'

'I am *non-bon*, mate.' James's legs buckled as he tried to get up.

Ferhat's eyes were ringed with black and his teeth clacked. 'Come.' He pulled at James and got him back on his horse.

It was Christmas morning, the twenty-second day of riding, and the two men began to climb a steep section of trail. James saw Ferhat peering up at the sky. Soon, a fresh load of snow started drifting down between the trees. He smelled wood fires, they must be close.

'Come,' Ferhat said. He was smiling, his teeth still playing castanets. They continued up the path. At the first house lay an enormous mustard-coloured dog.

It got to its feet, stretched its legs and lowered its bulbous head. There was a spiked iron collar around its neck and the chain chinked as the animal edged forwards and sniffed the air.

'Hello, mate,' said James. He clicked his tongue at the dog and it sat. Ferhat twisted around in his saddle, looking back. The dog was making a friendly whine in its throat.

'That Yoldaş,' said Ferhat. 'Bad dog.'

He pointed at a structure up above the village on the side of the slope. 'Honey house.'

The building's windows were dark.

Ferhat moved his horse on and James followed. Ferhat pointed to each building and spoke. He pointed to the drinking fountain and its beaten metal cup, to a group of barking dogs at the end of the street. Doors started opening and they stopped outside one building and Ferhat got down, calling out to the people inside. James tried to dismount too but his knees had locked and he was faint and he fell in the narrow road to lie flat on his back in the snow as night began to claim the day.

Chapter 4

I

At the beginning of 1990, Cem was twenty-three and a kind of shrug. He was one of the sugar men, but his sweetness was diluted in Melbourne.

'Yeah, it's pronounced Jem,' he'd say. 'The c's like a j.' He'd run a hand through his hair and look the other person dead in the face, legs open, jeans tight. Girls loved his name. 'There's something about you,' they purred in bars or at parties, in pubs and clubs. 'You're right,' he said. 'There is something: *Ben Osman*.' He raised his orange juice or his Coke in a salute to their puzzled faces and put a clenched fist over his heart, smiling around his teeth. The girls laughed.

'What?' they'd say. 'What's that?' And he'd explain.

'It means, "I'm Ottoman."'

The thrill of him made them stay, holding their own glasses frozen to bottom lips, eyes flashing and alert to the beauty of him.

In the kitchen, his mother wrung her hands in her thin apron and begged him to stay away from Australian girls.

'You do know,' his grandfather said, 'we had an Australian in the village, a long time ago.'

'Really?' Cem looked out the window, bored.

At meals, his father, Ali, tore at the bread and Cem nodded and chewed and avoided looking at his father's dirty fingers and his mother's tired face. After dinner he went to his room, took his poor tortured cock in his hand and thought about the neighbour's sister's mouth.

II

When Cem was small, he looked for his *dede* as soon as he came out of the classroom. He didn't see that his grandfather's suit was shabby and that he always wore it, even in summer, when the tomato leaves at the back of their house drooped in the heat. He didn't notice that Ahmet never stood with the other adults. His grandfather waited, alone, in the shadows at the periphery of the playground, always under the same tree. Cem would run out and there he was, flat cap shading his eyes: Ahmet Keloğlu, former child soldier of Atatürk, ex-shepherd of the Anatolian mountains.

'See this tree?' Ahmet would say. 'It's a wishing tree. We had one in our village.'

Cem ran his hands along the trunk.

'But there's something missing, isn't there?' his grandfather said.

'Wishes?'

'Yes, like dreams but different. You are like me. You will have big dreams, not the small ones of your father.'

Ahmet would pull a paper serviette or a strip of rag from his coat pocket and hand it to Cem. The boy reached up and tied it in a knot around one of the branches. Once, Ahmet had made him climb, pushing him up the tree with his cajoling words, but the boy had clung to the branch and cried, saying he couldn't. Ahmet scoffed. He said Cem wasn't a man, but he let him climb down again.

After school, they walked home holding hands, Ahmet making comparisons to the village back in Turkey. Cem knew his family had wanted to go to America (the better place, his grandfather had said many times) but for some reason to do with money, a reason that he wouldn't understand because he was too little, they'd settled in Australia instead.

'There are no such even and regular walkways back home,' Ahmet said. 'But on the other hand, there are no good rivers near here. When I was a boy our clothes were washed in the river.'

Cem looked up, worried. Sometimes he made brown stains in his underpants. 'Mum loves our Whirlpool. Did she have a Whirlpool in the village?'

'Your mother loves that machine too much. People shouldn't become too fond of electrical appliances.'

Ahmet noted the inferior gardens they passed and all dogs were deemed miserable urban creatures compared to the enormous Kangal beasts that worked the vast plains of central Anatolia. They would stop to peer at small white frothy things that yapped behind fences; Cem's grandfather called them sons-of-donkeys. He spoke about the men back home, men who filled their tea with cubes of sugar. He recalled mesmeric fairytales told from ancient doorsteps in the village. The talking animals, the *jinns*, witches and monsters. Zeynep, the dancer so beautiful she would make your eyes bleed and your pants rise in the middle. 'Here, your *yarak* goes up.' Ahmet plucked at the boy's crotch.

'Are they true stories, Grandfather?'

'Of course. I do not lie.'

Over time, the stories became as ordinary and familiar to Cem as the feel of his tongue against his teeth. 'Are the people still there?' he asked many times. 'Back home in the village?'

'Unless they've jumped down the well or rolled off the side of the mountain.' Ahmet hawked into the gutter. 'My cousin is an old man like me, but he's a liar and stubborn and only has one hand. He fell off his horse; he is a poor rider, not like your grandfather. I don't miss those people in my true heart. I was glad to leave all of them behind.'

'I wish I had a cousin to play with,' Cem said. He was often lonely. At home he had only his parents and his grandfather, and the hours at school were long and empty. He spent recess and lunch standing by the fence; the other children wouldn't play with him because his English was no good.

'Well, sometimes it's best to be alone in the world. Cousins can make trouble.' Ahmet's glance shifted to a cracked garden stake holding a bean plant. 'Look at this bean. These people don't know how to garden.' He reached over the fence.

'Why did you leave?' Cem said.

Ahmet straightened and reached for the cigarette packet he carried in his shirt pocket. He passed the matchbox to Cem. 'It was your mother, stupid girl. She did something bad so we had to go.'

Cem could imagine; he was ten and tired of his mother's fussing. She treated him like a baby with a peanut between his legs. He struck a match and held it out. 'Did she tell a lie?'

Ahmet exhaled smoke into his grandson's face. 'It was something much worse, but forget about that now. Let's go home and play cards. I have a new game to teach you.'

III

Cem went to his mother. First, he had to let her hug and kiss him. He was growing up too fast, she cried. She missed him and he never came to sit with her in the kitchen anymore. She held on to him as he asked his question.

'No, it was not me.' She laughed and wiped at her eyes. 'Your grandfather did the bad things, but these are secrets, so *soos*.'

IV

Ahmet listened carefully to the boy then sent him to bed. The old man finished his last cigarette for the night and stood to shut the window. He would talk to her tomorrow. He smelled the wetness of the garden outside and felt the chill through the glass. He got into bed only to lie awake a long time. Over the years, he had become scared to sleep. Something had followed him here. Was it Al Bastı who called her cats into the back garden? At night, when he heard them scream, he pulled deep into his heavy blankets. During the day, the birds would sing, making all their sounds as normal—but this terrified him too, because Al Bastı could speak to the birds and make them gather around the house. Make them do her dark, unsettling work.

V

Cem lengthened as he grew and began to lope when he walked, hands in pockets, chin dropped to the ground. He didn't look people in the eye because inside all of his stretched new form, he hadn't even begun to reach his own edges, and he was unsure about everything. He was on the verge of something, but he wouldn't have been able to say what. His family, though, never tired of telling him what kind of person he was.

'You're like me,' his father said and his grandfather too. 'Oh, we know,' they cried, passing him the end piece of the bread, the hottest of the peppers, not seeing that he left them beside his plate. 'You are always hungry; you are a dreamer; you are quiet.' The problem was that, as the person in question, the one who should know most about what it meant to *be* him, it did seem that they understood more about him than he did himself. He had no fucking idea.

VI

Somehow he finished university. His course hadn't been difficult, though he'd never got more than a credit in any of the subjects. It had been boring, endless, obligatory. A few months before graduation, he sat in the park opposite the Bureau of Statistics in Carlton. They were expecting him for an interview, but he sat on the bench and watched people going in and out of the building, and as he sat he felt himself shrink back to size. At first he'd swelled at the idea of getting a job, but now something was pulling away from him, becoming harder and harder to see. He'd thought a real job might mean he'd become visible, but now he wasn't sure, so he went up to Russell Street and played slot machines. He ate some hot chips. That night he went home and told his father the interview had gone well, that they'd probably offer him a job.

VII

The wishing tree hadn't been in Cem's mind for a long time but one night, in bed, before sleep, he found the tree and he found Zeynep too, the beautiful dancer, tucked away in his memories. He brought them out and let his thoughts turn and a yearning re-emerged, a desire for something wholly imagined and only half-known. Maybe he'd go to the village. It seemed as good an idea as any.

VIII

It was early summer and they were eating dinner outside when Cem told his family what he was planning.

'Lots of people go backpacking between uni and work, Dad.'

'What is this "pack-a-pack"?' his father said. 'What about the interview, the job you told me about?'

'He is like me: an adventurer,' Ahmet said, nodding in satisfaction. 'Who else would fight in a war at twelve years old? Who else would travel to a strange and faraway place at sixty? No one, that's who. No other shepherd has left the mountains, I am the first. Listen, my grandson. You will go to London and Rome.' Ahmet had never been to either. 'Paris. The high-class places with the high-class people. But not Greece; they are savages there.'

Cem realised it would be a bad idea to mention his thoughts about Naxos and Santorini, but surely no one could argue against him going to the village.

'I was thinking I might go to the village.' Cem shifted his chair, angled it towards his grandfather, glad for his support. He'd known his parents would respond negatively, especially his father.

'No!' Ahmet's hand hit the table. 'Not to the village. Why would you go there? It's dangerous and the people are not good.'

'But what about all the stories you told me? How great the village is, how majestic the mountain and the forests. The drinking water.'

'Now you're making fun of me. You're being disrespectful. Oh, my heart!' Ahmet clutched at his chest.

'Dad is right.' Ali lifted his fingers as he spoke to his son. 'You don't want to go to the village. They're all peasants there, old-fashioned people.' There was something wistful in his eyes.

'Exactly,' said Ahmet. 'Old-fashioned. They didn't have television until the late thousand nine hundred seventies. Refridges not until the *early* thousand nine hundred seventies.'

'I thought the Arçelik arrived in 1966, the year we left,' Ali said.

Ahmet said no, it wasn't then, and anyway, who cared about a refrigerator. 'They would ask for money,' he said to Cem. 'They think everyone who leaves is rich and can help them with their minor problems. They have no idea what a big problem is. Small bridge builders, they are. Sheep men, carpet weavers, coffee drinkers. They will try to make you do things you don't want to do.'

Cem opened his mouth to say something about heritage and identity, but his grandfather hit the table again. 'I have decided. You're not going.' His grandfather's nostrils were much wider than normal as he turned on his daughter-in-law and son. 'It's your fault he's like this,' Ahmet said. 'Always too sensitive. Too scared to climb a tree. Crying all the time, complaining about being lonely. This is the man he's become?'

Ali held out his hands in defeated supplication and Hanife started weeping.

'Mustafa is the chief now,' said Ahmet. 'With that head like a bear, telling lies about me. No, it is final.' He crossed his arms and looked at them.

'How do you know Mustafa is the headman, Dad?' Ali said.

Ahmet reached for more bread with twitchy fingers. 'Surely old Agha is gone by now.'

'Has someone been writing to you?'

'Of course not. You know I never learned the new writing.' Ahmet chewed. 'But it doesn't matter; he's not going.'

Hanife stood up. She held on to the back of her chair. Her eyes were still red but changed. She waited until she had everyone's attention.

'Let him go,' she said, once they were looking up at her. 'Perhaps it will help him.'

'What?' said Ahmet. 'What help does he need?' He wheezed, it was a laugh, and he held his hands up to his son and grandson, an invitation to join him in his amusement. 'Stop, woman, you making me choke.'

'It might help him to grow up,' Hanife said. She had been a crier as long as Cem could remember, and he'd never seen her speak in a firm and definite way, her wet cow eyes gone hard like this. 'You're always telling him who he is, how he is,' she said. 'But isn't this for him to discover?'

No one spoke. Cem watched his mother and felt both betrayed and loved. She walked away from the table, went straight-backed into the house. Ahmet was still laughing, but Cem was teary and turned his face to the garden. His mother hadn't looked back.

'What does she know?' Ahmet was saying.

'What money have you got anyway?' Ali said.

'I've been saving. I've got enough from the restaurant to go for six months. If I wait until next April, I'll have saved even more.'

'My son the waiter, you make me too proud. What happened with the interview?'

Cem swallowed. 'I didn't get the job. I didn't tell you because I didn't want you making it a big deal. They had a lot of people trying for limited positions.'

'It is a big deal; this is one life, no second time to do it,' his father said.

Cem said he knew that, he wasn't an idiot.

His father's face softened. 'If you do go to the village, you would have to be very careful—'

‘What are you talking about?’ Ahmet cried. ‘I am forbidding it.’

In the silence that followed, Cem got up and said he was going to bed. In his room he lay and thought about the wishing tree and about Zeynep. He thought about his grandfather’s reaction. He was definitely going now.

IX

That night, Ahmet tried to stop it but found he couldn’t, so he let the music come. The reed pipe and the *dum-tek* of the drum. The mournful voice that traced a man’s memories back over oceans and inland along cracked, dusty roads as it followed valleys and stretched across plains, until it finally came to rest in the Sultan Mountains, location of one tiny dot of humanity in the Republic of Turkey. It was a place where the sound of the lute was magical. Where music hung in the air, dipped a little, wavered, then became strong and pure. It was the sound of his dreams, of the east, the sound of the mountains, and it was there that his village was perched atop a crag of rock. Nearby were grasses lying open and moist in never-ending grace for the sheep, sweet rivers to wash the handspun carpets, where women walked from place to place with their drop spindles tapping against their legs through all the hours and days so the tufts formed the thread that they took to the looms.

Ahmet wondered if it was homesickness, this tightness in his chest which felt like a fist squeezing a fluttering bird. Later, he slept and, despite his sadness, one of the good dreams came. He was back in Hayat with his cousin. They were drinking aniseed liquor together, arms across each other's shoulders, doing the step-step-hop dance. They wept over lost loves and stood in the snow to piss, their streams as strong as young men's.

In the morning, Ahmet sat on the edge of the bed, willing himself to stand. The dream had comforted and upset him like a gentle finger prodding across time and space. He wasn't a coward, a murderer, a fool, a betraying husband; or, if he was any of these things, it had been for the best. He had left the village to become a superior man. Sometimes you had to crawl from the earth and find something to climb, something higher, it might be a tree or a mountain. During the trip to the new country, with each hour that had passed, he had felt his new life sinking deep into his bones, so that by the time they arrived in Melbourne, the village and all her bastard people had been pushed out of him and he was a new man. No, it was for the best. The boy would not go.

Chapter 5

I

In Istanbul, Harry Forest insisted Cem Keloğlu sit in the front of the taxi. It was five o'clock in the evening and Cem was flattened with fatigue after the journey. At the airport, he'd forgotten to ask the taxi driver to activate the meter, and climbed in, nodding when the driver said, 'Sultanahmet?'

The foreground of the road spun under the bonnet of the yellow car, the accelerator pushed to the floor as they shot along the coast road towards the tourist centre in the old part of the city. The driver had a black walrus moustache and passed his fingers across it every time they were stopped at a red light.

Cem had been sitting next to Harry on the plane. The older man introduced himself as Dr Harry Forest, historian. When Cem asked what kind of history, Harry had said, 'Australian,' sounding a little defensive, but Cem didn't know much about history and said so.

'Recent Australian history,' Harry added. He was an intense type. His kept his fingers tightened on the brown briefcase that remained on his lap throughout the flight. He drank too much and became overly talkative, bombarding Cem with information that wasn't interesting. He was a tall man with long thin shaky hands and greying hair that stuck up in waves across the crown of his head. He mentioned an obsession he had developed, an idea he 'shouldn't say anything about, I'm sure you understand'. His wife had become tired of it, Harry said. 'Well, forty years is a while to endure, I suppose.' Then he told Cem about his bad back, how he had been left in agony after a car collision (sacral region, around S2; Holden Barina, silver-grey). 'Terrible pain, it comes and it goes. But I haven't suffered with it for a few years now. It would be awful if it were to come on during this trip. It's inhibited my investigations in the past.' He fluttered a hand at the flight attendant for another drink. She saw him and walked in the opposite direction. Harry's shoulders slumped and he stared at his briefcase.

Cem wanted to nap, but Harry began talking about his wife (Marlene, lovely hair, the colour of *wheat germ*, do you know wheat germ?) and her predilection for Chinoiserie (small Chinese-style lacquered bowls and drinking vessels, have you seen them?).

The hours passed and Cem managed to sleep, only occasionally disturbed by an elbow or knee as Harry tried to find a comfortable position or summon the hostess. Towards the end of the journey he'd been jolted awake by movement at his side, and he opened his eyes to see Harry mopping at his brow with a serviette.

'Are you okay?'

'I shouldn't have mentioned the accident,' Harry said. 'Sitting like this for too long seems to be reactivating it, calling it if you will.'

'Sorry about it,' said Cem, and looked out the window.

The taxi drove along the coast road and ships strained across the horizon out on the grey-blue water. The taxi driver's leather jacket was well-worn and the crease in his pants was sharp. His face showed a hint of beard, the shadow greenish against his skin. Cem scratched at his own chin; there were a few bristles there. He ran a hand down his wrinkled t-shirt, lowered his nose and lifted a shoulder to sniff. He needed a shower. He looked over his shoulder to the back seat where Harry was asleep against the window, mouth open, very pale. They'd decided to take a taxi together—or, rather, Harry had suggested it, and Cem had agreed.

The driver put the radio on and Cem heard the melancholic music of his childhood.

'Cigarette?' murmured the driver in Turkish, holding out a packet of cigarettes.

'No thanks, I don't smoke,' Cem replied in Turkish.

'You Turkish? *Almanya? Yeni Zelanda? Avustralya!*'

Yes, he was from Australia, his parents from Hayat, Cem said.

The man shook his head; he didn't know it.

'Western Anatolia,' Cem said. 'Near Izmir but in from the sea.'

'Ah, Izmir.' The driver rapped his fingers on the wheel. 'Izmir figs are supreme.' He bellowed a lyric, something about a broken heart, something about a girl called Fatma who was lost in Izmir.

'I am İbrahim,' he said in English, twisting in his seat to include the sleeping Harry in the introduction. 'Do you have hotel yet? I take you my cousin place. It is comfortable with western toilet, breakfast also including.'

They slowed at a set of lights and turned left towards ancient city walls. İbrahim pointed out restaurants and shops, major streets and landmarks. They pulled in at a building that had a garden out the front and a sign saying HOTEL ANADOLU.

Cem got out and stretched and the air pressed against him, against his ears, as if he'd gone too deep into water. He stood feeling dumb as the place breathed over him, recognising him. İbrahim was getting Cem's pack from the boot and levering Harry's old-fashioned suitcase to the pavement, but Cem couldn't move. The taxi driver put the bags down and clapped Cem on the shoulder.

'Ah, you are feeling it, I think? You are feeling *hüzün*. Little bit like sad but not quite?'

Cem knew the word; his grandfather had used it. It was similar to melancholy but different, with no real English equivalent. No, Cem said, he was fine, just tired from the flight. He tried to pay, but the taxi driver clicked his tongue in the negative.

'For my brother there is no cost,' İbrahim said. 'Today Monday, so we will go to dinner on Thursday, I think, and I will be your guest. We will drink *rakı* and eat too much and you will pay. We will talk about *hüzün* and how once it comes to live in your heart, it stays forever. After, we will go to my friend's supper club where there is very beautiful *danseuse*. We will have drinks and you will pay for it also. I come here at ten to gather you and your friend. So not tonight, you tired. Not tomorrow because tomorrow night you will go to Gelibolu for day trip. So Thursday it can be, when you get back.'

Cem was confused. 'Gelibolu? Where's that?'

'Gelibolu, the special gathering for the war. All the Aussies love it very much.'

Cem said he wasn't going to Gallipoli. He found history boring, he said in a low voice, looking at Harry, who had woken up when the car stopped and was now waiting propped against a wall nearby.

The taxi driver gestured to the historian with his chin. 'He is okay?'

'I don't know.'

They went into the reception and İbrahim introduced his new Turkish friend from Australia to his cousin. A reduced tariff was elaborately announced. In his room, Cem lay on his bed, too tired to strip or wash. It was the jetlag that made him stupid, making his brain cottony. The call to prayer began from a minaret outside and Cem smelled the wool of the oily blanket as he turned over in the narrow bed. His eyes went dark and he slipped into sleep.

II

It was cold and the afternoon was becoming dark as long shadows stretched down footpaths. Cem walked the city and was overwhelmed. By the monkey in the market, its eyes pinned in its skull as it flew with a shriek at the bars of its cage, making him jump back in shock. Beggars with half their bodies gone resting on the footpaths, holding out postcards, matches, single cigarettes for sale.

Men who came out of shops wearing tasseled shoes, well-groomed and pushy about rugs and kebabs and Bosphorus tours, and while they clamoured for his custom, there was something in the air that was heavy like smoke, something that pushed against him and filled his chest with a sensation that he had to admit did feel like sadness but not quite.

He found himself sitting in the thin sun on the grass in the Hippodrome, eating a piece of salty boiled corn. A group of girls stopped and asked him where the cistern was. Their English was slow and carefully enunciated.

'I'm not Turkish,' he said. 'I'm Australian too.'

'I told you.' One of the girls pushed at her friend's arm.

There were three of them; the two who were standing there staring at him, and another who hadn't even looked his way but had slumped to the grass with a scowl.

'Can we sit?' the first girl asked. They all looked at the friend who was already down. 'Sorry,' she added. Cem said it was okay and they sat. They were Sally and Beeb, the two jolly ones, and Jenna, the one on the grass. Beeb was short for Barbara, the tall one explained. Cem couldn't work out if she was talking about herself or the girl next to her, but it wasn't important.

They talked, two girls giggly and keen, the other silent and remote. Sally and Beeb told him where they were from and where they'd been and where they were going. They told him about the good restaurants they'd found, and where to get an international student card. Cem only half listened. While their chatter puffed in clouds above their heads, he watched Jenna, lying across from him on the other side of their small circle. On the air, along with the food odours and the pungent cigarette smoke of someone walking past, he thought he could smell her; she smelled like the small white flowers that grew on the side fence at home, behind the garage. When he was little, his mother had hoisted him in her arms so he could press his face into them. He knew that Jenna would taste earthy and delicious, if only she'd let him. He'd never done it before, had never wanted to, but now it was all he could think of, burying his face between her legs. As he imagined putting his mouth on her, she sat up. He looked away but she held a hand out to one of the girls, who dug in her bag and produced a packet of cigarettes.

'We're sharing the pack,' she told Cem.

He watched as Jenna drew a cigarette out of the box, long and slim, white filter, the hairs on her arms pale as she cupped the flame and brought it to her lips. The other girl offered the pack to him and he said he didn't smoke.

He saw how it could be. Him stepping out onto a hotel balcony in Cairo, say, ducking under Jenna's dripping bra and knickers which she'd hung there to dry.

He stands and looks out over the city, hands on the railing like the captain of a big white yacht. The streets darkening below with a soft purple light, and the aroma of rosewater, spiced lamb and fresh tomatoes drifting on the air. The time for love is approaching, their favourite time of day. She would be soaking in the bath, calling out for him to bring her a cigarette. Or maybe she'd come up behind him and sneak her arms around his waist so that he could feel her body pressing against him through her thin robe—or, better, a towel—or, better, naked. A mosque's amplifier crackles into life and they listen to the muezzin begin the call to prayer and she presses her sharp chin to his back. Cem imagined that in that moment he would take notice of it all and be truly happy.

Jenna lay back down on the grass and smoked her cigarette, occasionally flicking the ash to the side. Men walked past and Cem saw them notice her. Here was this Jenna from the northern suburbs of Sydney, stretched out like a creamy blonde cat in the grass, in her baggy denim jeans, baggy green top and scuffed brown hiking boots, her hair all messy, laid out in front of him but ignoring him, with her amazing skin and those two tiny, dark freckles on her right cheek, little flecks of dark chocolate. He tried to concentrate on what Sally and Beeb were saying. He smiled as their mouths smiled and nodded when they nodded. They talked about the Grand Bazaar and they talked about Taksim. They talked about taking a ferry around the Black Sea to a monastery or maybe going south to Marmaris and then to Greece, but they weren't definite about it yet. They talked about Gallipoli, which was definite. They were going that night.

'Are you going?' Beeb or Sally said.

The other girl kept passing him her bag of pistachio nuts and didn't seem to mind that he was eating heaps of them.

He looked at Jenna. 'Is something wrong?'

'She's got a headache,' Beeb or Sally said. 'Usually she's more fun.'

'I am,' said Jenna. It was the first time she'd spoken and her voice was deep and slightly hoarse, her words ponderous. Those two words and the way they were uttered let Cem know she was a girl who rushed for no one, a person who was comfortable in whatever place she happened to find herself. 'I am extremely fun except for times like now, when I have my period.' Her long hair was pulled over one shoulder in some kind of a bunch and she was pale with lips that were the colour of coral. Cem didn't think she was wearing any makeup, but it was hard to tell as he sat there on the grass, shot through the chest by something that hurt, something that made his thoughts fizz and spark. Not even the mention of her period turned him off, and usually he was squeamish about that type of stuff.

'You all going tonight then?' Cem ate another nut.

'Yep,' said one of the girls, Sally or Beeb, one of the not-Jenna girls. 'We're on Ekrim's tour.'

Jenna rolled over with a groan, settling on her other side, arm now straight out under her ear on the grass, one leg bent forwards as if she was mid-hurdle.

Cem looked at Jenna's arse and asked where he could buy a ticket for Ekrim's tour. He tried to concentrate on the directions they gave him. He would go straight there. He was going to buy a ticket and go to Gallipoli that night.

III

The bus was filling. Ekrim was walking the aisle, dispensing lemon cologne and promising there would be singing. Cem put his small pack on the seat beside him, but as more people climbed on board, noisy and excited, a lanky guy asked if it was free. Cem said yes and moved his bag. They nodded hello to each other and Cem said his name and held out his hand. The guy was French and his name was Pascal. Pascal thought old war cemeteries were very interesting, he told Cem; he had been to several in Europe. Cem hadn't suspected this was something a person might boast of, but then he hadn't met anyone from France before so maybe this was what they were like. After five minutes he reckoned he had the measure of both the man (pushy) and of his brain (small; almond-sized, or maybe walnut). He was one of those guys who, if you said something, they had done or known something bigger, better, older.

By the time Pascal got around to asking about Australian politics, Cem was disengaged and wondering how to complete the disconnection. He kept looking at the door of the bus. If they didn't come, he'd be stuck here with this dickhead for the next twenty hours. But just before the bus pulled out, the three girls from the Hippodrome arrived. Jenna was in front, clearly recovered from her headache, with Beeb and Sally trailing behind as she strode down the aisle of the bus, looking for seats. She had her hair up in some sort of mushrooming platinum bomb and her lips were twisted to the side as she moved past, her gaze flicking over the top of Cem's head. It was the first time he'd seen her face properly. Her nose was long and fine, her cheeks sharp and hectic with spots of colour. He waited for her to see him but she didn't, though Beeb and Sally waved as they went past.

Pascal twisted around and watched the girls find seats at the back of the bus. Cem heard him say *oh la la* under his breath, and then he introduced himself and Cem to the couple behind. Cem said hey to Phil (boring, protruding teeth, from Canberra) and Miriam (narrow watery eyes, Queensland somewhere), and for the next half-hour Pascal lectured the three of them about Australian politics. He had read the prime minister would be there, at Anzac Cove, and his wife, and old soldiers. The whole thing was very interesting. Miriam kept blowing her nose.

They drove into the night. People went to the front of the bus and sang along to music, mostly American rock. Ekrim was a conscientious host, standing up the front smoking and regularly coughing into the microphone between songs, explaining the history of Çanakkale and the peninsula. People had beer and were swapping seats, but Cem didn't see the girls again until later, when they stopped for a toilet break which led to a game of cricket in the street.

It was three am and cold. Cem got off the bus and stood huddled in his jumper. Phil and Miriam were standing together and Pascal was with the group of three girls. Jenna was wearing a green beanie and drinking a bottle of beer. Cem looked up at the black sky, avoiding eye contact, but Pascal called out to him and waved him over, so he went and stood with them and said hi and Jenna said hi, and he said they'd met and she said really? She couldn't remember. They stood, silent, while Beeb and Sally and Pascal engaged in intense conversation about *Neighbours*.

'It's cold,' Jenna said after a while. 'Aren't you cold?'

He was freezing but said he was fine. He'd left his coat on the bus but didn't want to go and get it, didn't want to lose his position, not now she was finally talking to him.

'Listen,' she said, tipping the bottle into the air and finishing it. Her lips were wet. 'Can you tell me one thing?'

Cem nodded and stepped forward. Here we go, he thought. Anything, he wanted to say. I will tell you anything.

'Do you think you're a nice person?'

It wasn't what he expected, but he answered without hesitation.

'Of course.'

'So you're decent, kind, all that? I'm not talking about with kittens or children.'

She moved, taking a tiny step towards him. He would remember that step and how he thought it was encouragement when, really, it had been a concession, an attempt at discretion. Her voice was low, intimate.

'It's not going to happen. I know your type. You think you're a nice bloke but you're not, not really. You think we are all so easy.' She did something with her lips, a kind of twisting that was a faux softening, an almost apology but not. It was a full stop, a conclusion, and with it she turned away and went up the steps to the bus.

Cem wanted to follow her, grab her arm and ask what his type was, whether she could please explain it all to him. That his parents and grandfather seemed to think they knew too, everyone was certain about something when what *he* felt was that his mouth and nostrils were at some sort of Plimsoll line. It was like his body was a desperate machine, and he was working hard to keep above the surface of the water. Beyond that, all he was aware of, all he was sure of, was that he'd been hot and urgent for her but hadn't known how to make it happen, and now she had said it *wasn't* going to happen and it was devastating. He wanted to follow her and say he would do anything she asked of him, if she would please just not say no, not disregard him. But he didn't speak and he didn't move, just allowed himself to hate her as she walked away. He waited five minutes more then went and found his seat and pretended to be asleep as they drove the final kilometres to the war site.

Once they got there, he would have preferred to stay on the bus and sleep; he didn't want to see any fucking graves. But he was hustled off the bus by Sally or Beeb, he still didn't know which was which. Whoever it was pulled at his arm.

'Come on,' she said. 'It's your heritage.'

He said wait a minute and pulled on his jacket. His shame made him follow them onto the beach, where they stood in cold silent groups, their breaths frosty in the black night. He'd hated Pascal for being cocky but he was no better. He'd been so sure of himself.

When Sally said she was thirsty, Cem passed her his water. When Beeb said she wouldn't mind some chewing gum, he found someone who had a piece to spare. He waited for Jenna to ask for something, so he could show he wasn't what she thought he was, but she asked for nothing.

After the ceremony, after the bugle, the speeches, the poetry and more music—respectful tunes, not Ekrim's Bruce Springsteen—they went to the cemeteries to read the headstones. One had an inscription by Atatürk, and Cem stood in front of it, sick with resentment. He didn't read the words that made the others sniff; he didn't care about any of it. He waited as they read. He thought about all sorts of other things: whether people ever ate kebabs for breakfast (he would, definitely); when he would be able to go to the toilet (a bit of back-up was in process); whether he should try one of the other two girls (maybe, maybe not); why it was he should feel embarrassed or ashamed about what had happened, when she was the one who'd been a bitch to him.

He stood, hands in pockets and shoulders hunched, kicking at stones while Beeb and Sally wiped their eyes on their sleeves. Pascal wouldn't shut up about how he could feel the *emotion* of the place, infused as it was with *memory* and *pain* and *heroism*. That even if you hadn't been there as the bullets punched into the flesh of young men, you could still *feel* it, couldn't you? Beeb and Sally agreed. Jenna didn't say anything, but she raised her eyebrows and once, just once, caught Cem's eye then looked away. He couldn't feel any of the heroism and emotion, but he was in pain, standing there, swaying on his feet with tired anger. The Frenchman's urgency intensified and he stepped towards Cem, asking the question again, so Cem said yes, sure, he could feel it, all the pain and heroism.

'I think you don't, you are just saying that you do. I think all you care is about her.' Pascal pointed at the three girls walking away. 'It's only about girls for men like you, isn't it?' He smiled but in a nasty way. He turned to walk back to the bus.

'Fuck the girls,' Cem called after him.

Up ahead, the group of girls turned around and Jenna opened her arms and curtseyed, a movement that told him he had proven her point.

Everyone was back on the bus, sitting in different spots, having made new friends, formed new groups. Cem found an empty seat and dozed all the way back to Istanbul. The party, it seemed, was over, and even tour guide Ekrim seemed to know it as he roamed the aisle in a diminished state, disconsolate as he offered thermos tea to anyone who was still awake.

Back in the city, standing on the street beside the bus, Cem waited for Pascal. The Frenchman had been sitting up the back with the girls, and their loud laughter had punctuated the quiet of the bus on the long journey back. Pascal was hand in hand with Sally, or Beeb, and Jenna was with them. Cem called out to Pascal, who came over.

'You know what your problem is?' Cem said to him. 'You make people think you're a nice guy, but you're a bit of a bastard, if you ask me.' Cem smiled hard, his eyes were stinging.

'Me?' Pascal laughed. 'I'm a regular person. I do the right things, I don't hurt people.' He turned towards the girls who were standing waiting for him. 'See?'

Pascal rejoined the girls and the four of them walked away.

Cem stood for a while on the street watching them go. He was sad and furious and something else as well. It felt like fear.

IV

That afternoon, when he went to the girls' pension to ask about them, the manager had a sly smile on his face as he told Cem that the girls had already left Istanbul.

'She's very beautiful, that one,' the man said, touching his moustache. 'The one with the golden hair. Like rice pudding.' He moved a hand over his chest.

Cem walked to his room and lay on his bed. Everything was wrong. He wondered where Harry was. He wondered if he should eat something, but he wasn't hungry. He sat on the toilet for a while, then climbed into bed and went back to sleep.

Chapter 6

I

On Thursday night, as arranged, Cem and Harry went to dinner with İbrahim. They drove in the taxi, the road spiralling downhill from the hotel. The darkness at the bottom of the winding road seemed to draw Cem in as he sat in the front seat, determined not to think about her.

'Bosphorus is good for fish sandwich,' İbrahim said, as he steered with one hand and pointed at the water with the other. He was speaking in English to include Harry. 'You can find boat there. Turk cost is eight hundred lira, but they try ripping you and him both.' He waved at Harry, who sat in the back, red-eyed, his briefcase clutched between his knees, glasses slipping down his nose. Every few hundred metres he pushed them back into place with his index finger.

'Ah,' said İbrahim. 'To live without fish in bread is to not live at all. I am writing poems about fish in bread.' Cem suspected the taxi driver was revealing an earnest and intimate part of himself; not just as poet but as lover of fish sandwiches. 'They are God's work and proof of the True Sublime.'

Cem had hoped to avoid any conversation about religion. He didn't feel up to socialising, still bruised by Jenna's rejection. He'd started to think he might be feeling lonely.

Harry had spent the previous day resting in bed, he'd told Cem when they'd caught up at breakfast that morning. Harry would come to this dinner, he said, but he was keen to leave the next day; he needed to be on his way. He'd tapped the top of his briefcase as he said it.

'You don't believe?' İbrahim was saying as he swung the taxi around a large roundabout, past another mosque on the left, and drove onto Galata Bridge.

'In the fish sandwich?'

'What does it say on your ID card?'

'It says Islam. Of course.'

'Yes, of course. Does your mother cover?'

Hanife hadn't worn a scarf when he was little, but she did these days, and Cem said so.

'She does?' İbrahim blew out smoke. 'You have good family then. That is supreme.' He put a hand on Cem's shoulder. 'I am religion.'

They went over the bridge and passed a taxi rank where monster Cadillacs idled, their drivers lounging along the sides, men who were whippet-thin and wore mostly brown slacks. Cem's head craned to look at the cars.

'Who does not like Caddy?' İbrahim said, noticing the cars. 'Very beauty, supreme auto. You can buy here and drive to your village.'

'Really?' Cem said. 'They'd be expensive, wouldn't they?'

'Oh yes, too much.'

Cem looked out the window at the street winding up in front of them, not thinking about Jenna.

II

At the restaurant, the waiter brought a bottle of *rakı* and a tub of ice with a spoon, a bottle of water, a basket of bread. Cem reached for the bread, but İbrahim took the *rakı* and started pouring. Harry's hand was shaking as he reached for his glass.

'Bottoms up, this will help,' Harry warbled and drank it down.

'Cheers! Health and power to the mighty Saddam!' İbrahim took a tiny sip and, without prompting, began to tell them his story. Like many other workers in Istanbul, he had moved to the city when he was eighteen.

'My family,' he said, speaking through a mouthful of bread and olives, 'they laugh when I said I want to become driver. In my village, my father never drive anything but donkey or maybe trap cart. One time he goes on farmer tractor, we can never make him stop to talk about it. How many horses it was equal to; how comfortable the saddle; how red the paint. When I said my dream becoming taxi driver in Istanbul, they laugh at me and my father, he laugh most loud. They say I lucky having my own pack donkey, that I should stay blacksmith learner. This make me too much angry. When I eighteen my mother give me one gold wristling. She saving that wristling many years from wedding dowry. Waiting to give me for my dream.'

İbrahim drank from his milky glass and a fat tear rolled out from under one eyelid and came to rest on the end of his nose. Cem looked wildly at Harry, but Harry was staring out across the street.

'My mother has very beauty heart.' İbrahim ate a stuffed vine leaf and reached for another. 'But I very angry, with all these feelings. I sell wristling for ticket to Istanbul. I catch bus with little bit money in my pocket. All we men in this country has is big hopes with empty pocket. Some days I think for us to stay small, in our shit villages is better. This city, she making us too sad.'

Cem started to agree, but Harry interjected. 'No.' He was half standing, leaning over the table, the taxi driver's wrist caught in his hand. 'You were right to follow your dreams. The first and most important thing a man must do is identify his quest. The second thing he has to do is complete it. You have succeeded already, don't you see?' Harry released the taxi driver's hand, sat down and held up his briefcase. 'On the matter of dreams, all will be revealed.'

İbrahim grabbed Harry around the neck and kissed him on his cheek.

'Harray, I not understand your speaking, my friend, but you is clever man! I am believe you! We live in this crumbling city, we have black feeling in our hearts. Music makes it blacker, all the broken people around us, but still we are proud, and still there is honour.'

He poured more *rakı* into their glasses.

'So, you,' İbrahim said to Cem, his face serious. 'What is your dream, little brother? What did come like pushy pigeon into your heart when you little boy?'

‘I don’t know,’ Cem said. Sometimes he wanted to fight and sometimes he wanted to fuck and they were about the only two firm thoughts that seemed to ever drop out of the swirling morass of stuff that was inside of him.

‘How can you not? You must to know who you are and what man you want to become.’ İbrahim leaned back in his seat. ‘You remind me of someone. You are like poor man being given cucumber who says no because it is crooked. Ah, I know! You are Karagöz, shadow puppet. A flat man.’

Cem’s grandfather had called him Karagöz and he had hated it.

‘I’m not a fucking puppet,’ he said.

‘You say fuck to me?’ İbrahim squinted at Cem. ‘I say fuck to you. You are old enough for big dreams now. Do you know what sort of woman do you want to marry? Are you even heterosexualist? These are the questions a man must think about.’

Cem couldn’t trace how this had happened. Instead of eating, drinking and watching out for girls on the street down south somewhere, they were talking about difficult things. A mad taxi driver and an old man from Wangaratta. With a briefcase.

‘You want woman like your mother?’ İbrahim was eating salad now, forking it up to his mouth.

‘Maybe not everyone has a plan,’ Cem said, ignoring the question. He couldn’t bring himself to say the word ‘quest’.

‘Of course they do. But know who you are, this is the first thing,’ Harry insisted, his eyelids fluttering as he concentrated on forming the words. ‘You must stop floating and begin to swim.’

İbrahim slapped a hand on the academic’s shoulder and laughed. Harry flinched but the taxi driver threw back his head and the veins in his throat were rigid. They were the neck veins of a real man, Cem thought. Even Harry, who was shuffling vaguely much of the time, with his thick glasses that made his eyes look too big, even he looked sure and somehow impressive in that moment.

'But it takes time,' Cem said. 'To work all those things out.'

İbrahim lunged forward. 'That is chicken shit. I say to you it is making excuse. I know who I am when I am ten.'

'Oh, yes,' agreed Harry. 'We have to find something that matters. Know ourselves.'

Cem thought about knowing and he thought about mattering.

'In fact,' said Harry, pushing his glasses back up his nose with a shaking middle finger, 'it's not the goal that's the most important. Can it be the getting to it?'

No, Cem wanted to say. Harry was talking in circles and not making sense.

İbrahim said, 'I start as oldest shoeshine boy. Everyone laughed to me and gangs of eight-year boys kicked me from too many street corner. I have to find new corners for my working. I working too hard, five years and slowly my English improving. It is not always supreme quality your ears enjoy tonight.' İbrahim pushed his tongue into his cheek and rubbed at a smear of baba ganoush that had dropped onto his shirt. '*Sheizen*.' He licked his thumb.

Cem was drunk. There was something he wanted to say, something about neck veins, something about a quest, maybe something about identity. There were thoughts in his mouth, emotions that tasted familiar, something to do with the legendary dancer Zeynep or another girl—no, not her. He looked up. Harry was studying the cobblestones and İbrahim was talking to his left arm.

'I work as commission man for carpet shop and slowly I come to be salesman,' the taxi driver was saying. 'Everybody like me too much. I work in bathhouse, I am good massage man. I buy gold and some American *dolar.* I meet rich foreign ladies, I take them dancing and I make fuck to them. All this time, my plan is to be taxi driver. What more better job is there in this city? Everyone else crawling like snake on their stomach to rich tourist, bastard carpet boss, museum operator, polices. But to be taxi driver is big honour job. Of course there are bastard drivers. Listen to me, this important. You cannot sell carpets without lying; you *can* drive taxi and be honest man. It can be very possible.'

Harry looked like he'd dozed off, his glasses propped up on his head with one arm still draped across the briefcase.

'Ah,' said İbrahim. 'Here is our fish. We start with sardines; these small beauties are the little brown birds of the sea. What do you call the little brown birds? To them you giving bread.'

'Sparrows?'

'Yes. Sparrow. They are plain and we don't think important, but for God, everything is important. For us everything must be have value. You have to understand. Ah, my friend. Look, look fish. Look this sparrow fish, it is so beauty. Supreme. We eat, we drink, we go to dancer.'

Cem looked at the table. The food, the cigarettes, the drinks. The chef appeared and placed another platter on the table, a single large whole fish.

İbrahim pulled off the head and slid it onto Cem's plate. 'For you, the best section. You have a sickness, you have *hüzün.* Here let me check you.' The taxi driver's fingers closed around Cem's wrist. The bastard was taking his pulse! He tried to peel İbrahim's fingers off.

'Now,' said the taxi driver. 'I can feel the beat. Tell me her name! I will diagnose you.'

Cem pulled away.

'You have the black pain,' İbrahim said. 'It came with you, yes, it's always been inside like a seed, but now it is watered with the air of Istanbul. Smell it!'

Cem inhaled and coughed, a piece of bread catching in his throat.

'What is your fear, my little brother? Because it is there, I know it is. You tell me and I give you cure. We will find something to fix you. You can walk the Bosphorus like tragedy man or you will find some street and look at the building that are broken like your spirit inside, like in every old film.'

Cem pushed the hair off his forehead and sipped at his drink. He ignored İbrahim's raving, ignored the fish head. In the morning he'd pay his hotel bill and leave. He would swim not float. He'd go to a beach. Find the heat and spend some time lying near water during the day and drinking beer and eating kebabs at night. He picked up the fish head. He would say goodbye to the historian and he would grow a beard. He would start smoking. He looked at the fish head. He would suck the brains.

There was a sound, the final call to prayer for the night. Cem sat and listened. İbrahim was sliding to the side, draining his glass. Harry was still dozing in the corner, his bony hands clutching the briefcase. The sound of the mosque lengthened through the night air, then the moment was gone and all that was left was the clinking of cutlery, the shifting of wooden chairs and the sounds of people eating and drinking and talking and laughing. Cem came to himself and realised they were right, that Jenna was right. He didn't know anything about himself. All he knew was that he was sitting in a busy alleyway in Istanbul holding a fish head.

'I don't know how to make things happen,' he said, but nobody heard him.

He looked at Harry and İbrahim. 'I don't know how.' He looked at the fish head in his hand, and felt what he guessed must be despair. 'To make things happen,' he told the fish.

III

The sun came through the window and hit the bed. Cem stood under the shower, which was alternately fiercely hot and dribbling cold. Then he dressed and went to the garden for breakfast, his hair dripping and his neck stiff.

The tea arrived loaded with sugar and he tried to flick it out of the glass with a spoon before it dissolved. Last night, shortly after he'd dropped the fish head under the table, they'd gone to the supper club, where the promised *danseuse* had been tacky and ordinary. They'd reeled from the club, drunk and rowdy, and he and Harry somehow found their way back to the hotel, but not without Cem sliding down a wall which moved as he stopped and leaned against it, knocking his chin on his knee as he sat on the footpath. With Harry weaving over the top of him, telling him to get up, get up, he finally, embarrassingly, vomited in the gutter. Cem had apologised to Harry, who'd merely said, 'Oh dear, my boy. No need to apologise.'

Soon after, İbrahim arrived and sat down. He was freshly shaved, cologned and impossibly robust.

'Good morning. Today we buying you car.'

'What?' Cem squinted up at the taxi driver. The sun was bright.

'To drive to your village. We talked it last night. My friend has brother selling supreme car. We go and look. You can drive, Harry said he will take bus to his. I offer to take him but he say no. Maybe Harry village near your village, then you can go together.'

Cem had no memory of any of this and began to say he didn't want a car, that he didn't have any money, but İbrahim said they should wait for Harry, so Cem put some cheese on his bread and took a bite. He ate an olive. He needed some sunglasses, maybe some fake Ray-Bans. That would be his plan. Where had the girls said they were going? Black Sea or Rhodes via Marmaris? Or south? He might go there too.

Harry came into the garden. 'Well,' he said, rubbing his hands together. 'Nice to have a plan, isn't it?'

Cem didn't respond. When he'd finished breakfast he was going to explain that he was going his own way. He would take a bus, he didn't need a car.

Harry put his briefcase on his lap and clicked it open. He pulled out a map and spread it on the table, pushed his glasses back up his nose and looked at Cem, magnified eyes blinking behind the lenses. Cem slipped another olive into his mouth and İbrahim stood over them and sipped tea.

'If our villages are in completely different directions then we have a little problem, but if they are close maybe we can manage something with the car.'

Cem relaxed. There was no chance the villages would be near each other.

İbrahim scanned the map. 'Hayat, Hayat, you say near Izmir—' he whispered. 'Here.' He placed a finger. 'Now, which is your one?' He looked at Harry questioningly.

Harry stared at the map. 'I don't believe it,' he said, taking off his glasses. 'Kismet is too gentle a word. This'—he gestured at the map—'is fate. It seems a larger arrangement has been made by the universe and we would be fools to meddle. I have been researching something for almost my whole life. The reason I became an historian was because of a few old stories from my childhood, some neighbourhood talk.'

Harry's face had become quite red. He patted the briefcase. 'Such a cliché, isn't it? "Long-lost papers about an exotic land. Unbelievable revelations. A secret that will explode so many of Australia's notions about—" Well, I can't say any more just now.' He glanced at İbrahim, then back at Cem.

Cem sat, confused. It was a huge coincidence. He felt the promise of lazing by the beach fading. Maybe he'd forget the village, tell them he'd changed his mind.

'This very good,' said İbrahim. 'Two friends, same village. I don't must to worry about you mens.' He lit a cigarette. 'You will look after yous together.'

This was the moment to say he'd changed his plans, Cem decided, but before he could speak the taxi driver had stood up, swinging his keys around his fingers, flipping them like worry beads. 'Now I drive you my friend-brother workplace, at the bus station, we buy car, we say goodbye and I will cry too much. Bring your bags, you will drive into village like kings in Caddy.'

'What?' said Cem.

'Yes, it is Cadillac. Very beauty auto, supreme.'

The sun grew even brighter.

'I suppose we can look at it,' Cem said, eating the last olive and standing up. There was no harm in having a look. A Cadillac. And at the bus station, once there he could decide. Whether to get on a bus south or not. 'Why not?' Cem said. 'There's no hurry.'

IV

The bus station was crowded and boys carried trays of tea, weaving in and out among smoking touts who shifted like water and shouted their destinations to travellers. Everything was an assault. Harry and Cem were introduced to a man called Çetin and they shook hands.

'Let's go, car is this way,' he said.

They followed Çetin through the bedlam and out the other side of the bus station. Around the corner was the car. It was a 1953 Eldorado Cadillac, İbrahim told them, and it stood beautiful and glossy with all its panels straight. It was perfect. Cem walked around the front, looking at the double grille, the V-shaped piece under the insignia, the hood ornament. The taxi sign was still on the roof. They climbed in and he smelled the leather polish. There was a blue charm hanging from the rear-vision mirror.

'How did it get here?' he managed to say. İbrahim was standing in the open door.

‘My friend’s brother, he work in Adana near US base. He a-fuck crazy. One day he come Istanbul for find the girl he love. It is too stupid, driving all that long way without making telephone, and of course, when he arriving the girl is married. Car now has bad atmosphere. He selling.’

Cem saw it all. The road trip, the radio playing, the wailing songs of yearning and heartbreak, crying all the way to Istanbul to find his love long gone. The man strolls through the old parts of the city, or stands on the bridge watching the seagulls. It was one of the traditional narratives of this country, this place where love and loss were somehow the same. His grandfather had described all the old movies to him when he was a boy.

‘Wow,’ he said, thinking he wouldn’t do something like that. He’d find another girl.

‘Yes. We Turkish.’ İbrahim bent his head and the back of his meaty neck was shiny in the sun. ‘We love to love.’

Cem looked into the man’s eyes, saw that they were moist with some remembered emotion of his own. He looked away and held on to the steering wheel. He stared out the windscreen, straight ahead.

‘No, it’s too big,’ Harry said over his shoulder to the taxi driver. ‘We can’t drive this. It’s too yellow. And a taxi? People will try to flag us down all the time. No, I don’t think this is the car for us.’

Cem started to speak, but Harry kicked out and caught him on the shin. The older man’s eyes were wild and circling.

‘But you can switch off the sign,’ said İbrahim. ‘It is here.’ He reached forwards, pointing.

‘How will it go up mountains?’ Harry said. ‘How can we be sure this vehicle is compliant with safety regulations? Are there registration papers? Where are the seatbelts? I'm not convinced this car conforms to international legislative requirements.'

Cem ran his hands around the white steering wheel, which was cool under his fingers. This car was all hope and all desire. He tried to work out how much money he had: some in the bank, some travellers' cheques. He could get a job. He had an ID card. Maybe he could work in a carpet shop, or a kebab shop. His Turkish wasn't great but it would probably do. He could work to buy this car. He had to have this car. He had never in his life wanted a thing so much.

'You are joking to us,' İbrahim said to Harry. 'Is too beauty car. What is your offer?'

'We don't offer anything. We don't want it.' Harry got out of the car and shut the door on Cem. 'Let's smoke,' Harry said.

Çetin climbed out of the car as well, speaking to İbrahim in rapid Turkish.

Cem's hands were locked on the wheel. He couldn't get out. He looked over at Harry, who was holding a cigarette awkwardly between his third and fourth fingers, his hand lifted to chin, palm upwards, looking regretful.

İbrahim and Çetin's arms were windmilling, scraping through the air, hands chopping rapidly from right to left and back again as they pressed their common point home to the older man. Fingers were pinched together to form inverted bird beaks and vibrated in front of Harry's face. Harry remained calm, shaking his head, shrugging every thirty seconds as if to say *what can I do?* He flicked ash from the cigarette to the ground and put the tip to his mouth, took a small puff and blew it straight out without inhaling.

Cem prised one hand from the wheel and let it drop to the seat. The upholstery was firm to the touch and he wanted to slide down onto it and cry. He felt sick with disappointment. The door opened and Harry climbed back in. His face was grey. He reached out to the indicator controls. His fingers were trembling.

'Irregular flashing,' Harry said loudly.

'Harry,' Cem moaned.

'We've got it.' He opened his hand and Cem saw the car keys.

Çetin popped his head in the window, smiling. İbrahim's face was pushing in as well. Çetin handed Cem a small bottle of cologne. 'All journeys require *limon kolonya*.'

Harry slumped back in the seat.

'You'd better drive, Cem; all this excitement has triggered my back and the pain is not good. We'll need some alcohol, as soon as you can stop. I'm in a bit of a spot now and it'll only get worse.'

They pulled out of the bus station, their bags in the boot.

'Auf wiedersehen,' İbrahim shouted, waving. His nose was red and streaming and he was patting his eyes. 'Goodbye, you two mens. Goodbye, goodbye.'

As they drove, Cem whooped and shimmied his shoulders and clicked his fingers and sang *na-na-na*. Then he stopped. He had no idea where they were going. They were heading back from the bus station towards the old part of Istanbul.

'Here,' said Harry, pointing. 'Stop.'

'What?' Cem stopped the car and looked across. Harry's face was waxy and grey.

'It's like a leviathan swelling from the deep.' He wrenched his torso and clutched at his lower back and said 'blast'. 'Can you get me a couple of bottles, please? Something strong.' He pointed at a shop nearby then looked back at Cem with enormous eyes, and Cem again registered the shakiness. He had noticed that sometimes when Harry talked his eyelids fluttered as though he was losing consciousness by being so deeply in thought, or perhaps by being in distress. His eyeballs were starting to roll now. Cem went into the shop and came back with two bottles of liquor in a plastic bag. As he reached for the door handle, a man opened the back door.

'It's not a taxi,' Cem said and waved the man away.

They drove a little further up the street. At a red light, two women wearing scarves tried to get into the back and Cem said again that it wasn't a taxi, speaking to them through the open window.

'But it's got a sign,' one of the women said, gesturing at the roof.

They went through the streets with people trying to flag them down, Harry saying he thought that turning the taxi light on meant they were unavailable, and Cem saying he believed it was the opposite. They argued, and Harry moaned and clutched at his back intermittently, until they reached a motorway that was signposted to Izmir.

V

They stopped to eat at a cafeteria in Yalova and Harry went to the bathroom. Cem saw a familiar-looking girl at one of the booths and he went over and stood beside her. She was alone, but on the bus to

Gallipoli she'd been with a guy, the boring one with big teeth. He said hello and she looked up. He could tell she didn't recognise him. He ran his hand through his hair.

'Are you okay?'

She said she wasn't. He sat down opposite her. There were scrunched-up tissues in her hands and she was picking her fingernails. She dabbed at her eyes. He wiped his thumb across his chin.

'You don't remember me?'

Cem reminded her about where they'd met and she said maybe she remembered him, but she didn't look sure. She told him that Phil had stayed behind in Istanbul. Cem asked what she was doing, where she was going, and she said she didn't know. She'd been on a bus but had got off because it was hot and made her feel sick and one of the bus workers kept staring at her and trying to talk to her.

'Guys can be idiots sometimes.' Cem smiled, but she didn't smile back. She was drab and limp under the fluorescent lights and her hair was dirty. Every time he looked at her she seemed different, but he quite liked her droopiness. She would never grab his elbow, shove a cigarette into his face or press anything on him. She wouldn't push him to put sugar in his tea.

'Do you have a plan?'

'Not really. I was going to go to Izmir. I don't even know why, but that's what I decided. I might go south. Maybe Phil will come to Izmir.'

Cem shifted on the seat. At university, he had gone out with a girl, Anna. He had never been sure why they were even together, but it had happened somehow. She'd taken him in hand, this severe, practical science student with perfect skin, soft lips and a surprising honking laugh that made her even more attractive, but somehow she'd remained out of his reach. She'd broken off their short relationship when he asked her to make him a coffee.

'I refuse on principle,' she said. 'I will not kowtow to your Islamic patriarchy.'

Cem had been puzzled as he drove home that night, his mind circling the word. Kowtow. He'd made her coffee twice while she was studying for an exam. That night, the night of *his* coffee, it was the first time he'd ever asked for anything from her. He hadn't told his parents the details of what had happened, just that they weren't going out anymore.

'What do you expect from an Australian girl?' his mother had sniffed, pleased. 'Don't marry Australian. They are lazy and cannot cook. Even a Greek girl would be better, but don't tell your father I said that.'

In the restaurant, Cem considered Miriam's shiny forehead. A hand dropped onto his shoulder. It was Harry, who sat down next to Cem, still moving gingerly but looking slightly revived.

Cem introduced Miriam.

Harry said how do you do and she said good thanks. The older man smiled politely and flipped open his briefcase to go through his papers.

'Do you want to travel with us for a while?' Cem said. Harry looked up. 'We're going through Izmir, we've got a car.'

'I'm not sure,' she said. One hand went to her hair, to her scalp, and she started to scratch. She put her hands across her face and her shoulders started to shake. Harry exhaled and slowly got up so Cem could slide out and go around to her side of the table. He sat next to her and was wondering what to say when she launched herself at him and pressed her forehead to his chest. Cem patted her. Her hair smelled of apples and cigarettes.

'I had a fight with Phil,' Mim said. 'I don't know what I'm doing. I saw the other Australian girls—do you remember them? They were on their way to Izmir. I should have gone with them.'

She tipped her face up to him and all her ordinariness was gone. She was almost lovely with her weepy eyes and red nose. Cem felt a beat in his throat at the mention of the others.

'You should come with us. You can ring Phil from Izmir. When did you see the others?'

She let go of him and took a sip of water. 'Okay,' she said.

'Was it today?'

She started to get her things together.

Outside, they stood in front of the Cadillac.

'This is your car?' she said. 'Bloody hell.'

VI

In Bursa, in the hotel lobby, Cem told Harry he and Mim had agreed to share a room. At first, Cem said it was because she didn't want to be on her own. Then he said it was because Harry snored, even in the car. Then he admitted, as he shuffled on the spot, that he thought he might be able to kiss her. He said this in a whisper and Harry held up his hands and said it was fine with him, far be it from him, etcetera etcetera. They went to their respective rooms for naps before dinner. Cem woke to find Mim sitting on the edge of her bed, watching him.

'Have you ever been in love?' she said.

He turned onto his back and stared at the ceiling, saying nothing.

'I'm not going to ring Phil. I want to keep travelling with you and your dad. In that car.'

It took Cem a moment to understand who she was talking about.

'That's not my dad. He's just someone I met.'

'Whoever. Can I stay with you two for a while?'

'It's okay with me.'

The next morning, they were on their way. Harry had slept well and his back was settled he announced. In the front passenger seat he had his briefcase open and was looking at papers, rapidly clicking his ballpoint pen in and out. Mim was quiet and unhappy in the back and Cem drove, bored, wondering once more how he had managed to get himself into this situation.

In Izmir, the hotel's rooms were overheated and had thick pink satin eiderdowns on the single beds. Cem went out for a walk, to check the streets. He bought Mim some spinach and cheese pastry. She said it wasn't as good cold but ate it sitting cross-legged on the bed anyway, licking her fingers one by one and wiping them dry on the bedspread.

He sat by the window and looked out to the street. A group of travellers walked past. Three guys and three girls, the guys joking, showing off and wrapping their arms around each other's necks, laughing back at the others who trailed behind. He recognised none of them. He'd know her even if he was looking down from the moon she was that bright, that apparent. The group disappeared around a corner. Behind him, Miriam was lying down again, making disgusting sucking noises as she tongued the pastry from around her teeth. He turned away from the window.

A bit later, she began to cry. She was starting to give him the shits.

'Do you want to talk?'

There was no answer, only sniffling. Eventually the noises stopped and he realised she'd fallen asleep. He stood and went to the window and rested his head on the glass, gazing at the car. Then he opened the window and leaned out. He heard a small cough. It was Harry, at his own window, leaning on his elbows.

'She's asleep again.'

'She sleeps a lot, that girl.'

'She's always in the toilet, too. I heard her spewing.'

The two men considered the car as the call to prayer started. When it finished Harry said that he was going to bed. Cem said he would too. They said goodnight and pulled their heads in.

Cem found it hard to sleep and lay awake for a long time looking at the ceiling. Any time Miriam shifted in her sleep or made small noises or sighed, he looked over, but as far as he could tell in the dark, her eyes were always closed.

VII

Mim was going to stay on in Izmir. She paid for another night at the hotel and went out to buy a big bag of pistachios and a supply of Coca-Cola. It was the only thing she wanted to drink. They said goodbye; Harry edgy and keen to get away, Cem horny and sullen.

They drove off, Harry calculating aloud the expected distance and time, and Cem surprised by how angry he felt.

VIII

They were headed east, a package of cheese and parsley pastries on the seat between them. As they drove, Cem told Harry his grandfather's theory of the Eleven Strings of the Oud.

'There's this dancer in the village. Her name's Zeynep. My grandfather said she is the best dancer he's ever seen and totally beautiful. Men don't usually see females dance but Zeynep is different. Her father is rich so she has more freedom than other girls and her mother is powerful, like a man herself my grandfather said. He also told me an oud player said that Zeynep was the only eleven-string dancer he'd ever seen.' Cem couldn't believe he was going to see Zeynep the dancer at last. 'There are eleven strings and this guy said for each string there are eleven parts of beauty which can be given to a dancer.'

'Eleven parts?'

'Right. Things like feet and chin and hair, the stomach . . . The stomach can't be flat, it needs to be curved. The point is, Zeynep was the only eleven-string dancer the musician had ever seen and he'd been travelling with wedding bands for forty years. I've wanted to see her since I was little.'

'Perhaps she is your quest, she of the eleven-string perfection? She whose ears must be just so, hips just so too.'

'I don't think there was anything about the ears,' Cem said. He was annoyed at himself for even telling Harry. When the idea of Zeynep was inside of him it made sense but became wrong once the words had been spoken aloud.

They drove on. They saw the great Kangal sheepdogs of the Anatolian plains sitting on rocky inclines with sharp haunches, dirty-white as they roamed beside the roads or huddled on the small rises with their backs to the hills, sheltered from the wind that raced through, denuding the land of grass and plants. Sheep stood nearby, under the watchful eyes of their grumpy and rheumatic canine overseers. Sometimes the dogs rushed at the car, getting so close that Cem could see the nicotine-tinge of their fur and the ferocity of their teeth.

'Big as lions,' Harry said. 'Goodness.'

By early evening, with the sun setting, they were crawling the final few kilometres up a steep mountain road. As they drove, the road narrowed to a roughly-sealed stretch. In the near distance, there was a village, a random scattering of buildings, the houses built right up along the boundary of the road. Cem saw a central square and a building strung with lanterns as decoration, already lit in the darkening night air. And that was when Harry told him to pull over and said he needed to tell him something.

'I have to tell you what brings me here,' Harry said.

'Okay,' said Cem.

When Harry was done, Cem laughed at the thought that Ned Kelly had a son. But after he stopped laughing, he sat in the car looking at the dog, aware of his breathing and of the thumping in his chest.

II

A Turkish rug is woven with an eye to symmetry. The field must be balanced and regardless of whether medallion or animal motifs are used, regularity is important. Some weavers talk of the 'intentional mistake' where a change in colour or pattern might be apparent because the belief is that only God can create something perfect.

PROFESSOR OSMAN HEYBELI,
DOBAG CARPET PROJECT

Chapter 7

I

My name is Berna, but it can also be the wind that wraps the mountain and the trees that surround it. I am as old as our hills. See my hand with its wrinkled back and veins large and ropey. I like my skin for it is my good and loyal friend. It keeps the insides of me from spilling out. My hands and face are friends too. They keep me fine company during the long hours of silence. It has been a quietness so complete I have listened to my hair grow white. I am an old woman now.

This concerns the past and I remember it well. Do not be deceived by this face for my brain remains magnificent. The dates are all there: my brother lost his hand in 1929; in the forties he won a large cash prize in the Turkish Aircraft Association Lottery, but it was too late by then. Too late for Ayşe.

I am old, but when you are invisible you learn much and all the narratives of my village are woven in front of me, not flat with two dimensions like the simple kilims that the girl children knot; no, these are as elaborate as the plushest hundred-percent-silk carpets, with their pile short cut but dense, as intricately crafted as clouds in the sky. See the base with its warps and wefts, the foundation built upon from there; the loops of thread, purest thread, the colours and motifs creating a form of which only I know the entire pattern.

It is true. I am the village's eyes and ears, but there is a collective heart outside of my own chest that beats in all of us. It beats here on top of this mountain in this village in Anatolia. It beats from the youngest, baby Sufi, who lies bound and clasped to her mother's leaking breasts, to the oldest, my brother Mehmet, who sits beside me on his fancy city-bought chair. It is true that most know my husband was a brutalist of the worst kind and that our headman Mustafa is a good man who needs a new wife. This is what we all know, but other things are only for me. I know that the beans this morning were wrong, but I know also that the beans are never wrong forever. I know that two men are coming up the mountain, at this moment, including the boy from far away. I wonder what my grandson's face will look like.

The children call me witch. Ever since I got bent and thin they have called me that. They think I fly through the night as a bee or walk on water as a frog, but I'm not the vengeful Al Bastı, I'm not the one who visits men in their sleep and makes them crazed. I don't twist trees as they grow or make the horses lather with foam, but that one, oh, she is coming. She will come and she will stir the boy's dreams too with her snake-hair and iron teeth. I know the boy is innocent, that it's his family soul which is guilty. Yes, I was left behind, but I am glad about it. I am sorry for my friend Ayşe, who died down the well. I promise I will tell you about her when it is time.

II

This morning, as the two men drove towards us in their yellow car, I read my brother's fortune. I try not to do it too often and I avoid telling all of it. No matter what they say, there are some things people prefer not to know.

I was sitting by the window when Mehmet arrived.

'I have a thirst for your tea and a reading,' he said as he came in. He settled at the table while I fussed at the stove. Then the girl Kehribar knocked on the door with some eggs she'd collected for me. I'm not too old to stoop, but she likes the work. I was not happy that she was there.

'Can I watch?'

I said no, but she stood in the doorway. She's a one, that stubborn rabbit, standing there, looking at me with her strange yellow eyes.

'Can I, Aunty?'

She takes advantage of me, a poor old woman without much power. In the corner my brother stopped himself from making a sign with his fingers. He never wants to hurt the child's feelings but superstition is strong. It isn't her fault that she has the eyes of an animal, but sometimes he forgets himself.

Looking at the grounds in a cup or the lines on a hand or the fall of the beans in the dirt, I can see a thing with perfect clarity, and the whole fate of the person is laid out in front of me. These days, I keep from looking too closely and try to squint at the truth so that all that forms in the air are the ordinary details. I talk about bread that won't rise or perhaps a spoiled bowl of yoghurt. These are the things I am happy to share. Any of the other village matters that fall through the net I keep to myself; the affairs, infanticides and lies. The darkness that people carry around inside of them. I will keep his thing to myself. Life is better with surprises in the recipe.

This morning, the problem was the girl. Kehribar can read the beans as well as me, maybe better, and she thinks people should be told the truth. We discuss it often, this idea of truth and its opposite, how to be kind can also mean not telling everything; that even when things are under our noses sometimes it's better to let your eyes slide away. This girl is always asking, wanting to change my thinking.

'But what if it is our headman, your father, and you had to tell him about an accident?' I say. 'How could you speak such words?'

'He would understand,' she says. 'People need to know the truth. How can they believe in life if they don't know the future?'

The child is only that. She hasn't lived long enough to learn that people want to be lied to, that even when they are told the truth they tell themselves lies. One day she will understand how the world turns. That faith does not spin on truth; that it spins on belief.

Mehmet called Kehribar over to the table and she sat down. I frowned at him, but he ignored me. My brother and I are close and we don't need words. I sat to throw the beans. He told me not to sigh. I told him to *soos*. The foreigners were coming closer in their big yellow car but were still several hours away. I reached for the beans and tossed them on top of the table.

I began with my usual sweet stuff, making sure to sugar the words. I told the old man he would live many more winters in good health, but something caught at my eye, something green and slippery, and before I could even look at her, send her to the stove to check the kettle, Kehri's mouth had dropped open and the room became still.

'Tell me,' the old man said. 'Tell me everything, Berna.'

'See, Aunty?' Kehri said. 'He wants the truth.'

I put my hands in my lap and held them there. Mehmet turned to the girl and asked her what she had seen. My own mouth moved but the girl spoke, and it was too late because she talked quickly, saying the words she shouldn't.

'There is a seven here, seven birds falling from the sky. One bird might be an hour or a day, it could be a week, or a month even but I don't think it will be that long.'

'Don't think what will be that long?'

'It's to do with time. Seven is the amount of time until something happens to you. A green darkness is coming and your breath will end. Probably this means you will die. In seven days, I think, not hours.' She paused. 'And there will be a bird.'

I swept the beans away to make a pile at the side and stood. I went to take the kettle off the stove. Maybe some apple tea would hush her, I thought, but madam said no thank you, she'd better be getting back to her sisters, they needed help in the house. She kissed my brother's hand and pressed it to her forehead. She did the same to me but wouldn't look at my face. She left, waving at us over her shoulder as she passed through the door. Impudent child.

'I'm sorry.'

'Don't be ridiculous,' Mehmet said. 'This is marvellous. Get me my stick. I have a week to make sure everything is finished.' He was delighted and rubbing his hands together. I watched him walk up the road from my doorstep.

Chapter 8

I

Cem stopped laughing and turned the key in the ignition. The car moved towards the village. The dog lunged and Harry gave a yell and leaned in towards Cem.

'You told them you were coming?'

'No.' Cem wiped his hand across his mouth. It was stupid to be arriving late in the day, with no warning, and with a man who believed Ned Kelly had a son. They drove into the square.

'How's your Turkish?' Harry said.

'Not great.'

They parked near the building, which Cem could see was a tea house with a garden to the side of it.

The man who'd been sitting outside walked forwards to meet them and there was a loud crackling noise overhead, the hiss of an amplifier, the intake of human breath and then a shuddering cacophony as the call to prayer played from a tiny mosque nearby. Harry paused at the sound, smiling, but Cem wanted to put his hands over his ears. In Istanbul the sound had come in waves from a distance, soft and muted; here it was an oppressive screeching from above.

People crowded out from the building and a tall man came towards them, pushing barrel-chested through the crowd. He had the head of a bear and Cem knew exactly who he was. He put out his hand to say hello.

'I am Mustafa,' the village chief confirmed.

Cem introduced himself as Ali and Hanife's son, and Mustafa grabbed Cem's hand, pulled him forward into a hearty embrace and kissed him on both cheeks with vigorous affection. Cem introduced Harry and he received the same violent welcome. While the villagers were clutching at Harry, Cem looked around. Located on a narrow road, the festively-decorated tea house stood facing a row of buildings that had to be residences. Built right up to the edge of the street, with white-washed or turquoise doors, the houses were modest and neat. There was a central open area, where a fountain was situated, constructed upon a stone base. The tea house itself had rough plaster walls, patchy with paint that had faded to pastels, and Cem could see the lanterns had been tied onto vines that spread across the front wall.

They were taken inside and Mustafa led them to chairs and waved a hand for tea. An old man with a stick was ushered into the group.

'This is Ahmet's son?' said the old man, who was introduced to Cem as Old Mehmet. 'My cousin has another son?' The old man was missing a hand. Cem's grandfather had talked about this cousin who'd lost his hand in a riding accident. He told the old man he was Ali's son, Ahmet's grandson. The old man handed his stick to one of the younger men who stood around the table. He reached forwards to grab Cem with his good hand.

'This is my grandfather's cousin,' Cem said to Harry over the din. 'But in Turkey all the older men are called "Uncle".'

Old Mehmet held on to Cem and kissed him and cried with happiness to see this boy here in the village after how many years? He turned to Mustafa with tears on his cheeks.

'How long has it been?' he cried. 'And why didn't *you* say anything about this?' He was shouting at an elderly woman standing nearby but she just lifted a hand, as unconcerned as if she were testing the weight of a cotton seed. Her eyes were fixed on Cem.

'It was the year of the Arçelik,' the old woman said. Everyone fell silent. 'That was when they left, when the first refrigerator arrived. It was 1966.' Heads nodded.

'This is Ali's boy,' Old Mehmet said to the old woman who had taken a seat. Around the table, men touched their moustaches. 'Can you see?'

'I know who he is,' she said.

'Ahmet's grandson? Why has he come?' someone said. 'Trouble always finds this village.'

Mustafa got up from the table. The old woman was staring at Cem but her face was blank. Nobody introduced her. 'I know who you are,' she said again.

There was silence. Cem didn't know what to say so he looked around the room. It was spacious and the walls were furnished with embroideries and small kilims. The Turkish flag was positioned at one end, along with a picture of Atatürk. Small clusters of wooden tables were scattered about, and it seemed there was some kind of function happening. Maybe a wedding, he thought, or a circumcision party, but he couldn't see any small boys with feathered hats and capes nor miserable-looking brides and their terrified-looking grooms. That might be why females were there too, such as girls carrying trays of food across the wooden floor, one of whom had stopped in the middle of the room and was staring at him right now.

Mustafa was beside her, speaking into her ear, telling her something while tipping his head back and pointing at Cem with his chin. The girl's expression of surprise changed to one of fear, starting in her eyes then bleeding across her mouth, causing it to gape and stretch. Mustafa walked away and she stayed standing in the middle of the room, until a younger girl came and pulled at her arm to make her move again. The two of them disappeared through a door at the other side of the hall.

Mustafa sat down again and Cem turned back to the table. Food was brought and he ate. Drinks were brought, tea and *rakı*. Harry stirred from his silence and accepted a glass of the aniseed spirit.

'That was my daughter,' Mustafa told Cem. 'She has good eyes and is a careful girl. Did you see her?'

Cem nodded slowly.

'Ali's boy has come home to us,' the old woman said, and then the villagers were all talking at once, asking him questions, clamouring to know: Was he married? Had he been to military? Did he have a sweetheart? Did they have a big house in the other country? How many refrigerators were there? What did he think Saddam was up to?

He did his best to answer between bites of food. He told them he had deferred his military service, because of university. That their house had three bedrooms. That he wasn't married. A young man came and stood by the table and was introduced as Cevap. Cevap took Cem's hand and shook it, then kissed him on each cheek, smiling as he welcomed him. He offered to take Cem on a tour of the village the next day, but Mustafa stood up and interjected, escorting Cevap outside. Cem watched the headman in the doorway, holding up a finger in front of the young man's face. Harry was smiling and nodding, not understanding anything that was being said around him. Cem remembered Zeynep, the dancer.

'Is Zeynep here?' he asked Mustafa, who had sat back down and was lighting a cigarette. The headman snapped his lighter shut and exhaled smoke. He looked down his nose at Cem and said that she was. Then Mustafa sighed and said his business never seemed to finish for the night, and gestured with a hand over his shoulder, saying she was back there with the other women. Cem looked again. There were the young girls, but they all looked under eighteen. He saw no older woman with a face as beautiful as the moon and eyes that were like deep velvet pools.

Mustafa called out to the room, 'Zeynep, come.'

The woman who walked towards them was wearing the same baggy clothes as the others and her scarf framed the shocking plainness of her face. Her nose was large and while the hair that fell out the back of the fabric in a plait was indeed as thick as two men's wrists, just as his grandfather had told him, the colour could not be described as burnished and it was not as glossy as Black Sea oil. Zeynep gave a formal welcome, and though her teeth were white and strong, like an animal's, they were somehow dangerous behind her lips. Cem said hello and told her that he'd heard about her dancing when he was growing up.

She was serious as she told him that the wedding season was over and there would be no more dancing, not until the next winter. Zeynep said she had work to do and left the table and Cem watched the back of her. She was hulking and squat, and he was overwhelmed with disappointment. She'd been one of the reasons he'd come, her and the tree, two childhood memories that had been planted as seeds when he was little, memories not his own but pressed into him and tended by his grandfather. Somehow, these seeds had grown into things of great beauty and importance in his mind. There was a small boy who lived inside him, and Cem realised that boy had been desperate to see the belly dancer who made people's eyes bleed with desire. The boy also wanted to see the wishing tree and tie a wish on it, but now he was frightened of what it might look like.

Mustafa stood and said it was time for the village to go to their houses, but that they could celebrate the arrival of Ahmet's grandson and be happy he was finally here as promised. Cem opened his mouth, to ask what had been promised, but the village chief continued, 'Cem has come to make everything right. Ahmet said he would fix things and he has kept his promise.'

People pressed around Cem and shook his hand and kissed his cheeks. He was rotated in a circle as people grabbed at him, congratulated him for his strong sense of responsibility to the village, for his honour, for his strength of character. He was smiling and confused. What had the headman said? Why did they think he was here? He looked at Harry, but the historian was also smiling, clapping along with the villagers who were now singing a song, glad that the community was receiving his travel partner with such enthusiasm.

'What?' Cem almost had to shout for the headman to hear him over the noise of people talking excitedly. 'What did you say about my grandfather?'

'He promised to send us his first grandson and he has kept his promise!'

'First time that's happened,' someone said, and Cem was rotated and congratulated some more.

Finally people began to leave. The old woman kissed Cem. She held his face between her hands and said she had much to tell him. Then he was passed over to Mehmet and Harry was given to Mustafa so they could be taken to their rooms. Harry was installed in a small stone and wooden building up in a paddock beyond the village's main street and Cem was taken to Mehmet's house.

Lying in bed, he found he couldn't sleep though the room was large enough and the bed comfortable. It had an overstuffed mattress and soft white sheets and on top, a thick eiderdown with a shiny golden satin cover. Pillow cases with ties at the corners, and patterned with small embroidered flowers. He thought about what the village chief had said and the behaviour of the old woman. What did they want from him? What did they mean when they said he was there to fix things?

He got out of bed and turned the light on, which was a bare bulb hanging overhead. The room was painted a pale blue, but about two-thirds of the way up, it changed to white. In one of the corners near the ceiling were two holes with wires sticking out. The drawn curtains were white with little wooden beads threaded onto plaited ends that fringed along the bottom. His mother had similar curtains at home but it seemed they and the bed linen were the only things that were pretty in the room.

His grandfather had described the village houses as being like palaces. Perhaps elsewhere in the village he would find these mansions. He edged the curtains open. He could see the place where Harry was staying, up on the hill. A light glowed from the shuttered window and he imagined Harry setting out his things on a bedside table, moving quietly around the room, excited about what he might find here. Cem hoped the other man would be able to cope with his own imminent disappointment better than he had. And then there'd been the girl, staring at him as if he was a ghost. The old woman who knew him before he was even introduced. He switched off the light and got back into bed but lay awake and listened to the dogs. His grandfather used to talk about the howling dogs in the village and that there were superstitions surrounding them, but as much as Cem tried to think of them, and he lay for a long time more, still he was unable to recall what they had been. Sometime during the night, much later, he fell fast and hard into a sleep that was restless and hot and unlike any sleep he'd had before.

II

In the morning, he woke tired. In the middle of the night he had woken with fingers travelling down his body and he recalled what his grandfather had told him about the dogs: that the howling meant death was coming. He'd gone back to sleep but in the early morning with light behind the curtains had been pinched awake once more, his grandfather's urgent voice in his ear: *They will try to make you pay.*

Was any of it to do with why his mother sometimes cried so much that her nose bled? He looked at his watch. He had been in the village fifteen hours. He remembered his grandfather's hand slamming the table and wondered whether it had been a good idea to come. He lay awake in the bed, sweat drying, trying to keep his mind from turning to Jenna.

III

Harry was on the bed with a book on his chest, looking at the ceiling.

'Breakfast is in a while,' Cem said, hovering in the door. 'There's some sort of meeting.'

Harry told him to come in, so he sat on the floor with his back to the bed.

'I slept well and my back seems fine. Now how soon do you think we can talk to that big man who has the head of a bear?' Harry said.

'I suppose today.' Cem looked at the rug, at the designs woven into the pile. All the hopes and dreams of a village girl's heart, his mother had told him when he was little. The comb was for marriage, she'd said. He found a comb with his finger and traced it. He'd never been interested in romance, or matters to do with love.

'With your wife,' Cem said, 'did you love her more or less when you got to know her?'

'Significantly more, naturally. Marlene is a wonderful woman.'

Cem was silent.

'Why do you ask?'

'The more I know of a girl, it seems, the less I can like her.' He was sure that if he'd gotten to know Jenna, this would have been rapidly proven. He remembered her directness, and how bold she was.

'That doesn't sound quite right to me. I'm sure it's meant to be the other way around.' Harry held up the book he was reading. 'Listen to this. It's a dreadful novel, an absolute bodice-ripper.' He turned the cover over. '*The Secret Son*, by Frances Adams. The wife, left behind during war, writes to the man: "I kiss your eyes." That's only the first page and I fear it won't get any better, but it tells the story. Of the son. It has to be him.'

Cem lay on the carpet. 'What makes you think it's true, Harry?'

'Have you ever believed something, believed it absolutely, known that for it to be untrue is simply impossible? I realise there's no logic to it . . .' Harry's voice trailed away. Cem thought of Zeynep. He thought of Jenna. Harry continued, 'You can think a thing for so long that it becomes inconceivable to let go. It sticks to your brain and, even if you find direct evidence to contradict your belief, you can't quite give it up. You keep finding ways to make your belief true.'

After the long night, the thin sun had risen and lit the scene outside of his window, and Cem had seen the village in the morning light. He had seen the skinny dogs in the street and, in the distance, a man walking up the hill. The buildings were a mix of stone and wood, doors with their faded paintwork, the single road through the village muddy and uneven. Buildings were being constructed or pulled down, it was hard to say which. There was no correspondence between the reality of this place and his grandfather's descriptions, just as the real Zeynep bore no resemblance to the Zeynep of his imaginings.

'Then,' said Harry, 'once you find the truth, the magic is broken, yes? But you still have small sneaky thoughts that prevent you from completely letting go of it? It might be that I won't find my answer here, but will that stop me believing? I can't say with certainty that it would.'

Some sort of magic had broken for Cem. He considered telling Harry about Zeynep; about how the village in the raw sunlight was not what he expected, but didn't. It felt too private. He lowered his forehead to the carpet. There'd been no chance of magic with Jenna, it had never even gotten started.

Harry was still talking. 'I can't quite believe it, but I am here and I might get my proof. I can understand your doubts, of course. Another man might have called it ridiculous. Other men *did* think it ridiculous, people laughed at me. But I listened as a small boy. I listened when the woman next door said something precious of Ned Kelly's had been left behind at Gallipoli.' Harry's voice cracked and Cem looked up. Harry was leaning forwards, urgent. It was, Cem realised, a life.

'And then, a few years ago, I got my biggest lead, I suppose you could say.' Harry described how his old supervisor, Professor Somerset, had 'turned around' on the matter. Somerset had for years denied the possibility that Ned Kelly had had a child. But one day, decades after they'd first met, and having been scoffed at repeatedly all that time, Harry had received a summons from the dying man and had gone to visit him at his home. He was ushered into the man's bedroom by a harried-looking wife with wispy hair, and no sooner had he stepped through the door than Somerset had made an announcement: 'Ned Kelly had a son who fought at Gallipoli and lived out the rest of his life in Turkey—and maybe married a Turkish woman.' He seemed surprisingly robust considering his expiration was, apparently, imminent.

'I have a book!' Somerset lurched up and held out a slender volume. Harry took it and turned to the imprint page. The book had been published in 1953 and this was a first, and probably only, edition. It was, Somerset reported, a hideous novel (but with a most significant author note at the conclusion) about a young Australian whose father was a notorious bushranger. Though presented as fiction, the book was clearly about Ned Kelly. In the story, the young man had fought in Gallipoli, but was left behind by the army. He married a Turkish woman and lived out his life in Turkey, dying on an island off Istanbul. The novel was about success and failure, ends and means. About intention. It was about a son trying to rehabilitate a father's reputation, an agonised adjunct to the whole notion of Ned Kelly (Patrick O'Ryan in the book) as misunderstood political activist. Kelly had been a rebel, not a simple police killer, so went the argument.

Somerset was rambling, in pain, Harry said, but transformed with the energy of death. He was sorry not to have been more supportive of Harry's obsession. He'd found the book in a second-hand bookshop, in Benalla of all places. Somerset would drive up to Kelly country on weekends to potter in second-hand shops, trying to unearth anything about the Kellys. As Harry had! It was a wonder they didn't cross paths, Harry told Cem. In the book, Adams mentioned a planned republic of the north-east of Victoria and into

New South Wales, a territory stretching from Mansfield to Bathurst. The notorious bushranger, O'Ryan, had been carefully considering the idea of establishing a republic for about twelve months before he was injured and arrested after the shoot-out. There had been a founding group of people—'and note here I am carefully not saying "men",' Harry told Cem—linked through a series of hotels. The Americans had achieved independence and the Irish were hopeful of it. It was about to be accomplished in the Boer War. Rebellion was infectious, Harry said, and Ned and the others couldn't have been the only people who didn't like the British.

'He was born in the same year as the Eureka uprising,' Harry said.

Cem lowered his head again to the carpet. He was hungry and imagining fresh bread with tomato, white cheese and olives.

'And there's a connection to this country, as well, sort of a political birthing parallel as well. A new-born republic, emerging in 1923, a colonel at Gallipoli, war hero and future father of Turkey. One man whose plans were to be realised and another, back home, whose plans were ultimately thwarted.'

Cem lay unmoving on the carpet.

'And Remembrance Day—yes, but remembrance for what? Think about the politics. Think about the *history.* It's not only about the official wars. It's not a *coincidence* it's on that date, one hour after he was strung up. People say it's not possible the government enacted a memorial for a man like Kelly, that's what they've said any time I've mentioned it.'

Harry got up from the bed, slowly. He told Cem he'd asked Somerset about the significance of the author note, at the back of the book.

'You'll read it yourself,' Somerset said, holding the book up for Harry to take. 'But it says the story, while fiction, was based on factual events and real people. That it was sincerely written as an adjustment of the mythologising of a man. And finally that, as in all things, the truth was likely to be found somewhere in the middle, among myriad contradictory beliefs.'

As Harry was saying goodbye to the old professor, he told Cem, Somerset had laughed until the point of choking. 'I am telling you, you need to go to Turkey and find out once and for all if this is bulldust or credible.' His laughter descended into a dreadful coughing fit and Mrs Somerset had come in and ushered Harry out of the room. It was all rather awkward, Harry said.

'Right,' said Cem from the floor.

Harry finally stopped talking about Kelly.

'Do you know what they're meeting about this morning?'

'They keep going on about Saddam Hussein,' Cem said.

'I'm confused. The old man with the stick is your grandfather's cousin? And the man with the big head is his son?'

'No. He's Mustafa, the chief of the village. There's a family connection but I don't understand it. The old man and my grandfather are cousins but they grew up as brothers.'

Harry asked if they could go down yet; he was keen to talk to the chief. Cem said he supposed they could, but lying on the rug he had become sluggish as if the small amount of energy he'd had was leaked away. He even seemed to have lost his hunger.

'Imagine if there were original letters or photographs even,' Harry said almost dreamily. 'I suppose you can't appreciate the magnitude of such a thing.'

Cem yawned.

'I'll get dressed,' Harry said.

Cem went outside to wait. There was a girl walking at the bottom of the paddock. She was throwing something out of a bucket onto a pile and as Cem stood there she turned on the spot and took a long look up the hill. It might have been the girl from the night before. She turned and walked away just as the door opened behind him and Harry came out, holding his briefcase. They went down to Mustafa's house for breakfast.

IV

Mustafa was cooking eggs in the kitchen and Cem and Harry were shown into the salon by a daughter, a younger one with strange yellow eyes. Harry settled himself in a chair, legs crossed, and Cem kneeled on the rug next to a large silver tray on which were small plates and bowls. Still more dishes were being brought in by daughters: fresh bread and dried beef sausage, tomato and cucumber, honey and jam, olives, cheese and pale butter. Harry drank lots of tea and kept looking at Cem and exhaling heavily, but Cem wanted to eat before asking Mustafa about anything. Half an hour later, he still hadn't mentioned Harry's request and Harry was hunched over his food, pushing it around, looking miserable. Cem finished eating. He sat back and stretched, leaving the overly-sweetened tea on the silver tray. Harry accepted another glass and tried to put his hand over the top, but still Mustafa managed to get three cubes into the glass.

The headman said something and pointed at Harry's lap.

'What's he saying?' Harry asked Cem.

'He says your wife will like it more if you have sugar.'

'Like what more?'

'I don't know,' Cem said, going red.

'What does *yarak* mean?' Harry said. The village chief was repeating the word, pointing at Harry's lap and nodding fiercely, holding up sugar cubes.

'It means, um, your . . .'

'Oh, dear,' Harry moaned and arched his back.

'Are you alright?' Cem asked.

Harry said his nerve was getting chatty and he didn't know how long he could sit and could Cem *please* ask the headman about Ned Kelly's son.

Cem said he would, but that Mustafa was talking now about the village and something about a bridge and he didn't want to interrupt, it would be rude. Cem tried to listen and was almost dozing off when he smelled lavender and opened his eyes. One of the daughters was next to him, stacking empty plates onto the silver tray. She was introduced as Meral, Mustafa's oldest girl. It was the girl from the night before, the one who'd stepped back when she'd seen him. She had heavy black eyebrows and a crooked smile that she withheld from him yet gave freely to her sister, her face turned away from him, as she and the younger girl stacked the breakfast things. Her eyes were so black they looked purple. Two sisters with strange eyes.

'Mr Keloğlu,' Mustafa said, once his daughters had left the room, 'how are the things in your country, with marriage arrangements?'

'Young people make their own choice,' Cem said. 'Sometimes parents get involved, for Turks, and Greeks and Italians, I guess. Indians maybe, I don't know.' He was struggling with some of the vocabulary. He didn't really know about marriage, how it worked, or why were they even talking about it.

'Do you have a sweetheart?'

Cem inhaled and coughed.

'You cough because not enough sugar. Here.' Mustafa tipped two cubes into a fresh glass of tea. 'You do have one?'

'No,' said Cem, stirring. 'I'm only twenty-three.'

'I was nineteen when I married the first time.'

'What's he talking about?' Harry interrupted.

'You have no wife,' Mustafa said.

Cem agreed that he didn't. 'Can we ask him now?' Harry said to Cem.

Cem was happy to change the subject. He told Mustafa that Harry wanted to ask something important. The headman composed himself, ready to receive the request.

'So,' began Harry, 'tell him how much I appreciate his hospitality, that it is a wonderful thing to be welcomed into his home.'

'*Sağol*,' Cem said to Mustafa. 'The professor says thank you.'

'What is this business he brings me?' Mustafa asked.

'This man,' Cem said in clumsy Turkish, 'this Harry Forest is a history man, and for long years he has been reading and studying and trying to find out about another man. This other man has an important name in our country but he is not important here. His name was Kelly, and his father was a famous man in Australia. This Kelly, the son, maybe came here to fight at Gallipoli, and

Harry thinks he never went back home. He either died at the war or, Harry thinks, he stayed in Turkey. What he would like to know is if there was one time a foreign man who visited here in—' Cem broke off and switched to English. 'When would he have been here, Harry, what year?'

'It would have been 1915 or 1916, maybe even up to 1920.' Harry's voice was faint.

As Cem translated the dates the younger sister came back in with a tray. Her eyes were yellow, the colour so thick you couldn't see the whites.

'So,' the headman said. He wiped his moustache. 'This important man in your country? He is like Atatürk?'

'No,' Cem said. 'Not like him.'

'What did he say?' Harry asked.

'He wants to know if Ned Kelly was like Atatürk, I said no.'

'But it's possible he was. More of a failed Atatürk though.'

Cem looked at Harry. His face was grey and he had dried spittle around his lips. It seemed possible the man really was mad.

Mustafa finished his glass of tea and reached for a cigarette.

'Mehmet will have to come and speak about it. This is not my business.'

Cem translated this to Harry while Mustafa sent a daughter to go and get Old Mehmet. 'Harry,' said Cem, 'Why do you think this is all real? It was a novel your professor found, so that's fiction, right?'

Harry said yes that was so.

'I told you, in the hut. Just before. There's a note in the back of it stating it was based on a true story. And my research confirmed that a man, a journalist, saw the handbill about the North-Eastern

Republic of Victoria. He saw it in London, on display. It's disappeared now, of course.' He rubbed at his back.

'Oh dear,' he groaned. 'It's finally clicked out.'

Mustafa poured more tea and edged the sugar bowl closer to Harry.

About ten minutes later Mustafa's daughter returned with Old Mehmet, who walked in slowly, raising his chin in greeting. He handed his stick to the girl and settled into a chair. He accepted some tea and three sugars and listened to the headman's summary.

'Yes. It would be so.' He patted his arm where the jacket sleeve was folded and pinned over his missing hand. Cem translated for Harry.

'He says he will talk to you about it maybe tomorrow, probably the next day. He needs to think about it and remember the important things. I don't know what he means by that but he is inviting us to take a walk, a tour of the village, later today.'

Mustafa broke in to say to Cem, 'If someone called Cevap makes trouble, ignore him. He can have a hot head.'

Once they were outside, Harry clutched at Cem. He needed to lie down flat, the pain had become horrific. Could Cem help him back to the hut? It took a long time for them to make their way up the meadow. They didn't speak while they walked, but Harry made all sorts of sighs and clicks with his tongue. Cem began to really wonder what he was doing there. It was nothing like he expected and being in the village seemed to mean being surrounded by difficulty. He could be on a beach doing his own thing, free, but here he was, stuck on a mountain, in someone else's plan. He could have visited the village later, after going to the Greek islands and beaches down south.

Once he was on the bed, Harry asked whether Cem could pour him some water and Cem handed him the glass. He went to the window. Down the hill he could see people were moving about on the street. He saw, too, that Meral was outside, about to knock. He opened the door. She was holding a satin eiderdown and it looked heavy in her arms. He took it from her.

'Thank you,' he said.

'You're welcome,' she replied. Her face was mournful, her cheeks wide and pale. She was a girl whose misery had sucked the colour from her face. Her eyes constantly shifted from side to side, watchful without properly settling. It created an impression of longing. He stood in the doorway and watched her walk down the path, aware of the way the breath was coming from his mouth. There was some sort of opportunity here and he felt pulled by her vanishing form.

He said goodbye to Harry over his shoulder, called back in answer to Harry's plea that yes, he'd remember to ask about aspirin, and followed Meral down towards the village. The morning air was cold, and his shoes slid on the wet grass. When they were on the flat he tried to pick up his pace to catch her, perhaps he could ask her a question but he couldn't think what, but she walked faster. As she passed a house, a young man stepped out to talk to her, raising his arms to stop her: Cevap the troublemaker.

Cem saw Meral put her hands up to where her ears would be under her scarf and, with a growl, she dodged Cevap and rushed down the road. Cevap lowered his arms and turned to look back at Cem, who was standing about fifty metres away. Cem lifted a hand in greeting and Cevap's brows pulled together. Cem stood in the road, knowing there was a situation here and it made him excited.

What was this thing between them? The other guy had been intense and almost desperate. Cem suspected it was a case of him loving her and her not loving back. He wondered what Mustafa thought about it. Perhaps she was being edged into an arrangement that she didn't want, by this boy, by her father.

He turned and walked back up the road to Mehmet's place, to his room, which smelled stuffy. He opened the window and lay on the bed, listening to the sounds of the street as the white curtains stirred in the breeze and the wooden beads at the bottom of the fringe clacked quietly against the sill.

Chapter 9

Mustafa calls Cem the foreign boy but in my heart I know him to be the son of the village, one of us. A sugar man. Our chief Mustafa scoffs and tells me, 'Berna, you don't know anything,' but I say it is he who doesn't know anything.

My brother Mehmet is on another path. All he wants is to go to the trees, to lie down in the forest and be calm in that green place. To look up to the sky and, if it rains on him, to say, 'Let it be so.' Let it snow too, he would say. Let the air cover him and let the birds come, seven could appear and line up on his legs. Let them peck or let them sing, he doesn't mind. He is ready, or so he thinks. I go to the stone step and wait for him, and in a little while he arrives.

I can see he is tired, but it is time for the true stories and the new endings. The children love the fairytales, the doings of *jinns*, maidens and warriors; all the old stories of talking dragons and phoenixes that lift you to the sky and carry you through all the planes of heaven. These are the tales that draw the young to the feet of my brother, and they will expect witches as usual, but today they will be disappointed.

I know he intends to tell the most important of all stories, about love. Too many men care for gold and power, and too many lie for both. Some push for war and think that is the place they will find themselves, but it is love that is at the centre of everything. If a man is good at war and bad at love, then he is a man who is lost.

I'm not sure how much of this the children will understand.

Mehmet settles into his chair; no cushion for him, he likes to say, though he has seen more than eighty springtimes and his backside is bonier than an old donkey's rump. He waits until the smallest child, a nervous boy called Sami, is sitting right at his feet. I can see my brother's question, how it hangs on the air just outside his lips. How to put into words the things that have never been spoken?

Kehri brings us tea. She tips four sugars into the glass, stirs and puts it down on the flat stone for my brother. She gives me my tea and goes to the back of the group. The spring breezes have started to stir and we have sunshine today, the first of the new season that is coming.

'I know,' Mehmet says to me. 'I know what to do.'

'Ayşe is dead. Stay with the witches and talking animals.'

'And the boy?'

'I am happy to see him.'

I pick up my work. He is watching me with those eyes.

'I'm not angry at him,' I say. 'Not like you. He is not his grandfather.' I start my spindle and feed the tufts into the thread as it whirls.

Mehmet tells the children he is going to start a new story. There are cries of 'no' from the children. He has to finish the last story first, the witch one, they shout.

'You never listen,' I say.

'Oh, *soos*. I will start a new story and finish it tomorrow. It's always best not to finish a story at once. This is what Scheherazade taught us.'

'To keep her head,' one of the older girls says.

'Yes. Now this will be a real story. Not made up like the *Nights* or "The Goat that Whistled". This is about two boys from this village and how they both loved the same girl. It's about a man with a monkey he loved as much as a friend or brother.'

Some of the children laugh and Sami the Small laughs the loudest, saying it isn't true. There aren't any monkeys in Hayat.

'I like the sound of that story, Uncle.' This is serious Kehribar, who sees too much. 'I like real stories and I like stories about love.' She looks at Sami. 'You get scared by the witch stories, they make you cry.' The boy denies this vehemently.

Mehmet clears his throat and the children become quiet.

'Now, two boys—Ahmet and Mehmet—grew up,' he says. 'One fell off his horse and cut his hand. That was Mehmet.' My brother holds up his pinned sleeve. 'It was because the other boy made his horse bolt. Mehmet rolled off a cliff and lost his hand, but the other one married a pretty girl.' My brother doesn't say that the other boy shouted at her and said that she was a child, that she had a tiny crack in the place where a man needed a large cave. That her breasts were bee stings, tiny eruptions that no man could adore. No, my brother doesn't say that the other boy was cruel. That part is not for children.

Mehmet looks at me; I can feel it even though I have my eyes closed and my face turned to the sun. We are an old sister and an old brother together, and the lines are deep around our mouths. My friend Ayşe has been dead for a long time and Mehmet thinks it's only his heart that has counted each of those long years.

Our headman arrives at the doorstep and stands there a moment, casting a shadow over us. Mehmet squints into the sun and I keep spinning.

'Ah, Mustafa, how is our chief?' Mehmet says. 'We are talking about love today. When the heart is released and starts to flap outside of the rib cage, beating its wings so strongly that all feel the breeze. Sometimes it crashes to the ground with a heavy thump and leaves a bigger hole than anyone could imagine. How could such a large crater be caused by something as small and soft as a simple human organ?'

'I don't know what you're talking about, Uncle. I must keep walking.'

'You don't wish to listen to our story today, Headman?'

'What's wrong with the old stories? "The Seven Layers of Heaven"? "The Talking Goat"?' Mustafa shakes his head and walks on, and Mehmet turns back to his audience and continues. 'Someone we know has love starting right now, but so deep in his heart he doesn't even realise it!'

He gets half through the new story fifteen minutes later and stops, thirsty and tired. The children are restless. I put down my work. My brother needs to rest.

'That's all for today, my darlings,' I say.

Children begin to get up and move away. Everything is coming, in its own true time. My brother knows it is time to move, but still he sits a while longer. Something falls from the sky and drops into his lap. It is a dead bird.

'Look what God has sent us,' Mehmet says, and I see Kehri's golden eyes, watching us. 'This is a sign.'

Yes, no more witches, I think.

Mehmet gets to his feet, holding the dead thing out to Kehri and she takes it in her skirt. He waves his hand for his stick and she passes it to him.

Mehmet turns to me. 'The history man is asking about Jim.'

'Show him what we have.'

'Very well. Also, Cevap will try to make trouble.'

'If he feels he must, then it will be so,' I say. 'At least he is clear about what he wants.'

'You think? Fine. Now I walk. We do the "visiting". It's all very inconvenient.'

'But it is time for all that too. This is the moment.'

Mehmet sighs, but I can tell he knows it to be true.

Chapter 10

I

James woke at dawn. He was in some kind of shed with bare walls, lying on a mattress that was on top of an earthen floor. He had tried to rise once during the night but had been unable. Outside there was a sound; a small beginning that built to a crescendo of noise. He lay listening and it took a while to know that it was a man, singing in a voice that strained and tapered. There was a small cough, an intake of breath, and the voice wavered like a kite on the wind, seeming far away, closer, and fading back into the palette of pre-dawn sounds, where in the distance dogs howled behind the sound of the wind in the trees. It seemed to be finishing when it started again.

Later, he woke once more. There was a smell of animal in the room, but the mattress was comfortable, the best he'd had since leaving Australia. Better than the damp dirt tunnels with their still, icy air. It took him a while to stand. His legs were weak and there was a dull weight across his chest. The room was indeed a shed, with tack for horses in the corner and a couple of feeding bins mounted against one of the walls. He went to the window and looked out. The sun was shining and he was, he realised, terribly ill. He looked at the sky and saw the horizon was clear but, even so, he would be there a while yet. He could not go down the mountain.

He'd imagined Ferhat had been taking him to a city, and by the time it was clear that they had travelled far from any city and were in fact heading up a mountain, it was too late. During the night and through all of his fevered thinking he'd come to know what a mad thing it was for him to be there, but there'd been no choice. He should leave. No one knew he was here other than the villagers, and technically he was their enemy. He didn't fancy a truck arriving, a cohort of soldiers, to escort him off the mountain and into gaol, where he'd be forgotten.

He went to the door and opened it. On the ground was a tray with bread, honey and black tea. Stepping outside he looked around. The stable was located near a house and Ferhat was sitting nearby, hunched on a rickety chair, leaning back so it creaked, looking at the sky. He lurched forwards when he saw James and came over to him. Ferhat carried the tray inside and sat while James lay down again. He didn't want the food so Ferhat ate it and played with Alphonse, trying to teach the monkey to hold his nose and wave the other hand. Ferhat kept saying '*foof*' and holding his nose.

'I know, mate,' James said. 'It's a bit stinky in here.'

'Yes, mayte.'

Ferhat finished the food and went to the door with the tray. He called a name—*Saliha!*—and a girl came. When she saw Alphonse she tried to enter to get a closer look at the animal sitting on Ferhat's shoulder, but the boy shooed her out.

James slept for long hours and during that first day there were more song-calls that came from outside. Always the small cough before beginning, the rattle of phlegm as the man cleared his throat to start the song, the elongated sounds that stretched through the moment. It became familiar. He learned the tune, began to listen for the pauses. He wondered what its purpose was and, during the afternoon calling, he got up once more and went to stand at the window. Some of the men were walking to a round stone building which had a tower with a tiny balcony and a latticed wooden railing. At the top was a man in robes with a piece of material wrapped into a kind of hat. Men were at the base of the tower, washing their feet and hands at taps set into the walls of the building.

It was a church, James realised, and the singer a Turkish priest calling the people to the service. They had a song instead of church bells and gatherings all through the day and evening. Standing at the window, he became dizzy, and by evening he was shivering badly.

James lay in the darkened shed for the next few days. Around him he saw moving shadows at the window and dark eyes peering in at him. Children, he thought. Just children. Sometimes the door would open and he'd squint at the light and see Ferhat, often with other men's faces behind his shoulders, all pushing forwards to see the foreigner. Ferhat brought trays of food and sat with him, eating most of the food himself, passing cupsful of sweet water to James who lay on the mattress, silent and somnambulistic, listening to the man calling outside, and dipping in and out of sleep.

II

The villagers met at the coffee house to discuss what to do with the foreigner. Mad Arif waved a sharp-fingered hand at the men as they waited for Ferhat's father, Haluk, the village chief, to come and tell them what was to happen.

'I think he's an anarchist, or someone sent here to spy,' Mad Arif said. 'He has a beard but it's not a normal beard. I suspect he's a pamphleteer! We should take him and run him out of town—but we'll keep his horse, it's not a bad sort.'

'It's snowing again,' Huran said. 'A man can't be walked down the mountain and left in this weather. It would be inhospitable. Also, he is unwell, Ferhat says.'

Fresh teas were placed on the table and the men started stirring sugar in.

Arif waited until everyone else had sugared theirs. Once their eyes were on him he reached out, put five lumps in his glass and held a sixth between his front teeth. With teeth bared and his dark lips pulled back, he stirred the tea. Resting the teaspoon on the edge of his saucer, he lifted the tulip glass to his lips and sipped the tea through the sugar cube he held in his teeth. Letting it absorb the tea and soften, he sucked the syrupy lump into his mouth.

'You know what I think about strangers, especially ones with pamphlets. The headman's boy said it himself: the man is an enemy.'

'That's not what I meant,' Ferhat objected.

'You're a son of a donkey, Arif,' Huran said.

'Sick in the head,' someone else chimed in.

'Which city does the foreign man come from? Is he from Izmir?'

'You cannot trust anyone from Izmir.'

'He looks like he's from Adana. Good kebabs, but they like fighting too much, and you can't understand their accent.'

'He's not even a Turk,' Ferhat said. 'People aren't listening to me.'

'He is too tall for Adana anyway.'

Ferhat sighed.

'Enough, ladies.' It was the headman, Haluk, standing in the doorway. Haluk was a legendary man in the bed, his wife with a smile on her face all the time, people said. He had an unusual spray of red hair from a band of wild Gauls who had settled on the Black Sea coast generations before. Haluk held up a hand and waited for the men to settle. The rooster-who-pecked was standing behind him, looking around his legs. Haluk shooed the rooster away and walked to his seat.

Ferhat tried once more. 'He's from Australia.'

'Is that near Istanbul?'

'Austria, you fool,' someone else said, rolling his eyes. 'It's well past Istanbul.'

'Av-u-stra-ly-a.' Ferhat turned to his father, the headman. 'It's further even than America. His name is Chems. He was asleep in the ditch at the war and they went away on the boats. They left their own man behind. You said we must always be hospitable, that we have to be polite even to an enemy.' Ferhat looked at his father, upset. 'The English shot their horses, Baba.'

Even Mad Arif was shocked. 'Bastards,' he said.

Ferhat's father, Haluk, had to admit what his son said was true; there was nothing worse than to be a poor host. Even to be deceived and taken advantage of was better than refusing a man hospitality, especially a sick one. Lame Adar stood to speak. The other men muttered. Adar had been born deformed and determined in equal measures. He had a proverb for each occasion which had become an irritant to the villagers over the years.

'Did not the Koran specify that the house which receives no guests also never receives angels?' he said.

Haluk agreed that it did.

'You're right,' he said to Ferhat. 'You had no choice but to bring this man. He is our guest and we will help him. He has not entered our village in secret, has stolen neither land nor women. He is not a spy or anarchist or pamphleteer, any fool can see that.' Haluk looked at Arif. 'Tell your women and children to stay away from him but not to be scared. I don't think this will be an imposition for long. He will want to go back to his own country, but the weather is bad now and the snow won't stop any time soon. He may be here a small while.'

'And he is really ill, Baba,' Ferhat said.

'No one is to harm him and no one is to make him leave the village. Yes, I am speaking directly to you, Mr Arif.'

'Perhaps we could devise some tests,' ventured Lame Adar's father, the *hoca*. He was the man who made the calls to prayer and led the services.

'Oh, you and your tests,' grumbled his brother, a jealous man. 'Your God doesn't want tests. He wants charity and a good heart. And to see your stupid face in Mecca if you can afford it.'

'*My* God?' The religious man was disbelieving. 'He's your God too. He's everyone's God.'

'Enough, you two,' said Haluk Bey. 'Why is my village the most argumentative in the region? While we do have the best water, the highest birth rate, the most superior carpets and the best-looking women of anyone, we are home to fools who bicker at every opportunity. I don't know why you people can't be content. I don't think we need any tests. He won't be here long. In the meantime,' he said, turning to his son, 'you and Lame Adar go and take him a pot of tea. Sweet tea remedies all.' He looked at Lame Adar. 'And check with Meryem. Make sure he has everything he needs, including pillows. A man needs pillows. Are her animals over at Mesut's?'

Lame Adar said they'd moved the goats. He didn't bother reporting that Meryem had opened the window to air out the space. That she'd said more snow was on its way, and Adar had smelled it too, the scent of snow undercut with pine from the forest. She'd told her daughter to get a warm eiderdown from the cupboard, to get the one with the scarlet satin on one side. She swept the floor and put a kilim down and then a mattress, eiderdown and two bolsters in the shed.

Haluk stood and pulled a wad of *livres* from his shirt pocket. He paid for the teas that had been drunk and for the teas that would be drunk after he left. People lifted their glasses and tipped their caps at the headman as he strode away. The sky was beginning to darken.

Ferhat went to see if James was feeling any better and wanted tea while Lame Adar knocked on Meryem's door.

Inside, the house was filled with women crowded up at the back window, looking out at the shed. They were there to help with making pastry, but none of them were doing anything other than look out the window. The women surrounded Adar, accosting him with their questions. He was invited for tea but declined, saying they were taking a pot to the foreigner. The women wanted to know if it was true the prisoner's eyes were the colour of the sky, whether he was as tall as a tree. Was he from Adana?

'He's not a prisoner, he's a guest of Ferhat,' Lame Adar said. 'He's not from Adana, but it's true that his eyes are the same blue as the little flowers you find beside the river.' The women wanted to know how long he would be staying but Adar couldn't say.

'I'm leaving now.' Adar moved to the door. 'And Mr Haluk said to make sure the foreigner has enough pillows.'

Meryem tried to push the women out. She had cooking on the stove and the two boys were wrestling and running around the room. One was her son and the other her nephew and two years younger. His mother had died during his birth and some whispered that he had killed her. His father had gone to war with her husband, two of them brothers, off to adventure. Neither had come back, but instead of them, this man had. This foreign man with his stranger-blue eyes.

'If he killed my father at the war, I will kill him back.' It was the smaller boy, her nephew, six-year-old Ahmet, standing in front of her with fists clenched.

'Oh, *soos*, Ahmet. You don't know what you're talking about,' said Saliha, Meryem's daughter who was helping at the stove. Saliha chased Ahmet to the divan, where she sat on him until he squealed.

Over the next few days, in the manner of small children who stubbornly settle on a belief and cannot be dissuaded from it, Ahmet decided James was an enemy, a foreigner who had killed his father and probably his uncle Sevinc as well. He had come to the village instead of the disappeared fathers to steal their women and sheep.

'I bet that man killed them,' Ahmet said to his cousins. 'You gave him all our pillows, but he killed our fathers at the war.'

'Don't be silly, we don't know that.'

'I do know it,' Ahmet insisted. 'It's the truth.'

He went to the corner and crawled underneath a pile of blankets.

III

Meryem's dreams told her that her husband, Sevinc, wasn't coming home, but still she hoped. She wanted the stranger to have pillows. Maybe the man with the sky-eyes had seen her husband at the war. Had they lain on the same earth and seen the same stars? Was it possible her husband might be in another village far away, his body broken now? He might be sleeping on a cold floor and being fed thin soup and dried bread by some other woman. If so, she hoped the other woman was someone kind-hearted, someone with good food. And as that woman cared for her man, she felt her job was to look after this one, a man who was sick with travel and war, a shy person who had a decent face. A man who needed more pillows.

She refused to ask her daughter. She knew if she did, Saliha would tell her that the blood at Gelibolu had carried many corpses and that her father's had been one of them. Saliha was a girl who knew all the things that were impossible to know. She always had.

IV

The months in the damp trenches and the journey had brought him low, but each morning, when James woke to the sound of the man calling from the tower, he felt a little stronger. The song from the tower invaded his sleep until it seemed to be he who was called. It was his mother's voice that he heard as he lay half awake, telling him to stay there, that it was safe where he was. Other times, it was Cole's or Linda's.

In a letter that had reached him at the Dardanelles, she had written:

> One day I'll visit you by plane. After I fly to Europe I'll come and find you, no matter where you are. You'll hear the sound of my prop. Look up and there I'll be, flying all on my own.

In the shed he read the letter again. There hadn't been anything hopeful for him in these words, not back in his dugout and not now. He knew her energy was for adventure, that in her imagination, the more far-flung the place she had to travel to find him, the greater her amusement in getting there. Each morning James woke from his dreams and lay flat on his back, staring at the rough wooden ceiling.

Alphonse liked to wrap himself around his hand or sit on his chest, playing staring games.

'What is it you know absolutely?' James said to the marmoset.

All that way he had come, each step taking him further in the wrong direction. To travel to Constantinople would be a mammoth task in this weather.

It was colder than he'd ever known back home. Those dry winter mornings in Melbourne that were so still his breath had hung like a pennant, his nose running in a stream, even those moments didn't touch the freeze of the air here. And it was cold today, colder than yesterday. He realised the room was dark, that there was little light coming through the small window.

There was a soft thump outside and he went to the door. It wouldn't open. He heard noises and pulled at it and snow fell into the room. The doorway was gone and, at the top, Ferhat's face was grinning and waving. They dug him out and moved him up the mountain before the next fall came, installing him in the stone hut that nestled in a wide pasture. He liked the new spot. It didn't smell of animal, but instead there was an ancient sweetness in the stone, the scent of honey.

The hut was up the hill, away from the village, and the calling from the man in the church tower was fainter and sometimes became lost on the wind. James rested and felt strength building in his limbs as he lay thinking and not thinking, breathing yet holding it, watching the drifting snow through the window. He listened to changes in the sounds outside, the gradations from silence to the sniffling and giggles of the children. He held his breath suspended and noted how the light in the room moved, from night to day and back again, the low winter sun casting its feeble light as it struggled up and eased down to unseen horizons, rising just south of the east and setting south of the west.

He slept and woke to see children in woollen hats at the window, fronted by a boy who had the cheekiest face of all. It was a face like Alphonse's: small and impish. The children gathered and James showed them his hand ditties and games. They stood waiting with fingers raised to mouths ready to scream and run whenever Alphonse climbed onto the windowsill. When they got restless, James would read to them from his tatty *Cole's Funny Picture Book.* At night, when the lantern was lit, he made shadow puppets on the wall of the hut and it was the small boy with the cheeky face who sat closest and laughed loudest, the boy called Ahmet.

Ahmet brought the marmoset white cheese and put on James's army hat and marched around the room in a comic pantomime, before his older cousins Mehmet or Saliha arrived to take him away. The mother seemed to be the small woman who brought him food if Ferhat didn't. She had a smile that twisted her mouth as she left the tray and walked away quickly.

Sometimes James found Ahmet in his hut, waiting for him. The boy would be opening boxes or looking in his duffle bag, climbing up onto the shelf, always talking, speaking fast, hands moving. James would wave his own hands in apology, not understanding the boy's chatter, and Ahmet would stop and stare at him with a keen look of assessment.

With time, the sun's arc in the southern sky moved a little higher, and by the time the snow had gone, overnight it seemed, the day came when the sun rose exactly from the east and set exactly to the west and they had reached the true equinox.

V

As the weather warmed, he learned some more words. He and Ferhat pored over the *Funny Picture Book* and it was the maps that fascinated both of them. James studied the world, finding it difficult to believe how far he was from home. Ferhat traced his finger along a line from Australia to Turkey, across the seas and across the land.

'How much?'

'Five,' James said, showing him five fingers. 'Five weeks on a big boat.'

'Big bowt. Hm, bowt.'

'Right,' said James.

There were many things they didn't know about each other, but James learned that Ferhat had three sisters and no brothers and that he had started calling James the word for 'brother'. If he stayed too much longer, he knew, it would be difficult to leave, as he had been enfolded into the village life, welcomed by Ferhat, by Haluk and his sister Meryem—the woman who cooked for him and did his washing—and by Meryem's children. Meryem's husband was not in the village and James didn't know what had happened to him.

His name had become 'Chems' in the villager's mouths, so to make it easier, he asked that they call him Jim. Soon he knew the words for come, yes, no, please, more, chicken, bee, dog, horse, sheep, where, when, why and son-of-a-donkey. Ferhat tried to teach James some swear words but he resisted, blushing. He was taken on a tour of the village, along with all the men and children. The rooster-who-pecked went too. They took him up to the crest of the mountain and to the caves, including one so large everyone could fit inside. They walked around the mountain in a quarter-turn to where the two forests lay: the Big Forest and the Small Forest. Through the Big Forest the river ran, and walking back down the slope from that point, the first building they came to was his—the Honey Hut as Ferhat called it—and then, another five hundred metres below that, the village. Buildings surrounded the square with the communal fountain in the middle. The well was on the other side of the village, near a tree that was covered with rags.

One day, James was standing near the base of the church building when the man started to sing. Some of the men were washing their faces and hands and they took him and washed his face and hands too. They removed his shoes and washed and dried his feet, and led him inside for the service. Later, everyone in the village stopped him in the street to say *teşekkür ederim.*

'What are they saying?' he asked Ferhat.

'It means thank you.'

What Ferhat didn't have the words for was the communal pleasure felt by the village. They were proud of their mosque and happy that this stranger trusted them to show him their God. They'd seen the respect on his face, and no words or translations had been needed. The villagers looked at James sideways less and less. They still watched him, especially Mad Arif, but all he saw were smiling faces, hands swiped through the air, men pulling him to the tea house for a hot beverage or a smoke of tobacco.

As it became warmer, James and Ferhat would lie in the meadow, attended by a collection of sheep and dogs. They played with the yellow puppies, a tumbling mass of fur and flesh rolling on the grass. Even the rooster-who-pecked would find James and nestle amorously into his leg. The red-haired chief, Haluk, stood in doorways and laughed as loud as the rest. He was glad his son had a friend; Lame Adar had always been a poor option. The boy couldn't even walk properly.

James gave the children bareback rides on his horse, Blossom, and once the rooster fluttered up too, onto Ahmet's knee. The boy shouted and pushed the bird off and it went skittering down the back of the horse's rump and strutted away. James fished in the river and came back up the road with a clutch of slippery grey-pink mullet, threaded along a stick, their gills open in the air. He insisted that he be the one to cook them on the barbecue, confusing the women. They'd never known a man to cook. He carried the plate of finely-chopped salad over to where the women were sitting, separate from the men, and he stooped and served until Haluk said something to Ferhat, and James was made to stop and sit down.

He needed some sort of work and managed to make Ferhat understand this. They went out with the sheep, and he helped to tan hides, and after a day's work they would sit at the fountain in the middle of the street, James listening to Ferhat's chatter, exchanging words, learning more, noticing how the rows of houses were painted different colours: white, indigo, pale pink, light yellow and green.

He had found a community, something close to a home, but even so, he often thought of Beechworth, a place so distant yet fixed in his mind, a place where he had no one. For a long time, he woke from dreams about the particular type of grass that grew along the side of the track beyond the house that he and his mother had lived in. He dreamed of the bucket she used to collect the chook scraps; the shape of the handle of the tap over the gully trap outside the back door; the small pink flowers that bloomed next to the outhouse in spring. He would be roused from his dreams by the noises and sensations of clambering child bodies, of small fingers peeling his eyelids back, saying, 'Wake up! Wake up!' and he would open his eyes to see the boy Ahmet squatting in a corner, his eyes dominating his small face, on the verge of shrieking laughter or uncontrollable tears but always filled with high emotion.

'How long will Jim stay?' the villagers asked each other, impressed when he showed them how he could remove his thumb and put it back on again.

'As long as he wants,' said Ferhat, his arm around his friend's shoulder.

VI

James was going to tell Ferhat that he planned to leave before the next winter. It was unclear to him where the time had gone, yet it had passed by in what seemed like the same way that the wind blows leaves along the ground.

He and Ferhat were walking near the forest and James was thinking of the words. It was the end of summer and he was sorry but knew in his heart it was the right decision. He missed the bush and the paddocks, but mostly he missed how the bees sounded in the late summer and the way their honey tasted on rough slabs of bread and butter. He wanted to see Cole and perhaps Linda, if she was still in Melbourne. He could go via London, take the chance to see the city his mother had once urged him to visit. It might be a place to think about staying for a while.

They were walking across the narrow part of the river when he heard the sound. He ran into the trees and Ferhat ran after him, thinking it was a game. He found the tree and peered into the deep hollow. It was a fixed comb and he could see the queen cells, all pointing downwards. The hive was going to swarm and they had about a week to get ready. James tried to explain to Ferhat. He knew the words for 'wood' and 'house' and used his hands to signify boxes. He dragged Ferhat down the hill, his elbow locked around the younger man's neck, rubbing his knuckles across his scalp, trying to describe what they had to do, using his limited words and as many actions as he could make. 'Boxes,' James said. 'For the bees.'

They worked hard and boxes began to appear on the hillside, dotting the gentle slope at first. They worked until past dark each day and when they were ready, in the heat of the middle of the eighth morning, they shook hands in front of the tree before James performed the cut-out. With a knife in one hand he stretched both arms in and began to scrape at the connection between the comb and the ceiling of the log hive.

Ferhat stood back with his hands over his face, but James removed the comb and strapped it into the frames they'd prepared. It was a type of bliss, the happiness he felt when he located the queen and watched the thick yellow ooze across his fingers.

He would stay and get the colony established; it would be his gift of thanks to the village. Ferhat would have industry, and perhaps the boys too when they were older. It was important for a man to have something to do.

James stood in front of the main hive, studying the colour of the combs. It reminded him of something and he turned and walked down to his hut. He checked that both nuggets were safely where he had tucked them, wrapped in the material and pushed into the roof cavity. Twice he'd found Alphonse up there, sitting near where the nuggets were hidden, and he'd had to coax him down with cheese. He didn't want him to fall off the beam and get injured. He'd hate it if anything happened to Alphonse.

VII

Over the next few months the bee boxes started to make one long snaking line that crawled up and around the side of the mountain. Ferhat wanted to paint them blue and walked from box to box with a dripping brush. James went on ever-longer hikes up and around the peak to check the different vegetation. As the months passed on top of the mountain it was a time of expansion but also of narrowing. With the sky an open dome above him and all kinds of birds in flight, as the sun crossed and re-crossed the sky, James let himself settle. As he walked around the village and up onto the top hill and through the forest and along the river, his hands were open and tender. He had found something to hold him and a place of peace, but when Ferhat said to him, 'You are alone man I think, my Jim,' he'd found himself blinking away strange tears.

The bees held him with a tight stickiness and the late nights and early mornings were filled with the music of the call to prayer. And in the Honey Hut, James slept deeply and well. The summer blooms cycled into autumn and they migrated the boxes up and down the mountain. The days were long and the temperatures warm, so the bees stayed in the centre of the hives and were more easily moved.

The bees foraged the honeydew and the hazelnuts, the bay trees and rhododendron. James still didn't understand everything Ferhat told him, but it didn't matter as they worked side by side, chatting in their own languages, until Ferhat got bored with the bees and began to talk of other types of honey and ran down the hill to drink tea with Emine's parents.

VIII

The weather turned and Ferhat became an unreliable helper. Lame Adar was enthusiastic though limited physically. His high curved back and buried neck meant he couldn't lift his head properly and his crooked leg stopped him from being able to carry anything heavy up the difficult incline of the hill. But he stayed close to James and kept him company.

In the afternoons, Ahmet and Mehmet played with the yellow puppies on the grass as James rested in the meadow up past the Honey Hut. Though the boys were meant to help Haluk with the carpet dyes, they ran off to avoid it, especially Ahmet.

'Uncle Jim has bee work for us,' Ahmet would say to Haluk, and disappear before the headman could raise a hand to swat him. First Ferhat, now these boys, Haluk said to his wife. All for their Mr Jim and his bees. His wife gave him tea and he tipped the sugar in.

James no longer had thoughts of leaving. He had been in the village for four years and knew there was nothing back home for him. What would London be other than a metropolis swarming with people, sooty and cold? Here was a place where a man could stretch out with his hands behind his head and lie on a mattress of grass that smelled sweeter than anything he'd ever known.

Though older, the boys' bodies were still skinny and sharp and they wanted to climb all over him as he lay there in the meadow, tired after the bees. Ahmet demanded rides but Mehmet seemed to understand that sometimes James was too tired to play. Saliha was often there as well, sitting to the side, running her hands over one of the puppies or walking in a circle around them, spinning wool onto her wooden spindle. Sometimes the boys swam in the river at the place where the willow trees hung over the water making soft green curtains, or they lay on top of James's legs as they all flopped onto the grass together, laughing and telling each other to look at the sheep, look how funny their faces are, look that one is like a caterpillar with ears poking out of a cocoon.

Mehmet was going to be a shepherd because his father, Sevinc, had been one. Ahmet snickered and said he wasn't going to work with dumb animals, that he would be a famous pilot, perhaps the first Turkish villager to go into the sky. He would be rich and have a beautiful wife, maybe even three. James said that a man should only have one wife, more than that was wrong.

'Who said?' Ahmet smiled. 'You don't have any wife, how can you know?'

James said one day a lady friend might fly across the world to see them.

'A woman flying a plane?' Ahmet considered it. 'Is she pretty, this female?' He was a sensualist even at ten.

'She is indeed, my lion.'

'Is she prettier than my mother?' This was Mehmet, a fierce and protective son.

'No one can be prettier than Meryem,' said James, and it was the right answer.

Ahmet jumped up and shouted, 'Meryem, Meryem, Aunty-Aunty Meryem,' and wiggled his hips, showing how she danced in the kitchen with them clapping out the drum beats, singing 'ding diddle-ling-dang' for the brass finger cymbals.

Ahmet stopped dancing and turned to Saliha. 'I'm thirsty. Bring me water.'

Saliha said he could get his own water and Ahmet picked up a stick and went over and started hitting her.

'You are a girl and I am a man!'

'You are a pumpkin seed, nothing more than that,' Saliha said with a laugh, hand up, grabbing the stick and holding on to it.

'But you have to do what I say.'

'You're my little cousin.' She pulled the stick from him and snapped it in half, then stood with her arms crossed. 'And a bad one. '

'The other girls get their men water.' Ahmet wiped his eyes.

'I know how it works.' Saliha stood up and pressed her fingers into his cheeks, pushing hard. Then she grabbed him by the hair and lifted him off the ground. 'But I won't do it for you and you can't make me.'

Ahmet started shrieking and she dropped him. He was shaking and he called her a bitch.

'Enough, children,' said James.

'I'm not a bitch,' Saliha said to Ahmet. 'I won't charge money to my husband when we lie together, but you will have to find a slut to put your thing in. Now, goodbye, worm, I have weaving to do.' She began to walk down the hill. Ahmet shouted obscenities after her and James stood up and held the boy by the arm and shook him. He mustn't speak like that, he said.

'You're not my father! You talk like a baby.' He walked away.

'Your father would say the same,' James called after him. 'It's not nice to talk to people like that.'

Ahmet kept walking.

IX

Later, Ahmet snuck out. Jim, the man whose secret name was Enemy, was up the hill with the bees. In the hut, Ahmet found the small thing up near the ceiling, over in the corner of the room, a small bundle that was perched out of reach and looking at him. These days, when he snuck in, it didn't come to him as it had before. He tried to coax it down with cheese, but still it wouldn't come, so he had to climb up to get it. It scrabbled and chittered and clung on to some material that it pulled out of a crevice near the edge of the ceiling. Finally, he had its tail in his hands and he had the other things too. One was smooth and the other like a big finger. He supposed it was gold. He put them back and took the animal to the well. He sat a while on the warm stones, made a game with some sticks and leaves. He drew a bucket. He made the fur wet and it started making a noise, a pitchy scream that Ahmet hadn't heard before. He put more drops of water onto it and then its nails began to dig into his arm, which hurt. He flung it to the ground and worked at it with his feet.

Ahmet went home and crawled into the corner of the kitchen as his mother cooked at the stove. He crept under some cushions and went to sleep.

Chapter 11

I

Old Mehmet took Cem and Harry for the tour of the village. Harry's back had improved a little with rest, though he walked gingerly and listed to the left. Mehmet pointed out the fountain and the beaten metal cups in the village square. He showed them the mosque and told them when the tiles had been put on the roof. He mentioned rumours that Cem had spoken directly to some of the girls at the fountain. The villagers were unhappy about it, Mehmet said, but Cem argued that it was the girls who had been talking to him.

'That's what it might seem, but we know it's not true.'

Cem told Mehmet what one of the women had said to him earlier. She had grabbed his arm and said that he should pick her daughter to take back to Austria.

'Allah-h'allah,' said Old Mehmet. 'Which woman was it?'

'They're talking about a debt.'

Old Mehmet stopped walking. 'When Ahmet left the village,' he said, 'he promised to send his first grandson to pay what was owed.'

'Owed for what?'

'One of our girls died and Ahmet said he would pay, but he left without paying anything.'

'Paying money?' Cem remembered the talk about marriage that morning at breakfast. This was what his parents and grandfather had tried to warn him about.

'Who was the mother who talked to you at the fountain?' Mehmet said.

'I don't know. She had a pulled mouth.'

'That one's daughter will never find a husband, which is why she is making bold approaches. Don't talk to any of the girls or their mothers. Leave everything to us.' He peered at Cem. 'What's that face? You don't trust us to do it properly?'

Old Mehmet leaned heavily on his stick and reached for Cem as they walked up the slope. 'I am eighty-four and I walk well for a man my age,' he said. 'How does my cousin Ahmet walk? He is two years younger, it is true, but even so, how does he move?'

'He walks alright, but he doesn't sleep well.'

Old Mehmet said that it would be so.

'Who was that old woman I met last night? The one who came to the table?'

'That is Berna. She is my sister but not full. We had the same mother.'

'She said she knows me.'

'Yes, that is true.'

Mehmet started to list the village's finer points, making comparisons between Hayat and the other villages in the area. He talked about the water and the grass; he pointed to the forest and he showed them the river. They walked further into the forest until they came to a stone bridge.

'We can't use it anymore, it's old and dangerous,' he said as they stood next to the bridge. 'Broken.'

'Why don't you fix it?' Cem said.

'It's too expensive.' They walked a little further. 'How is your mother, your father?'

Cem said that his father was well, they were both well.

'And your friend here, he is a drunkard, yes?' Old Mehmet tipped his chin towards Harry.

'I think so,' Cem said. 'I don't know him well. I met him on the plane.'

'Yes, he bought the car, we know, you told us about that. We know you love that car very much.'

Mehmet crisscrossed them all over the village. He talked about the meadows and the sheep and carpets. Above them there was a rocky escarpment that stretched almost to the peak of the mountain, which was ringed with scrubby brush and boulders. There were caves at the top. Cem asked Mehmet about the wishing tree and the man sneered and called it a small feminine nonsense. He told Cem he didn't need to be thinking about such fripperies, that he needed to be thinking about his future. Cem said he'd promised to tie a wish on for his mother and Mehmet waved a hand, said that the tree was somewhere over there, near the well, but to be careful about the woods, especially the Big Forest, because it was a dangerous place.

He grabbed at Cem's arm and pointed down the mountain to where the plains could be seen in the distance. Fields were ploughed and furrowed, earth differing in colour from patch to patch.

'See them with their wooden ploughs?'

Cem couldn't see any people down there.

'Scratching life from their dry and inferior soils. While we'—Mehmet's hands were spread wide—'we weave and drink tea like kings.'

They visited houses and the meals began. Girls brought food on trays into rooms where the men sat; savoury pastries here, stuffed vine leaves at the next.

They drank coffee and ate sweet things through the afternoon and into the early evening. At each house, mothers and aunts peered around doorways, trying to catch a glimpse of 'the famous grandson', as they called him. At some of the houses, Cem saw postcards on walls, stuck into plaster with tacks alongside family portraits, photographs of proud-faced young men in military uniforms, and dour wedding photographs. He saw Luna Park and Melbourne trams, the edges of the cards curled.

'Now we go to my sister,' Mehmet said.

Berna gave Cem different tea to drink and sat down across the room. She asked him about his bowels and said she suspected he was blocked. He blushed and this seemed to be answer enough for her. She said travel could do that, that sitting still could bind a man, but she would take care of it, she wouldn't let him remain plugged.

'How is your mother?' she said. 'Does she weave?'

'No, they don't do that in Australia.'

'How can she be happy if she doesn't weave? Does she spin?'

Cem shook his head and took a sip of the tea. It tasted strange.

Berna said, 'Your mother was scared to go. Is your father gentle with her? What kind of man has he become?'

Cem guessed his father could be either gentle or not; how would he know?

He wanted to explain to her that his father was unknowable, a man without words, who worked long hours then came home to sit at the kitchen table and eat, and then moved to the lounge to watch television. He had never conversed or shared any opinions about anything other than disappointment when Cem had made mistakes (he failed his first driving test; had come home drunk one night and vomited in the backyard) and pride when he had succeeded (got into university; played a few games of basketball in high school). Until Cem had left to go overseas, his father had been mostly silent or absent, and since childhood his house had been a vacuum, with few words and little show of emotion from his parents. It had been his grandfather who filled the space.

'Uncle, why did my parents leave?'

Berna hissed, but Old Mehmet held up his palm to her.

'*Soos, kız,*' Old Mehmet said. 'It was your grandfather who decided to go. And he took your parents with him.'

'But why?'

'When was the Year of the Refrigerator?' Mehmet looked at his sister.

'How many times do I have to tell you? It was 1966. Ahmet pretended he wasn't jealous of that refrigerator. Mustafa's father got it once the electricity was put in, but your grandfather was angry and said he would leave and have a big house in Australia with three refrigerators.'

Cem agreed it sounded like his grandfather.

'He said the village was too small for him,' Berna said. 'That he needed a wider space. More people.'

Cem saw himself as a boy—the tree at school, his grandfather's suit, how Ahmet had made it seem he was choosing not to talk to the other parents in the yard. He was a better-quality man than they, he said.

'That's all it was. Maybe some bad dreams as well,' Berna said.

Mehmet turned to his sister with raised eyebrows. 'The boy says he has dreams there too.' He turned back to Cem. 'Listen,' he said. 'The village thinks you have come to pay the debt. All the women want you to choose their daughter. The woman at the well, those in the houses this afternoon. Some aren't happy about it, I have to say, but in the end it's not their decision, Mustafa and I will say yes or no.'

Cem swallowed the last of the bitter tea. *They* would say yes or no? He put the cup down. Outside the dogs had started howling again. It didn't matter if it was day or night, they seemed to roam the back streets and hills behind the village. They moved as if circling the village, barking. Cem looked at the two old people who were waiting for him to speak.

Harry sat at his side, trying to ask something, probably about his back or about the Kelly thing or whether he could get some more *rakı*.

There was something going on in the village, something serious and weighty, and for Cem it overshadowed any of Harry's imaginings about a secret son of Ned Kelly. He put his head in his hands. He knew what they wanted now. They wanted him to marry one of the girls and take her back to Australia.

II

By early evening, something had shifted inside and given him radiating cramps in his stomach. He decided he shouldn't drink any more tea.

What kind of man had he become? Old Mehmet had asked about his father.

It hadn't occurred to Cem that a man could become other than what he simply was, that there could be any sort of process to it. Did it mean that he too could become something other than he was? There was one thing he knew for sure: he wasn't someone who married a village girl. No matter how miserable that daughter Meral was, no matter how promising her eyes or how trapped she might be.

He'd found her in his room earlier, smoothing his pillow and touching his quilt, her slender hand moving on the fabric as if she were patting something small and furry. Before he could say anything, she left, and he'd gone to the window to watch her go out onto the street. Cevap was out there, trying to talk to her again, making her hurry away.

He'd stood at the window. She was being forced into a marriage with this Cevap. It explained her desperation. She was a girl trapped on a mountain with no one to help her.

Chapter 12

I look out the window. They have been here two days now. My grandson is at the fountain, sitting on the edge. He is smoking, which isn't good for his health or his reputation. My brother will say something to him soon, or, if not him, Mustafa will. Those two are as bad as the black crows who gather to gossip at Gül's house.

First came my father and now here are new people; the professor with many questions and the empty boy with none at all. The history man will get his answers, but it's Cem I hope who will start to think about what he wants from life. The men aren't happy with him and I'm not surprised. This is a boy in the skin of a man. He rolls along the ground like a thistle blown from its pod by the wind.

I stand at the window. It is time for me to tell my story and I am going to tell it to the world. Even though the man for whom my words are meant won't hear them, that doesn't matter. I go to my door and step onto the mat. It is a long while since the door has been painted, four years perhaps. Longer still since the walls were whitewashed. I am tired of doing all these things myself.

I stand on the mat. Gül isn't the only woman in the village with dead daughters. The talk of a girl going to Australia has made the young bride inside me roll over and become restless. I don't know what I am going to say, but I will tell it to everyone.

On the other side of the street, a curl of puppies writhes in the dirt. Yellow in colour, they roll and play with their sharp eyes and nipping teeth. They will grow to become protectors of house and village, scenting strangers, sniffing at the spoor of sheep and chickens. At night they will howl their own stories to the world, about how they have stopped killers and thieves in the night, men sneaking up the mountain to steal brides, others with feuds on their minds and cracked ancient handguns in their hands. The dogs howl about our births and deaths and protect us from our enemies, real and imagined. Their songs keep Al Bastı away, as well as the evil *jinns* and ghosts that roam the woods. We honour these ragged dogs in our carpets. We weave them into the wool, making them run, stiff-legged and rectilinear, with small triangles for ears and single-dot eyes, but on the plains or the side of the mountain, crossing the river at the old bridge, they are free and alive, energised by air and sunshine, liberated from tight woollen double-knots.

Now the boy is walking towards me down the road. Good, let him hear this, I am ready. My husband, that vicious old piece of goat shit, is far away, but he might hear my words in that faraway place. This boy might take my message back across the sea and stuff it into the old man's hairy, large-lobed ears.

'Good morning, sunshine.' My voice is loud and clear. 'And you dogs there. Here I am, old woman, and in front of God I stand. In front of you I have bent and prayed, alive now for almost seventy winters, an empty body and worn-out womb which has brought forth one live child and eight dead ones, may they be happy in Paradise. Five sons I gave that old goat and while all but one died, still he gave his thanks that the other dead babies were girls. He said it aloud! My poor little girls, sleeping now, thankfully spared from the misery on this earth that would have been theirs with a father like him.

'My friend, my poor Ayşe, and after her, it was me! I never dreamed it would happen, but I did my duty. I cooked three meals a day, brought wood for the stove for twenty-seven winters and twenty-seven summers. I hauled water for all the years before we got the pipes. I kept the stinking pit of a toilet watered, that place he emptied his bowels every day. I endured the slaps as I learned better how to chop the onion for the salad. He didn't like his beet juice chilled in the snow. The eggs must be almost set instead of solid, but not too runny! He would curse me with one breath and with the next remark what a fine day it was to walk to the tea garden and play a game. I kept on because he was my husband and it was my duty and well glad I would have been to perform it, to have done all of it, had he only been a slightly kind man.

'When he brought no money into the house during the Big Winter, when all he cared about was that the headman had beaten him again at backgammon or that his tobacco was running low, still I kept on. When I had an infection raging in my womb which took my fertility from me, still he wanted my bony bosom on the mattress, careful to curse me afterwards. And still I kept on. When he was thirsty for *rakı* to stop the dreams. When he stole my last gold bangle, the one I was saving for Ali's military service. He sold it and took the money and went to the cafe and bought all the men drinks. I cooked his meals and cleaned his toilet and opened my legs to him and said nothing.'

I look across the street. The boy is standing there, listening. I walk across.

'I'm saying it all and I don't care who knows. He can come back and crush my throat in the night with his dirty hands or kiss it with a grey-bladed knife. Put me in the well. I said nothing, but inside my kidneys and liver and lungs grew hot. The day he beat your father so badly his water was bloody, his face bruised and cut from his father's knuckles. He didn't even lift a hand to defend himself. I wanted to go to the shed to help him, but that one stopped me. The next day, when my son came inside, frozen, his lips purple, and kissed his father's hand and held it to his forehead and asked for forgiveness, my husband laughed in his face and called him weak. Still I said nothing.'

The boy is listening.

'I breathed his filthy cigarette smoke for ten thousand days. While ill with child in the early months, with smoke curling in my nostrils from morning until night, I smelled his breath, rotten in the mornings, and when I was pregnant, I had to leave and heave my stomach onto the cold snow outside in winter, the dry dirt in summer. And I cleaned—oh, how I cleaned. The window ledges, the floor, the soot from the chimney. The grey flecks that settled on the windows and the springy hairs that drop from the bodies of men. I managed the animal dung that collected in the garden and I dusted after the human beast as well; the mess that he let fall onto my floors, onto my rugs, onto my table as he sat there smoking, the ash growing long at the end to be flicked with purpose or shattered with a movement as he reached for the *rakı* bottle or the millionth glass of tea that I had served him, all without thanks. How many times he asked me if there was water, when we both knew there was. I would have been happy to fetch him a thousand glasses of water had only he once said "please" or "thank you".

'All the eggplants I peeled, fried, dried, stuffed and grilled. The chickens I plucked and boiled, the onions I chopped and sliced, the tomatoes I washed. A million cucumbers I have slit open and a million tomatoes have bled onto my fingers and still my job was not done nearly well enough.

'I ached and hurt and cried with gas and wind; monthly cramps, labour cramps, leg cramps, back cramps, head cramps. My heart cramped too. The nappies I changed, washed, wrung and hung. The clothes I scrubbed; the underwear, the outerwear, the stiff stinking socks and the black-collared shirts. For decades I washed his brown-streaked shorts, shirts with putrid yellow underarm stains. There was never money for new clothes so I patched and sewed and darned and renewed thread by thread, loop by loop.'

'You're my grandmother?' the boy says.

'I was, one of them, but they left me behind.'

'Who was my other grandmother?'

'The sister of a girl called Ayşe. I don't even remember her name now. Three girls they were, Emine, Ayşe and your mother's mother.'

'Is that why my mother sometimes cries in Australia?'

'That would be reason enough. Your grandmother howled for her sister and her sadness would have soaked into Hanife as well. These things can be inherited and I don't say any more than that.' I suck at my teeth. 'Are you kind to your mother? Please be a kind man.'

I can see he doesn't know what to say.

'Do the women in Australia have to bleed on the first night? I dripped red into the snow, pressed a handful of it against my swelling. Ayşe didn't bleed and she went down the well.' Look, he doesn't understand the verb for 'swelling' so I explain, using *kanamak*: to bleed. He understands what that means.

'How did he get to Australia?' The boy is standing in the shade. I take his face between my hands. I hope he can feel my love for him.

'You ask me how he went? My brother helped him. He also had gold, from your country, a round rock of gold but that was rightfully mine.'

'Where did he get it?'

'Stolen from my father.'

'Why didn't you go with them?'

'I didn't want to leave and I am lucky he didn't want to take me.'

'Why did they leave?'

'You've heard something about a refrigerator?' I wait until he's looking at me and I shake my head. 'But it was me,' I say and my voice is loud. 'I made him leave.'

I think I have been clear. I turn and walk down the road. I go around the corner and beyond the walnut tree, and from there I begin to climb the sloping road where the wild herbs and daisies grow along the verge. Many times I have picked leaves here to mix into my rice, things to make my potions. I am weak as if something that once filled me has now gone. I almost fall. I go up and over the hill, away from the village, to the wishing tree.

There I tie a strip of fabric and make my wish. I make one for Cem too.

I walk down into a shallow valley and pass along the river near the old stone bridge. At every winter meeting the men discuss replacing it, but there is never enough money in the village chest and the years pass and nothing is done. My father liked to come here and lie a while under the trees, especially when he was thinking about something.

I look for a long time under the trees for the thing that I need. I find several and put them in a piece of cloth and go back down the central road. Once home, I begin the preparations and make sure everything is perfect. When I am finished, I clean up and dig a small hole and bury the mess. The pot simmers on the fire. There is a thud at the window. Outside I find a bird lying on the ground. I see its yellow beak moving.

'Oh, little bird, what happened to you?'

Its tongue is the colour of a bruise. One of its claws opens and closes. The bird reminds me of the flying woman. As I get the spade I remember the day she showed me the world.

Chapter 13

Cem was walking to the Honey Hut. It was the morning of the third day and now everyone was watching him. Mothers at the fountain had tried to tell him about their daughters, to convince him of their special qualities. Whenever Meral drifted into sight, walking with her head down, radiating misery, someone would come and shepherd him in the opposite direction. He started to watch for her any time he was outside, or looking through a window, or standing at Harry's doorway gazing back down towards the village. She became like a beacon and he found himself seeking her form, alert to her location.

He ate with Mustafa or Old Mehmet, but not Harry, whose back had worsened. A boy took food on a tray up to the hut, so Cem knew Harry was being looked after, but Cem had come to be sick of the tea, sick of the talk, sick of Harry's stubborn delusion and the nagging about talking to Mehmet. He wished he hadn't come and had decided to tell Harry he was going to leave early.

He knocked on the door of the hut and found Harry down on the floor. His back had become 'demonic' overnight, Harry said, telling Cem to come in, come in.

'Today's the day but I'm in absolute agony, such a relentless griping,' Harry said, his voice thick. 'The alcohol isn't helping—in fact, it makes it worse—but I'm at the end of my tolerance. If I had some sort of answer I could bear it, but still I wait with high agitation and intense hope.'

Cem lay face down on the carpet at the end of the bed.

'Harry,' he said to the wool-on-wool double-knotted rug, 'I think they want me to marry one of the girls. They're saying something about my grandfather owing the village.'

'If you could leave the girls alone until I get my answer, I'd appreciate it, Cem.'

'I'm not doing anything with the girls. It's the village that wants me to.'

'Well, we don't want to upset them.'

'*You* don't.'

Harry sighed. 'Alright. Which one do you like?'

'You're not listening. I don't like any of them. One of them has a problem with her father, though, which is kind of . . . something. Interesting.'

'They might think it's your cultural duty to take one back with you. Or make an arrangement and marry later. Perhaps they see it as a community service.'

'I don't owe them, Harry.'

'I thought you were interested in Miriam? Or the girl in Istanbul—what happened to that one?'

'She was different.' He thought about Jenna. He was still angry about her.

'Anyway, if you could avoid upsetting them, I'd appreciate it. I don't think you understand how important this is. Just be patient a bit longer and then we can leave. I need to do something about my back before we go, though. I couldn't stand to go in a car while it's like this. The road was quite uneven as we came up and the thought of jolting all that way . . . Well, you know. Perhaps you could ask whether there's a person here who can perform chiropractic work?'

'I'll ask when I go back down to the village. Harry, I was thinking—'

'You did ask them about the aspirin, didn't you? I'm sure you said you did, but I'm having trouble remembering things. The pain's so bad, I don't know whether it's day or night. And another pillow would be splendid.'

Cem hadn't asked about painkillers, he'd forgotten, but he told Harry he had and that they'd said they had nothing to offer other than tea and rest. He felt bad about lying but when Harry sighed again, irritation replaced the guilt.

'Harry, I'm thinking I might leave soon. Maybe after breakfast.'

Harry's face fell.

'Before the meeting? But I need to you to interpret.'

'I'm sorry. This stuff that's going on. It's making me uncomfortable.'

'You have to stick with things in life, my boy. You can't just give up when things get a little tricky. Let me tell you about Marlene.'

'What do you mean?'

'Well,' Harry sighed. 'It's this. Marlene is living in Canberra with a public servant called Richard and our children are both married, with children themselves. My son lectures at the university and my daughter is a doctor.'

'Shit.'

'I suppose it is quite. She didn't stick at it, but I suppose I can't blame her. After my car accident, I became dependent on things to help with the pain. I tried opium, but it wasn't for me. Someone mentioned, as a joke, that I should try it, it was one of the chaps from the Asian Studies department. Nothing like it, he said. Well, he mentioned opium and I couldn't get it out of my mind, the idea of it. Like with the Kelly thing—I get an idea and it sticks, sometimes for decades. With the opium, though, I found I could take it or leave it. Now I can see I had notions of relaxed men in silk pyjamas, but I had a taste and the reality was different. Marlene was long gone by then. I think it's about working out when to keep going and when to stop.' He wiped at his eyes with his handkerchief. 'So, today is it: I find out if there's anything *to* find out. And I'm absolutely tormented with dread and anxiety. I'm preparing myself for it not to be true. If you could wait until after the meeting?'

Cem was surprised he felt sorry for Harry, and wondered whether the other man had told him the sad story about his family to make him so. That could be a lie as well, Harry was obviously a man who was not in touch with reality. Cem had never thought it might be possible for a person to trick themselves into believing something. Lying to others, he knew about that, but deception of the self? It was a new concept to him.

'Well,' Cem said, 'If it's not true at least you can forget about it.'

'I don't think it's that simple.'

Cem got up and went round to where Harry was lying. He hadn't moved, his eyes were closed and his glasses were propped up on top of his head. There was sweat on his forehead.

'Are you coming to breakfast?'

'I can't come down like this.' Harry lifted a finger. 'They'll bring me something on a tray, but I'll have a bit more of the *rakı*?' In the distance, the call to prayer began. Cem gave him the glass. It took Harry a long while to edge his head to the side so he could raise the drink to his lips. Cem stood and watched. He knew he should offer to help, but he didn't want to put his hands on the other man.

'I'm going down,' he said.

'Can you please remember to ask about the chiropractor? Check again about medicine?'

Cem promised that he would. 'Harry,' he said, 'have you heard any yelling? It happens when the dogs are barking, around midnight, but behind it I can hear someone shouting.' Cem looked from the door towards the village below. 'You'd hear it clearly from here. I hear a wailing and it stops when the dogs stop.'

'Perhaps it's someone in pain,' Harry said. 'I think you know nothing of pain.'

Cem wanted to say he did know about pain. That no matter how hard he tried Jenna would not leave his mind completely. That she had invaded his sleep, as well as a witchy woman with frightening teeth. He wanted to explain to Harry that he had never dreamed of a girl before other than Zeynep, when he was little, but they'd been boyish dreams, not the rich stuff of yearning that he had experienced every night since leaving Istanbul.

As well as his interrupted sleep, still his bowels were suffering. Last night Berna had arrived carrying a large glass of dark liquid. Old Mehmet had ushered her in and called out to Cem to come and take receipt of some poison. He was laughing, red-faced with his joke, but Berna was stern. Cem had become terribly constipated since arriving in the village, she explained to her brother, anybody could see it. She'd prepared a herbal potion, she told Cem, and he had to drink it fresh, just before sleeping that night. It would take effect by morning and he would see the end of the problem soon after that, but he shouldn't go too far away from the bathroom until the afternoon of the next day.

In the hut Cem thought about telling Harry what he knew of pain, that he was in pain himself, but he stood to leave and was just going out when Harry spoke again, in a whisper now. 'You will come with me to the meeting this afternoon?'

Cem turned. Harry had his glasses back in position, magnifying his owl-like eyes. 'Please? I don't care about the medicine, or the chiropractor, or the pillow, but I need you to interpret. I'm terrified I'll miss something crucial.'

'Okay,' said Cem. 'I'll be there.'

Just then, one of Mustafa's girls came up the path. She called out in Turkish to Cem, but it took a few repetitions before he finally understood that a lady with yellow hair had arrived in a taxi and she and the driver were down at the fountain asking for him.

Chapter 14

I

At the tea garden, the headman Haluk announced they were going to send a delegation to the new war. The Ottomans were collaborating with the foreign forces, intending to colonise Turkey, carve it up among the Europeans. It was to be the War of Independence, the biggest pants-stiffener of all.

'And Jim can go, now that we have papers for him.'

Everyone congratulated James. The women ululated out on the street.

'*Hopa!*' someone said.

'What?' said James. He was distracted. He couldn't find Alphonse. He had asked the boys if they'd seen him, knowing Ahmet particularly was fond of the animal, but they had both said they didn't know where he was. 'Papers?'

'Don't worry, I'm going too,' Ferhat said. 'And Meryem said yes—she agreed to marry when we come back.'

‘I thought you were marrying Emine,’ James said.

‘Meryem not for me, donkey—for you. You are man but no woman. You need a woman to wash and cook. And for love. You too old now.’

‘I don’t need a woman,’ James said. ‘And I’m not so old. I like being on my own. I’m fine.’

‘No man can fine without. Look.’ Ferhat held out his hand for the other man’s small notebook and pencil. He started a list.

‘Okay. No Sevre. No Duha. No Tulet. Big no Emine.’ Ferhat leaned towards James. ‘My love Emine,’ he whispered, then pointed at a beetle-browed man who was glowering at the two bachelors. ‘Emine dad,’ Ferhat whispered again and held his finger to his lips. ‘Greedy man.’ Ferhat sat back. ‘Emine sister Ayşe too young. For you: *Meryem*. My uncle.’

‘Aunt,’ said James. He sipped his tea. He must have forgotten to put his usual single cube in. He reached for another and Lame Adar nudged one of the men sitting there and pointed at James with his chin. James dropped the sugar into his glass and stirred and the men smiled. To Ferhat, James said thank you, but he didn’t want to get married, he was perfectly happy on his own in the Honey Hut.

‘Maybe I should go back home.’

‘You no go home. You marry to Meryem.’

James drank his tea. How was this going to happen?

Haluk reached forwards for more sugar. ‘My sister has no man and no one else wants her. Your people killed her husband at Gelibolu and there is responsibility. In the village no one is of the right age—sorry, Adar—except for you.’ Adar held up a hand to show he wasn’t offended.

James picked up the headman's hand and kissed it. He pressed it to his forehead. 'Please let me think about it,' he said. Then he left. He wanted to get up the mountain before anyone could see where he had gone. He didn't even want the rooster-who-pecked to follow him.

He sat in one of the cool caves, but after a while Adar came and sat with him in silence until it started to get dark outside.

'I'm sorry for the widow and her children, but pity isn't the same as love.' He leaned forwards to see Adar's face in the shadows of the cave. There was a dripping sound somewhere in the back. James got up and poked about at the edges of the cave, wondering if perhaps Alphonse was there.

'Maybe it's time to leave, Adar.'

James spoke in English but the other man heard his name and said 'yes'.

'Just now, when they suggested Meryem.'

'Meryem. Yes.'

James picked up a stone from the floor of the cave. 'I don't know what she'd make of it. Does she even want another husband?'

'Yes.'

'And I miss Alphonse.'

James sighed. It seemed he would have to accept that the animal had crawled off somewhere and died. He felt bad at the thought of him dying alone, so intensely sad it made him want to weep, but now it was clear he had something larger to think about. James sighed again and Adar sighed too. It seemed wherever James went these days he had the bent shadow of Adar behind him. People said that Al Bastı had been outside the window when Adar was born, that she had twisted him as she did the trees. But while the villagers dismissed him, and even Ferhat could be cruel to him, James had developed great affection for Adar.

He knew he would have been entirely happy had he never left Beechworth. He could have sold the gold, found some land, kept cows or horses. Chickens even, bees certainly. But here he was, over the other side of the world, perhaps the only Australian in this foreign land, having a new war suggested to him by a Moslem village chief, and now with an arrangement in place, not of his making, to marry a woman with whom he'd be unable to ever achieve true intimacy.

Perhaps he could travel with the other men down the mountain then make his way to Ankara. There'd be a diplomatic office there. He would find out what he needed to do to get to London and then home. He wasn't going to another war and he wasn't going to marry Meryem. He should have left long ago.

What would Cole say if he somehow arrived in the village, trundled in atop a lorry or perhaps on the back of some wheezing oily motorcycle, in a sidecar even, with his plane-mad daughter driving? What would the villagers make of them? And what would Linda say? Him going off to a war not his own and marrying a woman he couldn't talk to properly. He hadn't heard from the Coles, even though he'd written to say he was safe.

That evening, when James arrived at Meryem's house to begin his extraction from the village, a discussion was in progress. Haluk was there, sitting in the best seat by the fire.

'I want to go,' said Ahmet.

'What do you say?' Meryem asked her brother.

'Ferhat told me there were females at Gelibolu, and if Adar is going, so can my nephew,' Haluk said.

James must have misheard them. War was not the place for a boy. It was not even a place for men.

'It will be dangerous,' James said.

'Of course it will be dangerous, this is the nature of war and of life,' said Haluk. 'We used to love the pants-stiffeners with Yunan. As a boy I ran alongside the men as they rushed down the road, calling for arms. Behind us the women would make their noise and there'd be wild threats and accusations on both sides. "This man moved the boundary stick." "No, *this* man moved it!" "That man stole this girl for a bride." "No, *that* one did!" '

'Ferhat said the war will be Turk against Turk. Brothers killing brothers. Cousins shooting cousins,' James said. 'More than a pants-stiffener. Real weapons, real death, not just agitating over boundaries or donkeys.'

'I'd like to shoot a cousin,' said Ahmet. 'That would be velvet.' He put his hand in his pocket to play with himself. There was a little hole there his aunt hadn't found yet. James looked at the spot on the back of Ahmet's skinny neck. A child was not unlike a pupa. They need time to develop—but years of care, not mere days. They needed to be nurtured and protected so they could grow into hard-working drones. A small pulsing mass of tissue, wriggling and surging against the shell until the casing splits and the adult emerges metamorphosed from its waxed cell.

'God will protect him,' Meryem said as she spooned beans onto rice. She put the plate on the table. 'I'm only worried he won't like the food because he is fussy. Who knows if there will even be beans at the war?'

'He should go.' Haluk moved to the table and started eating. 'Beans or not.'

Meryem made a plate for James and he sat down as well.

'What would his father say?' said James.

Meryem served the children and took a portion for herself. Ahmet was sitting but not eating. He was staring at James with his lips pulled back over his teeth. James tried to make him smile by waggling his eyebrows at him, but Ahmet's face didn't change. Haluk chewed bread and kept his eyes on his food.

Finally, Meryem spoke. 'His father would have gone with him to keep him safe. You are to be his new father and you'll be there to look after him.' Her cheeks were red but she didn't look away.

James sat and ate with them and listened to their chatter. A little while later, he thanked her for the food and left.

That skinny fatherless neck. He had to go to Izmir and fight in another war to keep that skinny neck safe.

II

Yunan were sending three men so naturally Hayat sent five. The group comprised Haluk, Ferhat, Ahmet, James and Adar, who would drive the ox cart. The women threw pans of water into the dust behind the spokeless wooden wheels of the cart as it started to move down the sloping road. Children ran alongside and mothers caterwauled, terrified one would slip under the grinding wheels. Fathers told them to *soos*; once they spoke the words, the universe would hear them and make the tragedy happen.

Ahmet wanted to ride a horse, not go in the cart with Adar.

'A man needs to fall off twenty-nine times before he can claim to be a decent horseman,' James said. Ahmet said he was as good a rider as anyone and that he didn't want to go in the cart like a cripple. James kept the smile on his face and ruffled the boy's hair, but Ahmet was grim and his face tense. He said something that James couldn't catch and wouldn't repeat it when asked.

Saliha begged Haluk not to take Ahmet, saying if he had to take one let it be the older one, her brother. Mehmet was more deserving, she argued. He was not a troublemaker.

'Ahmet will be unbearable when he gets back, strutting like the rooster,' she said. 'And he won't be useful, he'll complain. Or take me. I can tell when people are creeping through a forest and I know what it means when the birds disappear. I could go to the village houses to ask for bread and cheese. I can read the beans and help keep the group safe.'

Haluk lifted his chin, raised his eyebrows and tsked with his tongue. The answer was no. Ahmet poked out his own tongue at his cousin and said that she needed a special piece of equipment for war, but Saliha reached forwards and grabbed his thing through his pants and said this wasn't the tool of a man. She told him he was an *eşek* and Ahmet complained to Meryem that Saliha had called him a donkey. Meryem told her daughter to leave Ahmet alone, that he was only a child. He needed understanding and soft words, not the opposite.

The cart rattled and shook its way down the mountain. As they travelled, Ahmet sometimes stepped off the cart onto the back of James's saddle from the cart and slid down behind him, gripping with his spindly arms. James felt the excitement of travel and was invigorated.

The journey took them through villages and across the outer plains of western Anatolia. They were in the last pushes of summer and the days were long and hot, the sun drying their lips. They ate eggs, yoghurt and black bread for breakfast, and stopped for an hour at the height of each day's heat and found cool spots for the horses to rest and drink. Streams crosshatched the land and along the road, fountains were set into the edges of hills, built into stone walls by one village or another. Haluk passed judgement on the different waters they tasted, but James could not tell the difference. To him they were all delicious and cold.

It didn't take long for him to settle into the pace and become dreamy with it. Slogging along beside the cart, leaning across to tuck the jute charcoal bag around the back of Ahmet to prevent the sun reaching his head, James listened to Haluk talk about how the French were fighting, and the English too. It was an unsettling thought, and James felt his bowels churn at the prospect of coming across an Englishman on the battlefield.

It took ten days of gentle travel over almost two hundred and fifty miles before they reached the eastern outskirts of Izmir. James leaned forward and rubbed Blossom's neck and the smell of the sea whipped into his nostrils in a surge of salt and brine. An hour later, just out of Izmir, a view of blue expanse appeared as they rounded a bend in the road, then a stretch of beach and sandy cliffs and houses nestled down by the water in the distance.

They stopped by medieval walls and heard the noises of the city. Political messages blared from the mosque minarets. Hilly streets were dotted with acacias in bloom, and old beeches stood as guards on either side of the city road.

'They say there is a British club here,' Haluk said, yawning to cover a smile. He'd become impatient during the journey, especially with James. 'And something called a beer hall, which sounds barbaric to me. But there is opium, oh yes. Forget the barley, the yellow dye, grapes and figs. Who cares for figs? Tobacco? No. Carpets from other countries? Inferior. Sponges from the islands. Who wants a sponge? Can you even tell me what a sponge is, Jim?'

James said it was difficult to explain.

'Try,' said Haluk. 'I'm not stupid. I think I can understand.'

But James was unable to make the other man know what a sponge was. If a person had never seen or held one, they couldn't understand. James smiled and said he was sorry, but the headman turned his back. On the street it was warm and James thought to show Ahmet the water. He asked Haluk whether it would be possible to go to the beach.

'When there's a war on?' The headman made a face at Ahmet, who laughed. 'Don't be crazy, Jim. It's not time for swimming at the beach.'

III

The next day, to Ahmet's disgust, he was left with an old couple at a house at the back of the city. The others went to a wide, stony field to engage in lukewarm battle. They fought alongside an army of irregulars, well equipped, albeit in an unconventional fashion. The clash was mild and James wondered why they were there. When he asked Haluk, the other man didn't answer other than to talk about civic duty. He chided James, asking him was he nervous, was he scared? Then a captain made a special fuss of James and took him by the arm to show him the cooled weaponry they'd stored behind the front line, and afterwards gave him a middle-sweet coffee cooked over a small fire. James asked the captain when the fighting had stopped.

'Two months ago. This is tidying. I was surprised when your group arrived.'

'You don't look happy, Mr Jim,' Haluk said to him that night. Ahmet was complaining and Adar was lying down because his leg hurt. Ferhat was quiet and withdrawn.

'Where is the war?' James said.

'There is still important work to be done.' Haluk was preparing for bed. James went to lie down near Adar. The five of them were sharing a large room; Haluk and Ahmet had beds each and the other three were on the floor.

'Why are we here?' James whispered to Adar. The other man shifted his shoulder.

'It doesn't matter,' he said. James saw Adar's good-natured smile in the dark. 'Here is just the place we are for now.'

'We're here because my father said we must come,' said Ferhat, lying down to sleep. 'He is the headman, he is the most powerful in the village.'

James was nodding, but puzzled by Ferhat's words.

'I know he is the headman,' he said.

‘And while the next headman will be voted, usually it’s the son of the previous chief who gets the position.’ Ferhat pulled his blanket over his shoulder. James didn’t know why his friend was talking like this. And what had been that strange look on Ferhat’s face earlier when the captain had given James the coffee? He and his father had stood a way off under a tree, watching. There was something afoot with them, James realised. Haluk had become terse and seemed angry all the time, and Ferhat was quieter than usual. What had caused the change? He couldn’t think, so he went to sleep listening to Ahmet wriggling on the bed nearby.

IV

They began to make their way home one September morning with a warm breeze at their backs. As James rode, the wind on his neck was a reminder of what he was leaving behind. A ruined town and an unvisited beach, but he’d found a hill and looked out over the vast blue of the sea, imagining Beechworth all the way across, with its papery trees and roaring koalas, the pinging bellbirds and oily eucalyptus smells. Melbourne with its trams and rushing people in hats, their speech filled with flattened vowel sounds. He’d stood a long while on the hill, straining his eyes into the distance.

They will drink more water and pass more villages before trouble will find them on the road back. Adar will begin to mutter his proverbs, things like, *Two captains sink the ship*, and become remote and watchful, and the atmosphere will tighten around them and become strained. Ferhat will seem to stop talking altogether.

V

When Haluk died, James knew it hadn't been deliberate on his part, but Ahmet's later testimony made him question the events, even though he had a clear memory of it. Even Ferhat would be noncommittal about what happened. One thing was certain: as they'd travelled back from the west, something had darkened in the headman and he'd become more irritable than ever, and finally there'd come a point beyond which it seemed nothing made any difference. The headman's usual jocularity had deserted him and he had become struck by cholera, a sickness that made him complain and find fault with everything James did, and everything that he didn't do.

VI

Two nights before they were due to arrive back at the village, they settled around the fire. The cold and dark pressed into their curved backs and no one spoke. The trees creaked and the wind built as the moon moved high into the sky. James couldn't sleep.

He smelled something peculiar and the horses nickered and stirred, their rumps bumping in the midnight. He got up and went to them. He put a hand on Blossom's long nose and leaned into her side, wrapping his other arm around the top of her neck. He brushed his lips against her coat and listened and, after a few moments,

Haluk came blundering into the clearing. His look was blank; wherever he'd been and whatever he'd been doing, he said nothing. He looked at James and his eyes were black hollows. The headman lay back down beside the fire.

VII

On the last night, all of them were beyond exhaustion. They lay, the fire lowering, and James heard Adar moaning softly.

'What's wrong?'

'My back aches in the damp air. The bone hurts because it's crooked.'

James tried to give the other man an extra covering, but he would only accept a jute bag.

'The boy needs the quilts; he's so skinny there's nothing of him,' Adar said.

James put another covering on top of Ahmet, whose narrow face poked out of the top, watchful in the dark. Then Haluk sat up with a curse and stoked the fire. He pulled out a small pouch. He said he was feeling too sharp in the brain and that they should all have some opium to warm them and help them sleep. Even Ahmet should try it.

'Who cares for figs?' Haluk said.

He had never spoken about his wife but now told the others how well he satisfied her in the bed. He asked James how he planned to love his sister and whether he would take his big thing and shove it in her from behind like a dog. Ahmet giggled from his jute-bag bed. James closed his eyes. Ferhat was rigid on his back and seemed to be asleep. The silence became larger. The waxing moon lifted high and, though it had one slight edge off it, Haluk became quite mad.

'Do you think the women talk about intercourse?'

James opened his eyes to the fire.

'They do.' Ahmet's voice was reedy in the dark. 'They talk about it all the time. How big men are, how small. They talk about good kissing and bad kissing and even about balls and arseholes. They complain about the hair from bodies and about smells. They tell how men put it in, how long a husband goes for and how much sugar he takes in his tea and how all of it is connected. Sugar and fucking, they say. They have a scale. The more sugar, the better fucker a man is. They talk about it more than cooking or carpets even.'

'Don't say that word, Ahmet,' said James.

'Especially the older women,' Ahmet said. 'The young girls go red, but the married women never stop talking.'

'*Oğlum*,' James said. '*Soos*.'

'I'm not your son.'

'How do you know these things?' Haluk lit a cigarette.

'Before I was a man I was stuck with the women and I listened.'

'Well,' said Haluk, 'they will like the Australian. They will talk about him soon.'

'You're talking about your sister,' James said.

Haluk came and loomed over him, fierce in the dark. He made James get up and James stood and raised his open palms as a gesture that he didn't want to fight. Haluk swung a fist and James sidestepped. The village chief twisted and fell down and hit his head on a rock. James called to the others. Ferhat and Adar came over and stood looking at the blood that was coming from their headman's nose, and they saw that his eyes were open with surprise. James started to explain what had happened in the darkness and Adar said it had been so, that he had seen it. Ferhat put his hand on James's shoulder and said he was sure it had been an accident and though his voice was quiet, James felt better, until he saw Ahmet's white face under-lit by the fire, and how in the night he turned and sniffed the air like an animal.

They talked about putting Haluk in the back of the cart, but Ahmet refused to sit with a dead man and said he would ride on Haluk's horse.

'We have to bury him once it's light,' Adar said. 'We should do it here, I know the words. My father showed me how.'

Ferhat said no, that they would take his father home so that the *hoca* could do the washing and prayers. 'We'll be home and can bury him by sundown.'

'But I've got a piece of white fabric I can use,' said Adar. He wanted to help. He had been a friend to Ferhat all his life.

'I said no.' Ferhat cleared his throat. 'I don't want you to do it, Lame Adar. And I want to tell the others my father died in the battle.'

'Okay, why not?' said Adar. 'Yes, it's better for him. People will remember him with more respect.'

'I disagree,' said James. 'We should tell the truth.'

'You're wrong.' Ferhat didn't look up

'But his body,' said James. 'They'll know he was recently killed, that we haven't carried him for days.'

'That's true,' said Adar. 'You know we must bury him before night falls. It won't make sense to say that.'

'They won't understand. They are fools, most of them.'

'Your mother will know,' said James.

Ferhat was angry. 'Don't talk about my mother. First you mention my aunt and then you mention my mother. You should not talk about other people's women.'

Adar stepped forward and lifted his hands.

'*In the name of God, Most Gracious, Most Merciful, Praise be to God, the Cherisher and Sustainer of the Worlds*,' Adar said to the sky, reciting the opening words of the Koran.

He looked at James and remarked that he was pale as a quince.

Chapter 15

I

In 1934, the Eskişehir Sugar Factory was opened and in Hayat, the early summer skies promised warmth for the day. In the new *muhtar*'s salon, the lighter lace curtains had been unpacked from a cedar dowry chest a few weeks before. Along the window ledges, ashtrays and the prized bottle of cologne from Izmir sat on lace doilies decorated with plastic flowers. The new headman knew exactly how many times the cologne had been dispensed into a cupped palm.

The villagers still called Ferhat the new chief even though he had been years in the job. Ferhat had told his wife, Emine, who had told Meryem, who had told James, that the new headman resented the position. He had to oversee and manage all official business of the village, receive visitors, raise taxes, keep order and bring criminals to justice. His first duty had been to formally reprimand Ahmet when Mehmet had his accident. It was a job he didn't enjoy. And then last year had been hellish, with what happened to Ayşe.

After Mehmet went over the cliff off his horse, people came to him and said Ahmet was to blame. Then there'd been even bigger trouble with the girl. For that, Ahmet had been sent to the new compulsory military service and he had never forgiven Ferhat for it. He'd said it was worse than the war, worse than anything else in his life, but still it hadn't managed to effect any transformation on Ahmet's character or morals.

James and Ferhat's friendship had not recovered. James had told several people the truth of how Haluk died, which made Ferhat angry, and Ahmet had said that James had hit Haluk, that it was his fault the headman had fallen over and hit his head on a rock. People retreated to their family units amid threats of a pants-stiffener, and the owner of the tea garden noticed a drop in custom for several weeks. It was a long time before the likelihood of intra-village violence subsided.

Ferhat, James and Lame Adar were in the salon, waiting for the rest of the men. Adar had arrived first, keenest to choose his new name. While they waited, one of Ferhat's sons brought a tray on which were several tea glasses, spoons and a bowl of sugar cubes. Ferhat leaned back, trying not to dislodge the dainty lace mats on the armrests of his chair.

'Damn these things. How on earth are we meant to conduct business with these bastards in the way?' he called to Emine.

'They have been there a thousand days, my pasha, and longer will they remain. They've never bothered you before,' his wife called back.

'God, how can you say it? I've complained about them every one of those thousand days. Bastards!'

The men started arriving. Ferhat tried to rearrange the headrest and the others looked around the room, not wanting to see their *muhtar* fussing with fabrics. Each man pretended to be interested in the kilim patterns; the stitching of their suit pants; the precise nicotine-shading of their index fingers.

James sat on one of the sofas, near Adar.

'Now then,' Ferhat said, 'there is an order from our government that everybody needs to make themselves another name. It's called a surname and we have to choose one by the end of the year. It sits behind your first name on official papers. Jim had such a name in his country. It's the usual convention in the west, he says.' Ferhat fiddled with a doily.

One of the other men, Orhan, shifted uncomfortably in his seat.

'So, Headman, these names—are they to be like the ones we already have?'

'I don't understand you, Mr Orhan-Bey.'

'Well, as a model of my meaning, I am Tall Orhan. For the additional name, do I add another name, such as, perhaps, Tall Orhan Barak?' Orhan was sheepish. 'I've always liked the name Barak. Its meaning is a good one.'

One of the other men, already called Barak, opened his mouth to protest, but before he could speak, Ferhat said, 'No, you fool, not another first name. It's the "Tall" we have to get rid of. It can be something like Sheepherder, or Woodman or Cotton-grower, or the name of an object, like "mountain". Thinks of something else, not Barak.'

Barak leaned back in relief.

'But we have other people in the village with the same names—'

'Close your mouth, Orhan, you are not following me.' Ferhat held his empty glass out to his son, who was pouring more tea.

'Thank you, darling,' Ferhat said. 'Now listen, you fools, both of you.' He pointed at Tall Orhan and Barak. 'This second name can be related to what it is you do, though I don't think "Fool" or "Time-waster" would be appropriate. It can be Pamuk for the cotton down on the plains, if that's where your family was from originally, or Ekmekçi after bread. Snake, even, if it be your inclination or strong wish. I have heard of people choosing volcano or bullet. As I said, mountain—'

'Oh, Headman, what name is it that you are choosing for your family?'

'I am not certain yet,' said Ferhat.

There was silence in the room.

'I would like to be Adar Aslan,' Lame Adar said.

'Alright,' Ferhat said, pointing to his old friend, 'your family can be "Aslan" for "lion".'

Adar tried to straighten in his seat.

'And you'—Ferhat pointed next at Ali, the harvest man—'your family should be Buğday, for the wheat. Barak, your second name will be Koyun.' Ferhat reached for his fresh tea.

'I know we are a long line of sheep men, but it is not a dignified name.' Barak had his hands raised in front of him in a plea for understanding.

There was a noise outside and James lifted his head.

'What is it?' the men asked each other.

James got to his feet and ran, stopping only to stuff his feet into his shoes outside the house. He went up the street, neck craning, looking up to the sky. He ran up to the meadow beyond the Honey

Hut. Villagers were following. Was it was another war? Was it Yunan come to attack? What was that machine in the sky?

James arrived at the meadow before anyone else. He was there to see the plane set down neatly on the flattest part, just below the caves. He walked towards the craft. It was small, no more than a pocket handkerchief of a thing. Through the window, he saw the colour of her cropped hair, her smiling face and madly waving hands. He stood back as the plane taxied to a stop.

II

She jumped out of the plane almost before it had stopped moving. She wasn't wearing a cap or a hat, just a scarf up around her ears. She grinned and ran across the grass to him, calling above the sound of the slowing propeller. He went to extend his hand but she flung her arms around him and clung to his neck. He breathed in.

'Sorry,' she said. 'My legs go to sleep on the rudder.'

James said hello and kissed her cheek. He asked if she was on her own.

'Do you see anyone else?' she shouted. 'Does it get windy here?' She was hectic, walking back to the plane. Had he said something as he'd hugged her? He couldn't remember, less than a minute afterwards. He said there was no wind at the moment and Linda shouted that was good, it meant she didn't have to stake the plane.

'Sorry about the yelling! My ears go a bit squiffy too! With the engine noise, it takes me a while to adjust to being back in the quiet.' She laughed and reached into the cabin to open a type of glove box. She pulled out a print dress, a pair of evening shoes, a thermos and a bottle of wine.

'Those shoes won't be any good here,' James said.

'Fortified table wine from Western Australia!' she shouted. 'It's in fashion at the moment, back home!'

James smiled.

'Dad bought a case for my wedding,' she shouted.

'How is he?'

'He died before it.'

'The wedding?'

Linda nodded, her nose red. James said he was sorry. He asked whether Cole had been ill or was it sudden, how her mother was, whether the shop was still open. All standing in the grass while noticing how the sun lit up her hair. Then he asked why her husband wasn't with her.

'I didn't get married in the end,' she said. 'It was a mistake. I think I was doing it for Dad. I wouldn't have been a terribly good wife. Men like women who make steak-and-kidney pies and knit baby clothes, who talk gently and are sweet, not ones who think about being in the air whenever they're on the ground and would rather strip down spark plugs than go to dinner parties. You would think he wouldn't have minded all the grease, though, him being a lawyer.' She grinned, but James shook his head, not understanding. 'He wanted me to promise that I would stop flying, but I knew I wouldn't be able to break the habit, so I stopped the wedding instead.'

This exchange had been shouted, but Linda smiled and her voice dropped.

'My ears are fine now. Sorry about yelling all that at you.'

III

Meryem scrutinised Linda and, even without being able to know things the way her daughters did, she understood everything in an instant. This woman was why her husband's heart was dull, yet it was clear there was nothing in it. Such was the way of love. A heart wanted what it wanted and could not be told, not by reason nor determination. This Linda was no threat and Meryem decided she would take care of her. If James loved her, then so would she, but Meryem couldn't help being brisk, almost irritated at her guest. Her husband was a good man and it seemed he had been badly hurt by this one.

Meryem bustled around the house. The evening dress was no good and neither were the shoes. Linda's pants and skirt needed cleaning, so Meryem gave her some of her own baggy *şalvar* with a skirt to go over the top of them. She tried to give her an apron, but the other woman said no and insisted on wearing a type of man's jacket over the top of it all. Meryem raised her eyebrows and clucked as she tied the trousers with plaited wool at the waist to keep them from slipping down.

IV

It was extraordinary to have Linda there. James hadn't realised how much he missed his own language. He had a slow start and struggled to remember words, stopping mid-speech and looking at the wall, trying to recall a particular expression and finally stammering out something inadequate and childlike. He was shocked that she had come all this way, navigated to this particular mountain in western Anatolia. When he asked how she'd found him, she showed him an old Jacaranda school atlas.

'I have a compass as well, of course. I knew which country to aim for and I followed the pink bits,' she said, turning the pages. 'I met some people in Ankara who told me which mountain this village was on, so I flew south-west and counted.'

'What about fuel?'

'When it starts to get low I look around for a town and a field to land in.'

She was far more energetic than he remembered. She told him her route. From Essendon she'd got lost south of Darwin. 'Not many features there or water to go by.' She went from Dutch Timor to Rangoon, from Persia to Damascus. Greece to England. 'And, as I told you, I stopped in Ankara. Oh, James, the pears they have are sublime.' She paused, looked at Meryem and then back at James. 'I expected you might die at the war. I'm glad you didn't. You were too nice for fighting; I always said so to Dad.'

James didn't know what to say.

'Your wife keeps smiling at me. She's a bit frightening.' She smiled back at Meryem, who kissed Linda and called her sister. James translated, but something inside of him was constricting.

'She likes you,' he told her. He supposed it should make him happy.

Berna came into the room and leaned against her father's leg.

'And this one here,' James said to Linda, 'is Berna, my daughter.' He kissed Berna's cheeks, twice on each side, making big smacking sounds. James introduced Saliha, who'd also come in.

'Saliha's a mute,' James said.

'Why?'

'Something bad happened and she decided to stop talking. No matter what we say, she won't speak.'

'Something bad to her?'

'No, to a friend. Last year.'

Saliha was settling in the corner to continue knitting some socks. She had lifted her head when she heard her name, and smiled at Linda, then bent her head back to her work.

Meryem spoke to James from where she stood at the stove.

'My wife wants to know if you get scared in the air.'

'Not at all; it's safe, like flying a kite.'

'I don't think she knows what a kite is.'

'Do you see God up there?' Meryem asked.

James translated.

'I don't see anyone,' Linda replied. 'But that doesn't mean He's not there.'

James went to the window. At the start of summer the smells of the trees changed and soon, he knew, the honey would begin to flow.

'I met a woman in Ankara called Halide,' Linda said behind him. Berna came and stood beside him, sneaking her hand into his. 'She spoke the most wonderful English and had an impressive collection of books.'

Linda talked about the English books the woman in Ankara had; how she had given Linda a couple to take away with her. She and

Halide had promised to keep in contact. Halide had been fascinated to know that there was an Australian man living on a mountain in Turkey.

'Don't be surprised if she turns up for a visit,' Linda said, laughing. 'She's a little like me. Adventurous is the word, I suppose.'

James turned from the window.

'What did you say?'

She laughed and said that it wasn't important.

'Would your wife like to come for a short flight?' she said to James, but when he translated this, Meryem said absolutely not, and so it was Berna who went up in the plane for a fifteen-minute flight, something that caused enormous trouble with Ahmet later, when he came back from the tea garden.

Once they'd landed, Berna didn't stop talking, trying to explain how it had been. She said it was like heaven to see the whole world spread out like that. She didn't say that while she was in the plane, with Linda leaning back and shouting things to her, words she couldn't understand, pointing out this and that, she had come to know why this woman was here. It wasn't her place to say anything about that, though, so instead, once back on the ground, she stood hopping from foot to foot like a burnt frog, talking to her father, in front of the house where half an hour earlier her mother had been watching, hands to mouth, as her daughter was taken up into the clouds in the flying machine.

Chapter 16

I

It was Miriam and İbrahim at the fountain. The taxi driver lifted Cem off the ground and spoke quickly in Turkish, Mim standing by, droopy and glum. As Cem had run down from the Honey Hut, he'd let himself think it might be another blonde, but of course it wasn't. He was an idiot for having thought it possible.

'İbo is here! When did you start growing a moustache? You need more than four or five days on it, my brother.' İbrahim touched Cem's chin, speaking Turkish. 'I decided to take a holiday and come to see Cem Keloğlu and my good friend Harray. I was driving near Izmir and I stopped for beans and rice. This girl waved me down outside a gas station. I tried to explain I wasn't on my taxi work, but she was crying too much, I had to help her. I gave her tea and I made her talk. She told me she'd made a big mistake, that she'd been travelling with two very nice people in a wonderful car and she'd stayed behind in Izmir and missed visiting an authentic

Turkish village. "What car?" I shouted at her. "Was it bright yellow? Was one man called Cem and very handsome?" She said yes, that it was a yellow taxi and you were the driver. She is very irritating, this girl.'

Cem and İbrahim both looked at the Cadillac parked nearby. İbrahim switched to English to include Mim, who stood quietly, her nose pink and eyes watering.

'Yes, I know it was you two mens. Is there 'otel here? You growing moustache or beard? It needs more hair here and here.' The taxi driver pointed at different parts of Cem's face.

'Hi.' Cem glanced at Miriam. Her lips were red and wet and her forehead less shiny than he remembered it. İbrahim rubbed his hands together. 'Have there been fight yet? Always in village there is argument, usually over some lady. It is like television operatic. Never boring in here. Now, where is my Mr Harray?'

İbrahim pulled out a cigarette and lit it, and Miriam stepped away, waving her hand through the smoke. Cem saw Berna nearby and called out to her, asking whether the girl could stay with her. Berna looked at the girl and saw everything in an instant. She raised her eyebrows at Cem over Mim's backpack, but Cem shook his head at her. Whatever it was, he didn't know anything about it and none of it was his fault. Berna led Mim to her house and Cem took İbrahim to see Mehmet, who sighed heavily and said he supposed he would take the new lodger.

'Let me wash my hands and face and make my toilet and we can drink coffee soon?' İbrahim said to Cem. He clicked his fingers and danced a shimmy on the cement doorstep. 'Where is Mr Harray? Does he miss me?'

'He's got a bad back. He's lying down.'

'Oh no! Nothing can be worse than this! Where is he? I will give him a massage. I worked in a Turkish bath, I am very skilled.' İbrahim cracked his knuckles, rolled up his shirt sleeves and stepped neatly out of his brown-tasselled shoes. 'You tell him I'm coming. I'll wash my hands then go to him. My poor Harray.'

Cem left as Mehmet started to recite the overly-formal words of welcome to the taxi driver, to which İbrahim bowed and delivered his lengthy and equally elaborate reply.

II

Cem didn't go to Harry. He'd tell him later that he'd found a 'chiropractor' in the form of İbrahim. He didn't go to breakfast either. Instead, he wanted to be away from people and started to walk up to the caves, wanting to think about things and what it might mean that Miriam was there. Maybe it was a second chance. But he didn't get to the caves. He became light-headed on the way. It had to be Berna's tea that he'd drunk the night before.

He'd been to the squat toilet about six times already with violent diarrhea, and now Miriam was here, and the taxi driver, and he was tired and unsatisfied and filled with a sense of claustrophobia. Harry needed him at the meeting, everyone wanted something from him, and each time he'd seen Meral, always from a distance, he could see her face was becoming sadder. She loved him. She wanted to escape. He was sorry for her, but it still wasn't enough reason to help her.

Emptied out by Berna's special drink, he was dizzy as he walked. Instead of going all the way up to the caves, he circled around the back of the peak and went down the other side of the rise, to where the forest was thick and dark. The river rushed around boulders and splashed onto the mossy edges. He drank from it and tasted the wild mint. There were fallen branches and birds and he came to a clearing where all was resoundingly quiet.

He remembered the claws his grandfather had made with his hands when he told him stories about the forest, the monsters and witches. He was standing by the river, still looking for a rock to sit on when he heard a noise. It was Cevap. Cem smiled and stepped forwards to say hello. This was an opportunity to talk to him, to explain he needed to leave Meral alone and show her some respect, but as he stood with hand outstretched to shake, Cevap rushed forwards, both arms out straight, and pushed Cem in the chest.

'Meral,' he croaked.

Cem's foot slid on some moss and he came down hard on the grass, striking his head.

Love to love.

He woke up alone. A beam of sunshine reached down through a gap in the canopy. There was a different quality to the sunshine. It was shiny and strange and somehow it contained all of his past and present, the essence of his whole life held in the rays of light that illuminated him where he lay on the ground. He felt the sun on his face and could somehow feel the warmth of a future too. This would be a lovely place to be in summer. He could fish and walk and forget about everything except what it might mean to love and be loved by a girl with purple-black eyes and beginning curves and small hands that would flutter against his chest.

Love to love. He shifted his head to the side and there was a yellow dog sitting nearby. It was time to think about what had happened the week before he'd left Melbourne.

He was with friends at a club and they were drunk. His mates insisted on buying him drinks to celebrate his leaving for overseas. He sat immobile, watching people dance. He didn't dance, hadn't since the time his mates teased him for being bad at it. They laughed at the 'village way' he moved and he'd got angry about it. In the club his friends bounced around, jumping on each other's backs, trying to get girls' attention. One girl with pale pink lipstick fell onto Cem's lap.

'Oops. Sorry.' She rocked against him. 'My friend said she likes you.' Her eyes were smudged with too much black makeup.

He smiled. She smelled nice, a mixture of fruity perfume and sweet sticky drinks.

'Really?'

'You should talk to her.' She leaned on his shoulder, spilled her drink on his chest. She didn't say sorry. 'I'll go get her.' She lurched up and walked away.

Cem stood up to go to the toilet. It took him ages to get there. He hoped he wouldn't spew. He pissed, washed his hands, and stood swaying in front of the mirror. Fuck, his hair was good. He left the bathroom and there was a screen outside, and on the other side of the meshed divider stood the girl and her friends. They were all weaving in a mass as they stood there, unsteady, and he put his tongue between his teeth, ready to jump out and scare them. That'd make them giggle and one of them might kiss him; it didn't matter which.

'No, Georgia. Did you see his friends?'

'What do you mean?'

'You know what I mean,' the friend said.

'But he's so cuuuuute,' Georgia said. Then the other girl said the word, to make it clear what she was talking about. Georgia said she guessed so and slumped back against the screen and it shifted a little. Through the gap that opened, Cem was revealed and they all looked at each other. One girl had gapped teeth and too-thin eyebrows, another had frizzy hair; it was the one with the teeth who had been talking about Cem and his friends. She grabbed Georgia and the third girl and dragged them away. He went back to his seat. His friends were still dancing. He sat and hated the blonde whitey bitches.

After that, things became like a dream. They were walking through a park and he needed to piss again. This was the other reason why he didn't like drinking, because you needed to piss all the time. He'd wanted Coke or juice but they'd pushed him, he had to celebrate his 'make pilgrimage'. They'd said it over and over until it wasn't funny anymore, if it ever really had been.

At the toilet block, Cem told the others to wait, that he had to go, he was busting. He stood in front of the urinal and could hear them joking around outside, telling him to hurry up, not to take a crap

’cause then they’d be there forever. While he was peeing, he heard a noise. There was someone in the end stall, next to him. Under the dividing wall were four feet, two of them bare and with nail polish. They were young feet. A pair of bright yellow thongs lay overturned on the wet cement floor. At first he heard nothing but then, between the spatter of his urine hitting the metal and his friends mucking around outside, he heard a whimpering. He stared at the bare feet and saw the toes curling and then one of those feet was lifted up off the ground and the pitchy sound became something that was ambiguous. Then two words, softly uttered, but clear and female: *Don’t. Stop.*

He shook his dick and zipped up. He didn’t wash his hands. He joined his friends and they walked through the park and continued on to the station.

By the river, he thought about those two words. He had convinced himself that there hadn’t been a pause, that the words had run into each other, but now, from this distance, he remembered the smell of the urinal and the shade of the nail polish and he admitted there had been a pause, a long gap between the two words.

He’d been angry at the other girls, not her. She had done nothing to him. He could have gone back, asked his friends to go with him and help, but he hadn’t. In the two weeks since, he’d allowed himself to think of all the reasons why it would have been a bad idea. He never once considered the single thing which would have made it a good idea, the best idea.

By the river, he thought about what he should have done. He pushes the door open and pulls the girl away. Takes her to the hospital, or home or the police—wherever she wants to go. Holds her hand, lets her cry and doesn't feel uncomfortable about any of it. He knows how and where to pat her, knows how to put his arm around her without it being awkward or sleazy.

He turned his head to the side again. The yellow dog was gone. He touched the back of his skull and there was a bump that stung. He started to get up but felt sick, so he lay down again. The tiniest blue flowers poking out of the grass. Five petals each and perfect. He smiled at one of the flowers and reached out to pick it. The boy Cevap loved Meral and wanted to marry her, but she didn't love him. She wanted to go to Australia; she wanted freedom.

As he walked down to the village he kept putting his fingers on the back of his head. The lump was getting bigger. On the outer edge of the forest, he met Berna. She took his arm and chatted, leaning into him, as they walked. Cem asked her about the wishing tree and she said it was on the other side of the village, near the well, and that she would walk with him.

'You don't have to pay any debt,' she said. She wouldn't say any more, only that the difficult business of punishment was not hers to talk about. They reached the well. Cem looked around for a special tree and in the distance saw a scraggly thing with paper and rags tied to it. Meral was at the well, standing in front of him with a bucket. She greeted the old woman and stared at Cem. He gave her the flower he'd picked. She tucked it inside her top, where it disappeared into folds of fabric. He helped her fill and raise the bucket. He took off his long-sleeved top and carried the bucket in his t-shirt and he kept looking down at himself to check his muscles were popping. One of Meral's cheeks was red, as if she'd been slapped. Then her sister arrived, Kehribar, the one with the yellow eyes, and she took the bucket with Meral and they went on ahead.

Berna and Cem walked back to the village. He stopped at the fountain and smoked two cigarettes and felt dizzy again. He drank a lot of water. Then, touching the back of his head once more, he went to Mustafa's.

The door opened and Meral stepped out into the street, both of her cheeks red now. Her father was behind her. She was in tears and Mustafa's face was crimson with anger.

'No,' said Meral, not seeing Cem who was to the side, near the window. 'I won't.'

'It's for the best,' Mustafa said. 'You must listen to me because I'm your father.'

They saw him then. Cem apologised for intruding and Meral kept crying; in fact, her tears intensified when she knew he was there, and her look became wild and yearning. Cem felt the urge to hold her—she was very pretty—and he actually took a step forward, but Mustafa came between the two of them and hustled his daughter back inside.

'What can I do for you, Mr Cem?' Mustafa said. 'Breakfast is finished.'

Cem could see the hem of Meral's baggy pants behind the headman, the rocking way she moved as she stood there with her hands over her face, almost swinging from side to side. Mustafa stood with stony chin, his arms crossed. Cem couldn't think what to say, so he asked if there were any more pillows, for his friend who had a bad back. Meral went and fetched one. It was in a scarlet satin cover the ends tied with knots. Cem said thank you and walked away, his heart beating fast. He reached back and felt his lump again. He went to his room and lay on the bed with the extra pillow underneath his head. It was very comfortable so he fell asleep.

As Cem lay down on his bed, Meral snuck out the back of her house to go and see Cevap. She had loved him since childhood and they had been promised to each other for the last three months. Everyone had been happy and it was all organised. But now this new boy had come to the village and was threatening to ruin things. Her father was telling her she should forget Cevap because there was a better prospect now. But she didn't want Cem, she didn't care about Australia. She loved her Cevap.

III

The afternoon was warm and after his nap Cem took Mim for a walk to the river. His head was sore and he was still sleepy. Miriam had been speaking non-stop but he let her words fall out of his ears. He had expected she might say something about his moustache, or that she was happy to see him, but she was self-absorbed and didn't seem to even notice it. He waited. He wanted to tell her about his plan to help Meral, but she kept going on about Phil. How Phil was the sort of man who didn't express his feelings. How she knew that he had them. That he sometimes got jealous and put her down, but only sometimes, in little ways, she said, to show that he noticed things and she felt it meant that he loved her, like, truly. When she stretched the truth in front of people they didn't know well, he pulled her up on it. And when she couldn't calculate the currency exchange in Paris, he'd laughed at her and had been quite mean. Divide by four, he'd said. It's easy. These things were proof that he cared, she said.

Carpets aired nearby in the sunshine and Cem was stretched out on the grass beside the water. He didn't even try to listen to her after five minutes. She was an idiot. He didn't think about Harry, either, or what he might find out at the meeting with Old Mehmet. He thought he might like to have a game of backgammon with İbrahim, have a smoke.

He studied the leaves above, noticed how they made a kind of tent roof. He listened to the bird and breeze noises which sat behind Miriam's droning voice, and he sensed some sort of connection, with life and with the world, the kind of connection he'd always supposed deep-thinking men might have, men who wore narrow-toed shoes with laces and shirts with collars, the ones who hadn't taken economics at university, but probably did arts, all the politics or philosophy subjects. He wondered if it was possible that Berna had put something else in the drink, or maybe the bump on his head had knocked something out of place. Either way, he liked this new loose feeling.

He imagined it was Mustafa's daughter there with him, instead of this droning girl from Queensland. Meral turning to him and putting her cheek on his chest, saying she kissed his eyes. Yes, Miriam would be easier and she was right here, delivered to him like a package by the taxi driver, but he found he wasn't too interested now. Then he realised what she'd just told him.

'What did you say?' he asked.

'I'm pregnant.'

'What?'

'I don't know why I came. I mean, we never even kissed. I knew you wanted to, but I was going a bit nuts and missing Phil and trying to work out what to do. I've never been pregnant before.'

'Right.' Cem's lump started to throb harder and he felt nauseous. Fucking Cevap; he'd punch him in the face when he saw him next.

'I rang him but we argued. I have to work out what to do.' She snuck closer and her hand snaked out to clasp his. He made sure their hands stayed hidden, deep in the grass. His nausea increased.

'You did want to kiss me, right? Do?' She parted her lips and her eyelids fluttered shut. He was confused by Mim's lips and by what she was saying. He thought he'd better go.

'Let's think for a second.' He squeezed her hand and turned to the side and vomited into the grass. Miriam pulled away and started to cry, and he reached back to pat her, saying *shhh*. He'd hit his head, it was that, he said, nothing to do with her. She sniffed and got to her knees.

'I'm going back. I'm so exhausted.'

'Sorry.'

‘It’s not your problem. Don’t worry about it.’ She made it sound like it was his problem and that she definitely wanted him to worry about it.

‘I’m not worried.’

She told him he was a dickhead and walked away. He lay there a while longer and then sat up. Old Mehmet’s wife, Gül, was standing behind a tree. She smiled and he saw her gold tooth. That tooth let him know he was in trouble. What the fuck was he doing? He would go tomorrow morning, go to the beaches down south. He walked back to the village, vomiting once more on the way.

Chapter 17

I

Linda was leaving, and when she told James she had something for him, he said he had a farewell gift for her too: a large ball of propolis. He waited for the puzzled smile, for her to ask what the heck *that* was, and he was ready to launch into a light-hearted explanation. She was distracted, said thank you, but that her thing was more important.

'What's more important than propolis?' he said. 'I don't think you understand the value of the stuff.'

Then Linda asked if he'd go to the plane with her while she finished getting ready. She needed to talk to him privately, she said. Her face was serious and he stopped smiling.

'No one in the family understands English. I wouldn't worry about it.'

Meryem came and set tea down in front of them.

'It's better that we're alone,' Linda said.

They walked up to where the plane was staked in the meadow.

'Look, Jim, it's big. I couldn't believe it myself for a long time.'

'You couldn't write about it?'

'No, I had to see you and tell you. It's why I came.'

James gestured for her to go on.

'I don't know how to say this—and I wish I didn't have to tell you.'

'You're being very mysterious.'

'I've got some things in the plane. Before you left Melbourne, you showed Dad a photograph of your father. He found out who he was; well, he knew straight away.'

'What?' James tipped back his head and looked at the sky and in that instant the colour of it would become the colour of the words that followed. Later, when he was an old man, when he thought of his father, he would see periwinkle flowers scattered across hills, shades of baby blue mixed with lavender.

'Your father was Ned Kelly.'

James laughed and it was an inhalation of air that guttered out of him in a staccato hiccup. Then he laughed properly. He bent over with his hands on his knees, his mouth wide, laughing at his boots.

'Jim,' she said and touched his shoulder.

He stood upright, pulling out a handkerchief to wipe his eyes.

'I have some things,' Linda said. 'I have his skull in the back of the plane.'

He looked at her closely. Too long in the sky? She seemed the same as ever: sharp and alert and serious. She was talking now, as if to get the words out before he could stop her, and he wanted to. He wanted to stop her talking, to put his hand across her mouth, put his lips there even. He stepped away from her. His head was giddy and he started laughing again and it was all he could do to remain upright, yet underneath the sound he was making, and her babble behind him, he heard what she was saying. That his father hadn't been a simple murderer but a political rebel. There'd been drafts of a declaration, a handbill outlining the intention to establish a republic. A Victorian republic. His sisters and mother had visited him in gaol; they'd smuggled in a wedding ring and there was a photograph of him, in chains, with the band visible on one finger, his hands raised in a boxing stance of defiance. He'd left no papers to suggest he was married, but he had been. There was mention in some letter, dictated at a bank. It was hearsay said some; fact said the family, a group of people who talked to no one. Her father had found someone he trusted, someone willing to talk for justice, not money, someone who trusted him too. A female relative who knew there'd been a son and who believed that son ought to know about his father. A beaten-down grandmother who'd seen her family destroyed.

James held up a hand, and felt ridiculous for doing so when he saw the look on her face, but he wasn't going to listen to this. A republic? Political oppression? Smuggled rings? It was ridiculous. He stood quietly beside the plane. He couldn't think or act; it was the same as when he was expected to marry Meryem, everyone giving him those sly smiles. When he was expected to go to the other war and he felt he had no choice. When the girl died down the well, and Saliha stopped talking and wouldn't say a word, not even to him, finally then had come a shutting down of all that he had been and all that he wasn't. It was the theme of his life, this inability to act.

'Murder is never simple,' was all he could say to Linda.

'That came out wrong, James. I'm sorry.'

Before her father died, he'd told her she had to find 'our Jim' and let him know. She had to give him the information and artefacts that Cole had been gathering after James had gone to the war. Four years he'd worked at the collection, Linda said.

'It's nineteen years since I left. It's taken you that long to find me?'

'It wasn't a direct route, so to speak.' She paused. 'Listen, I have a letter here from Dad explaining. I didn't look at anything for a few years. I needed to think about what to do, how to find you. That all took some time.'

'And there was your engagement.'

'That's not fair, Jim.'

'I'm sorry.' He blinked. 'This is . . . I don't understand any of it.' He remembered his childhood fantasies, the revolver in the house. The gaol in Beechworth and how his mother had refused to walk along the walls and crossed to the other side of the street every time they passed. How she told him not to play with the children at school, not to listen to their talk. How there was never any family and how alone they were in their isolation. There was a buzzing in his ears.

'I don't understand any of this.'

II

She was going and leaving it with him. Leaving him with the knowledge that his blood was tainted. He was no longer a boy counting cherry stones who thought that a bushranger for a father was an exciting prospect. As they said their goodbyes the space between them became more awkward than the time of the final Valentine card.

'I'm fine,' he said, answering her question, looking over her shoulder at the mountain behind them. He called the yellow dog and it came loping towards him, nipples swollen. He squatted and scratched around the dog's ears, both their heads bowed, but Linda's feet stayed in place. She didn't get into the plane.

'When he was sick at the end, Dad talked about fathers and how a man should know where he came from. He told me about his own father, and he'd never done that before.'

He was still bent over, patting the dog.

'He didn't understand why you didn't know. Didn't you see any newspapers as a child?'

'The ink made a mess, she said.'

Her feet came closer. 'But all that time in Melbourne. Jim, you worked at a paper.'

He stood. 'I'm not like your father, not an expansive man. He was open and wanted to draw everything towards him, but I don't lift my head too much. It's a simple life for me.'

'You're a stranger in a place that's not your own, speaking another language. Surely there's not a more complex way to live than that?'

'We talk about the rain, the grass, the sun and the sky. Luck and family, love and honour. We talk about sheep, food, fruit. Wool. There's a lot of discussion about vegetables. And bread.'

'Lots of nouns.'

'Correct. I have my daughter, and her brother and sister. I have my wife.'

'Another reason it took so long was that Dad left money for the lawyers, to keep gathering information. He was guilty about something too.'

The dog leaned against his leg.

'Guilty?'

'When you see the skull, you'll understand. There's this.'

She gave him a slender booklet, entitled *Phrenological Descriptive Chart and Human Science Register of the Mental and Physical Conditions of M— as Given by —.*

'Dad told you he was interested in phrenology?'

James said he remembered something about it.

'It's about knowing a man's character from studying his skull. Please don't judge him. It seems unconventional now, but it was thought of as new science, whether the morals of a man could be equated to the bumps and ridges on his skull. Dad wanted to know what made a man good.'

'I'll have a look at the pamphlet, but I don't want to see the thing itself. You should take that back with you.'

Linda said she couldn't. It belonged with him, she said.

'I want you to know I'm grateful to you both,' James said. 'You've gone to a lot of trouble on my account.'

Linda had an expression on her face he'd never seen before and there were tears in her eyes. As well as the papers she gave him the Colt revolver, still wrapped in cloth, telling him to put it somewhere safe. Then she handed him two books, saying the woman in Ankara had given them to her.

'They're in English,' Linda said. 'I thought you might like to read them.'

James took the books and held out his hand to shake hers. She started crying.

'You've done what your father asked,' he said. 'You've handed it all over. It's up to me now.'

'What do you mean?'

'It's up to me to deal with it.'

'The souls of men are not as dark as we like to believe, Jim. Even if men act poorly, it doesn't mean they're evil. There are people who think he was a good man; that he was for justice, like Robin Hood. His family was Irish. Do you know what that meant for people living back then?'

'He was nothing like Robin Hood,' said James. 'This is a man who killed policemen. He stole horses and robbed banks. This is an outlaw, not someone who simply acted poorly. You say there's no shame, but if such acts don't infect a person's blood, then—'

'Read the papers. There's always a context for a life lived, Jim.'

'I don't see how there can be any context to something like this. Bad is bad, evil even, and there can't be any excuses. A man can't hope to be pardoned for killings and the son of a murderer can't hope to be excused for what his father did. We inherit all of it from our parents. What little good he might have had in him doesn't count, not after what he did. Those things get cancelled out. Some bull about saving a boy from almost drowning? Just his name is a curse.'

'I don't believe in evil.'

'Well I do. I don't know how you can see it any other way.'

In the end, there was nothing for it other than a simple, short goodbye. Linda refused to shake his hand and insisted on a hug which she tried to prolong but he broke. He promised to write and she promised to travel safely. He stood in the paddock with the craggy top of the mountain behind him as she took off into the sun.

It was weeks before he could look at the skull. He did not take it out of the pillow case, only opened the top and peered in. Part of it was missing and it was this that made him sorry. The skull of his father was broken and it was this small missing piece of bone that made him sorry, not context or a son's forgiveness or anything close to love. Here was a man whose body had been desecrated after he'd been murdered by the state and it wasn't right. A man whose skull was not complete and had been separated from the rest of his body, which was presumably buried somewhere in Melbourne. It was unconscionable, what they had done to him, and he was sorry, but even so, there was no part of his heart that didn't remain cold at the thought that Edward Kelly had been his father.

III

He lay in the meadow and he lay by the river. He walked to the caves and up and around the mountain top. The sheep came close to surround him as he stared at the bright sky or turned blind in a slow circle, not knowing which way to go next. The sheep watched and waited for his direction but there was none and usually a yellow dog was with him, lifting its eyes to look at him every few steps.

Adar had to shake his shoulder to rouse him and tell him the sun had gone or that it was raining and what the devil was he doing out here? He would lead James down to the lights of Meryem's house and leave him on the doorstep for his wife to guide to the warmth of the fire or press a cool glass of water into his limp hand. Whatever the season, he was lost.

Meryem didn't tell him about the hardness in her belly and that it was hot and painful now. Something was growing inside her, something that wasn't child. Berna had refused to read the coffee grinds for her mother and had refused to throw the beans too, but even so Meryem knew what was coming and she turned away to make sure her husband wouldn't see her face. She needn't have bothered, because he saw nothing these days.

The woman had come from the sky and her husband had changed, but it wasn't love that Meryem saw on his face now. He didn't speak of it and she didn't ask. Not even when they had come back from Izmir with her brother Haluk dead in the cart and Jim excluded and something sour growing between him and Ferhat, not even then had she asked. He had been unhappy but had honoured his promise and married her and been kind to her and the children, even Ahmet.

When Saliha had stopped speaking after Ayşe died, James had urged her to find her voice, but in the end he had accepted her silence like all of them. It was what he did best it seemed, accepted things. But she saw now there was something he couldn't forgive and she was the one who had to accept that her husband had changed.

He kept being brought back to the house by the shepherds, by Adar or Mehmet. Sometimes it was Berna who led him by the hand as he almost stumbled across the nubby hillocks and bushes.

As summer began and the honey poured from the hives, the warmth loosening the flow as the bees flew to the blossoms, still he stumbled.

'What do you know?' he asked Adar one day.

'I know I will always be Lame Adar. No one ever uses my new name.'

'There must be other things that you know.'

'This is true. I know where the best flowers are for Saliha's constipation tea, also where the fattest fish huddle under the trees in high summer.'

'Have you always believed your father to be a good man?'

'Of course. He is the *hoca*.'

'But did you always know it? Even when you were small?'

'Especially then. He was patient with everyone, teaching religion, leading the prayers. He never made me feel bad about myself. He always called me only "Adar".' Adar lifted his head and looked at James, his hunch twisting his body and his bent leg at an angle. Adar put a hand on James's shoulder and he felt the warmth of the man's fingers and it helped.

IV

James asked Meryem this question one evening after he came home, his belly filled with sweet tea from Adar's father's house.

'What do you know?'

She shrugged. 'I know that the river never stops running and that the sheep must be shorn for their wool. That the loom never sits idle. These are the things I know. I know I'm going to die—we all are.'

'What about God?'

Meryem shrugged again. There was no God for her, but she wasn't going to say it to anyone.

'And you?' she asked.

'I used to know how the bees talk, but I find now I am forgetting.'

V

The bees were flying and the honey surged and James lay out in the meadow.

It was dusk and he smelled roses in the air. There were none in the village but the scent was carried on the wind from somewhere and it reminded him of Izmir. He'd bought Meryem some rose oil when he'd gone but couldn't remember if he'd given it to her or if it had been put to the side in the chaos of their return, but the scent found him now and invaded him as he lay animal-like in the grass.

He found the books Linda had given him; he'd put them in the chest in the small room off the salon. He read one and then in the middle of the other he found a piece of paper, a note from Linda, with the address of the woman in Ankara. He wrote to Halide and apologised for the abruptness of the request, he suspected it was both intrusive and rude, but he wondered if she would be able to send him some more books in English. He would repay her the money somehow.

Her reply came in the form of a package. Two more novels and a Koran, translated into English. Also enclosed was a letter which explained the religious book was a pristine first edition, published that year, and finally, a small bottle of lemon cologne. For reasons James was unsure of, he hid the cologne from his wife, but sometimes he would look at it and turn the bottle in his hands. He never opened it. Meryem would smell it straight away.

James read the books and went to the hives and handled the bees, and as they climbed across his fingers he thought about the woman in Ankara. He read the Koran and he read the Bible and in both found some answers. He began to know more about how to become a man who could say the words he wanted to, and do the things he ought. He stood with the queen's scent on his fingers and thought about Linda. These days there was a noise building inside him and it was the same distinct roaring the bees made if the queen was killed or absent. James knew if you opened the hive, the sound would be overwhelming.

He would destroy the things. He would put them into a pile and pour kerosene on them and burn it, all of it except the skull. No matter how ashamed he was, how disappointed, he could not do that. He would take it and walk through the Big Forest, follow the river far away from the village to the old bridge. He would carry the skull of his father away from the village, find a proper place and bury it. He would bury the skull of his criminal father. Get rid of Edward Kelly's skull so that no one would know it had ever been there.

Chapter 18

I

At the fountain, Mehmet is trying to calm his wife. I am nearby, waiting to speak with him. He has to be stern with Gül because she is almost hysterical, saying Cem had been at the river with the foreign girl. I look at her face and I see her glee. She is the most jealous person I have ever known. She does not want good things even for her own granddaughter.

'Come here, Berna,' my brother says to me. He wants me to help him. 'Leave him be, *soos*,' he says to Gül. He looks at me, exasperated. 'Who didn't ever lie by the river, thinking about a small kiss? Who didn't laze wretched and lonely in the pastures with the sheep and look at the ewes a little too closely?' He points at Olcay the sheepherder, who is walking past. Olcay lifts a hand and Mehmet waves back. 'No, let him be,' he says to his wife. 'This boy is harmless. There is no guile to be seen in his face. In the end, what does it matter? If there's any decision, it will be ours.'

'But she's pregnant,' Gül Hanım says, looking at me. 'He can't take one of our girls, it's shameful.'

'What?' Mehmet sighs. 'Where is my chair? This is how my last days are to end? Like that awful *Fathers and Sons* on the television? No.' He looks at me. I haven't seen him this angry since Ayşe died. 'Why didn't you say anything about this? It's not what was in the beans, it will not finish this way. Is this day three or four? I have lost count.'

I tell him it doesn't matter what day it is.

'My life at the end has become busier than all the years before. I still have to deal with the history man this afternoon,' he says. 'I'm tired and now I'm angry.'

Someone has brought his chair and he sits down. I say everything will be fine. He listens to me and nods once. He has decided. He speaks to his wife.

'Bring me a coffee, my precious. I shall continue my day. Bring it to me here on the chair in the sunshine. I have to finish the story.' The children are coming down the street.

'Before you begin,' I say, 'we need to discuss the plan. Things are moving closer.'

My brother says certainly, we need to. I go on.

'We don't know if it's possible. Whether university or school is better. Yes, she is intelligent, but there's the boy. She loves him, she is certain about it.'

My brother scoffs at me.

'It can happen,' I say. 'It just didn't happen to you or me.'

He frowns and his face becomes sad.

'Alright, it didn't happen to me. Her father is determined for her to go—such an opportunity, he says—but she won't have it. She slaps her own face, has a tantrum, and makes threats about going in the well. Mustafa is terrified, of course. But even if Cem agrees, and Mustafa can persuade her, we don't know how it works. She would have to stay with that family, Mustafa says, and we can't trust the Australians. But they are Turkish, I say. He doesn't agree. He is very protective of her.'

'As he should be,' Mehmet says. 'We know Ahmet. He can't have changed.'

'Mustafa believes it's not fair on the boy. He thinks the boy is not emotionally developed. I agree with the first, but the other, I think he is good enough, or he will be with time.'

'He owes us,' my brother says.

The children sit down. Sami the Small is ready, right up front, making his spit balls in the dirt.

'He doesn't owe us. His grandfather does. It has to be his decision and hers, with no pressure.'

My brother nods.

'Will you tell the witch story again?' Sami asks.

Mehmet tilts his chin and sucks his teeth, making a tsk sound. No, he is telling the real stories now, he says.

'Witches are real. We have them in the village. There's one who lives next door to me, that's what my mother told me.' Sami the Small doesn't look at me and my brother smiles.

'A less witchlike woman than that one you could not find,' he says, and it makes me pleased. They tried to shape my husband, to modify him. In the end, nothing worked, and he took power and I had to resort to curses and bad dreams. He had my father's gun and he had the gold too but nothing was a match for the dreams.

The villagers told him he would die if he stayed here and he knew I could do it too. He said he would shoot a wife who didn't behave but finally he left and it was a happy day for me, but miserable too, for I lost my son and daughter-in-law. An old woman without family is a woman with a harder life than most.

'Well,' Mehmet says to the children. 'To the story, then, if you insist.'

Sami the Small nods until I fear his neck might snap.

It is like having too many balls in the air and not being able to let them drop. My father had been good at it, but while no one in the village had learned how to juggle real balls, all knew how to do it with the invisible things made of air and emotion, the things that make up our lives.

I leave Mehmet to his stories and go to the tea house. Mustafa is there and he is agitated. He tells me he has asked for the television to be switched off and that the men aren't happy because *Şeker Şeker* is about to come on. He admits he has given in and asked that the volume be turned down. He says he has many things on his mind and I know Zeynep is in the mix as well as the other matter, the pressing matter of his daughter's future. Never has a father loved his girls so. The waiter brings tea and Mustafa tips in all the sugars on the small saucer. He takes a sip. He drops in another cube. Yes, he has noticed Zeynep, but that is for later. I tell him I need to talk to him about the boy.

The opening credits begin for *Şeker Şeker.*

'I think he will marry her,' one of the men says.

'No, you fool. She will marry the other one.'

'Where are we up to? I can't remember what happened last time.'

'Did he die yet? Is he out of prison? Does he know about the child?'

The men call for more tea and fall quiet.

I say what needs to be said. Mustafa listens, and by the time he has finished his second glass he is in agreement with me even if he is not entirely happy. But we have made our decision.

I see the historian walking down the street with the taxi driver, and he is moving easier. Someone has helped him with his back problem. I won't need to collect the special herbs for him and this is good because I have enough to keep me busy.

'We need to keep them apart,' I say to our headman. 'Cevap is becoming agitated.'

Mustafa agrees. He goes to speak with the historian and taxi driver. The driver tells him in a loud city voice about the Australian man's back, how he, the driver, used to massage men in the baths in Istanbul, that he is famous for giving the best and most vigorous massages, that he had many return customers. I hear Mustafa say he would be interested in a massage himself and could they arrange it and the driver is saying of course, that it would be his pleasure. The historian is standing straight and his face is relaxed, but he is nervous.

'We have the meeting soon,' Mustafa tells the taxi driver, who replies that he will be interpreting for his friend, Harray. 'And then we talk to Cem.'

'Talk to him about what?' İbrahim asks. Mustafa explains.

'Hmm,' İbrahim says. 'No one can rely on him, this is true. He is young and immature. My Harray needed him but all that boy can think about is girls.'

Mustafa's eyes narrow.

I go to check my cooking; after that, I need to be at Gül's. She is holding a meeting. The black crows are gathering and they think they are going to choose a girl for my grandson.

II

I sit in the corner at Gül's. Our hostess is the cold black sun around which the minor planets orbit. She never looks a person straight in the eye but has a dangerous watchfulness; a furtive glance that conveys some sort of emotion that is always false. She considers you and the glitter of her eyes is closer to animal than human. She will look away if you catch her but a minute later, her gaze will be back on your face, probing with malignant curiosity, wondering what she can find there to use, to take. I have never known a woman so jealous.

She is still beautiful. Her sausage-fingers are squeezed by gold rings. She never takes them off, those rings, nor the twenty-one solid-gold bangles on her arms. Once, she told us about a dream. A robber was standing over her with a knife and she was terrified, knowing he was about to cut off her arms to get at her gold, but even so, Gül was defiant and told him to begone! No, Gül would never take off her gold, not even if her fingers were slender, her arms thin.

Her daughter, her youngest, has similar qualities, if not looks. Zeynep might be a wondrous dancer and unscrupulous heartbreaker (once a shepherd was stabbed over her), but I've searched her face for her power and I cannot see it. If anything, her body is badly formed. Her shoulders are too high and her hips too narrow, and the second feature you notice of her face—after her eyes, which are green as a night animal's—are her eyebrows. They are thick and very black and meet over her eyes in a hard line. Her nose is fleshy, but when she smiles and dances, then the whole of her is transformed into something sublime that cannot be described with the words of humans.

'There's a western slut in the village,' Feride begins. 'And Gül says she's pregnant.'

Gül shushes her. 'Not yet. We have to wait for Hulya.'

While we wait, the women discuss their husbands, the sugar men.

'My Olcay is a fiver,' Fatma brags. She sways her shoulders. 'He's strong, even after a day out with the sheep.'

'You're new to it, Fatma,' said Bilal, married so long she can't count the years. 'One day you'll wake up and pray to God for a one-sugar man.' Everyone laughs, except me and Gül. Fatma's mouth turns down at the corners. Deniz, married two years, asks whether a man can ever *reduce* the amount of sugar he puts in his tea. Her Zuraf seems to want more every day, she says.

'Are you complaining or boasting, Deniz?'

I can see Deniz is anxious.

'When he visited my father's home before our marriage, he had three, and it was acceptable, but the morning after our wedding it was five and now he stirs six!'

More laughter, and Deniz becomes quite red in the face.

'I swear to God, before long there won't be any room for the tea in his glass.'

'Is he hurting you, my heart?' I say.

Her face becomes even redder.

'I'm fine, Berna—I'm just so tired!'

Gül leans forward to the group.

'Enough silliness. What of Mustafa? That big, sad face with the wet eyes don't fool me. You only have to look at the size of his moustache, not to mention the sugar, to know what he's thinking. And my Hamil, not in the ground three months. It's shameful. I only have one of my daughters left and he'll take her next.'

She makes a spitting noise between her teeth and calls to one of the girls nearby. 'Come.' She wipes a hand through the air. The girl puts her head down and walks over. 'Bring more pastries.' Gül puts a fist on her chest, where a heart would be if she had one. 'What sort of eyes are they? Who ever heard of such a colour, may God see them and protect us. She's got the devil in her, Satan's eyes, oh *God*!'

We've heard many times how Kehribar's yellow eyes are a throwback to some abominable mating between one of the women in Mustafa's family and a mountain lion. Gül looks around at the women. We have heard the stories about Gül, too; that as soon as she was born she crawled off the mat and went to suckle on the cat's teats. She cranks her owl-like head towards the woman next to her, eyebrows angled fierce and accusatory. 'Where's that Hulya?'

'She'll miss her own dying.'

The door opens and Hulya comes in. Her hair is messy and her cheeks purple.

'Satan take that wind, it's got worse in the last half-hour. It's a wind to freeze the wings off birds.' She walks to the fire and holds out her hands.

Someone mentions the pregnant girl again.

'You think Cem is the father?'

'I doubt it,' said Gül. 'He can't even fight. Young Cevap pushed him over, in the forest.'

The fire is popping as the gossip crackles through the room. Oh, ha, it is better than *Şeker Şeker*, the show with the two sisters who love the one man, and the father who killed his betraying brother.

'What is it about our village that attracts these foreign devils like iron filings to a magnet?' Gül says. She holds out her glass to be refilled. She thinks she is working with sheep and all she has to do is make hints and we will be shepherded. 'My mother told me about the man, the first one from Austria.'

In the hot room, I realise I am very tired.

'The boy thinks he will take one,' Gül is saying, 'the way he's been looking at my granddaughters, but I have decided no. He comes with his slim hips and wide mouth and strange pants. His hair like a woman's.' She puts her tea down and presses two fat hands across her face. She counts in her head to stretch the moment; she is a cunning fox. *One, two, three, four, five.* Oh, she is a one. If only she knew her show was for nothing.

She takes her hands away, her voice is soft. 'We have had minor postcards, stupid boastings from this country we know nothing about. Do they have religion? Do the women cover? I beg your pardon, Berna, but the old one was a dog. No, I don't think he should take any of our girls.' She looked around the room and her eyes stopped at me. 'Berna, what do you say?'

I have never left the village other than in my imaginings and they have taken me far and wide. In my real life, I haven't been past the top creek, over the mountain or completely through either of the forests, Big or Small. It's true that I have been the least curious person physically, but I have flown further from the mountain in my imaginings than I did in the plane. Life has to be different somewhere else and of all we women, it seems I have the largest mind to dream how things might be.

I put my tea down and turn to Gül and there is a new sharpness behind my teeth. My words have formed slowly and while they are heavy I speak them quickly.

I speak for Ayşe and I speak for myself.

'It's true, Ahmet was a dog and he cannot have changed, but if I had a granddaughter, and she wanted to, I would hope for such an opportunity. Who cares if there is religion there or not? The question must be: is there freedom? Miss Meral is a strong girl, anyway, she can look after herself.'

'What's wrong with you, Berna?' Gül is furious, as I knew she would be. 'Do you still have the change of life with you? Do you have a headache?' No one ever disagrees with Gül.

'My whole life has been a headache, but it is gone now,' I say. 'Shall I tell you what's wrong with me? I am awake.' I finished my tea. 'Does it matter what the family is like? Does it matter if a daughter wears skirts or trousers over there? If she learns to drive and read? These would be magnificent things, just to be off this damned mountain. Most women would be happy for their granddaughter to have a chance at a different life. But it's not your decision anyway; the choice has been made. They will tell him at the men's meeting this afternoon. Now, please excuse me, I have to get back to my cooking.'

'What if the baby is his?'

I stand and open the door. I feel like a queen, but I do not know why.

'It's not, but if it was, then many congratulations to him; then we would know his seed works.' I turn to go, then stop on the doorstep. 'And it's Australia. Av-u-stra-ly-a. I have to go to my cooking. It's something for the boy to take with him, for Ahmet.'

'Probably you will poison him,' Gül says. 'You have waited these years like a patient snake. The postcards to others but not to you. It must have caused you pain.'

'He's been punished, but now it is time for forgiveness.'

I go out into the wind. I wonder for a moment if I am mad and I'm thrilled to think I might be. Whatever invades me feels wonderful. I am strong and clear and free. I know the others will be saying that a *jinn* has found me in the night or that a shape-shifter has taken my body, and I am right about that; I will find out later from Bilal it is exactly what they are saying as I walk away. Refilling their tea, listening to Gül. *Maa maa*. Berna is insane. *Maa maa*. The sheep all drink tea together. But I don't care what they say. My name is Berna and I have decided to speak my mind from now.

I walk home and the feeling of power stays with me. In my kitchen, I check my brew. The wind has dropped and I sit in the backyard where there is some scrappy sun. We are almost there. Almost at the end of the truth.

Chapter 19

I

It was the time of the meeting and everyone was at Mustafa's, including İbrahim, who was pushing food into his mouth and smoking at the same time. Cem smiled at him across the room and the taxi driver looked back, his eyes heavy-lidded and cold. Cem turned his attention to the food. He'd vomited once more back at Mehmet's house, had a small nap and felt much better now, hungry even. There were honeyed pastries and sliced fruit and a crumbly cake, but he was also aware that there was a strange atmosphere in the room.

'Is there any Coke?' he asked one of the boys.

'That stuff will rot your teeth,' said Mustafa, tipping four sugars into his tea. One of the other men nudged another villager and tipped his chin at their headman. He wouldn't be a widower much longer, they suspected.

Old Mehmet was in the best position on the divan, with Mustafa next to him. The headman pointed at the carpet with his chin and Cem settled on the floor with the younger men.

'How's your back?' he said to Harry, who was on a chair with İbrahim next to him.

'It's quite extraordinary, the pain is completely gone.'

'You didn't help to your friend. This is not a good friend.' İbrahim spoke in English and Harry blushed and mouthed 'sorry' to Cem, who shrugged and reached for another pastry. He didn't care, but it would be rude to say that Harry wasn't a real friend, that he'd had other things to worry about. Cem had decided that he would make an announcement after the meeting; he'd tell them that he would consider an engagement to Meral now and marriage in a few years. He imagined they'd be surprised and happy to hear it.

'İbo is going to interpret for me,' said Harry, sipping at his tea. 'I know you don't like doing it.'

'No, it's okay,' Cem said. 'I said I was happy to do it.'

'Happy to do? Like with helping for his back?' İbrahim sipped at his tea, not looking at Cem. 'Harray could not move from the bed. That was very nice helping you did there.'

'I asked for a painkiller. I asked Mustafa.'

'I don't think you did asked. The headman didn't know anything about Harray's back. He said you didn't tell anything to him. They giving you pillow but where is this extra pillow?'

Cem was sure he'd said something to Mustafa, even if it wasn't specifically a request for aspirin or a chiropractor. He was about to say this when he remembered the pillow was still in his room. He turned and reached for a third pastry and the meeting began.

Old Mehmet waved a hand, the other handless arm tucked inside his long jacket sleeve. A wooden chest was carried in. It was the size of a small coffin and the helpers laid it on the rug, handles clanking as they were let go. There was a carving of a bee on the side. Using his good hand, Mehmet opened it. He began to speak.

'*When I was boy, a stranger man come to the village,*' İbrahim interpreted, adding as an aside, 'I say exact what the old man say. *He come with one of our village boys. They were fight together at Gelibolu, but as enemy. They becoming friends. This man was a good man, he tell us call him Jim, he coming from Australia but he helping us to fight other enemies; the English and France as well as bastard Greece. He never told us he had famous in his home place. He live here, he marry and have family. Berna his daughter. Your grandmother.*' Mehmet pointed at Cem.

Harry was trembling.

'*In this box there are some things that came with the sky-lady. Things we can't read. Pictures.*' The old man leaned in and pulled out a bundle of letters and cards. They were passed across to Harry, who held them. The top one was a photograph.

'That's him,' Harry said, and his voice cracked. 'The coif, it's unmistakable.'

'*The flying lady come to the village, in nineteen hundred and thirties year was. After Atatürk becoming Atatürk and after we got the new names. I'm not remember year but was sure before great man dying. The lady come in plane, driving herself through the air. She bring plane on this mountain. If I didn't see myself, I not believe this thing can be happen. She is handsome lady and tall. She wearing trousers! She having no chaperone!*' Old Mehmet's voice was incredulous and the taxi driver's mirrored the rising intonation. '*She didn't come because of loving Jim, he married to my mother that time. No, this woman coming to bring him the things.*' Old Mehmet clicked his tongue and spoke again.

'You can have all of them to take, he's saying, but you must stop crying,' Cem interrupted.

Harry said he was so shocked. But it still wasn't proof, he said.

'What?' said Cem. 'Of course it's proof.'

'It's not really, but it doesn't matter.'

Cem took a fourth piece of pastry.

'Leave some for the rest of us, Mr Cem,' Mustafa growled, but Cem ignored him, caught up in interpreting what Mehmet was saying, ignoring the taxi driver who was shifting restlessly in his seat.

'My uncle doesn't understand why you are emotional about these things. He asked again if this man Jim was a relative of yours, or whether he was a captain in Australia. I'm not sure what to tell him. I said he wasn't a relative.'

'No, not family,' Harry said, wiping his eyes. 'Just a small boy's dream.' He paused. 'You're the one with the connection, Cem. You said the old woman's your grandmother, and if her father was James, the son of. It's *your* family, Cem.'

Cem began to cough, almost choking on the pastry. Someone passed him a glass of water.

Mehmet slammed the lid of the chest shut.

'The meeting is over,' Mustafa said, standing up to usher people out. 'Cem, you stay.'

Cem cleared his throat and stood up.

'There's something I want to say.' He faced the crowd of men, speaking in Turkish. 'Meral can come to Australia. I have decided to accept an engagement.' He waited for the cheers and celebration, but the room was silent. His head was hurting again and the scene in the forest was still with him. Cevap pushing him over, him falling and hitting his head. Him walking away forming a plan, thinking it was a good thing to do.

Clearly confused, Harry asked, 'Why is everyone so quiet? Is it something more about the Kellys?'

'No,' said Cem and sat down again.

'The meeting is over,' Mustafa said. 'But Cem, you stay.'

II

Cem sat with Mustafa and Mehmet.

'So,' began Mustafa. 'We don't want you to take a girl. We know this is why you came to the village and we are thankful for your grandfather's offer, but we have decided it's not best for any of our daughters to go to Australia. It's too much risk so we say no to your request.'

Cem frowned but his uncle spoke again.

'Don't argue with us. It is decided.'

Cem wasn't quite following. Hadn't it been their idea that he marry Meral?

'But Meral is unhappy,' he managed to say.

The two men started laughing.

'That's not sadness, it's petulance,' Mustafa said. Then, when it was clear Cem wasn't familiar with the Turkish word, he explained, 'Childishness, anger. I've been encouraging her to consider going. I said it was an opportunity, that she could live with your family, as an independent girl, for education purposes. While America or England is better, still your country is acceptable and she can learn English there. I told this to my daughter but Miss Meral, stubborn thing, she loves a boy in the village.'

Meral loved someone? And then he realised: Cevap. Mustafa wasn't a bully seeking to keep his daughters indentured as servants in his house. He was a father wanting opportunities for them. Cevap wasn't an unwanted suitor. He was the beloved.

'You don't want me to marry Meral? That's not the debt?'

Mustafa and Mehmet were still smiling. They lifted their chins and clicked their tongues, indicating no.

'What will she do?'

'Marry her Cevap when she is older and go to Istanbul or Ankara. He promised that if she wants to learn something, they will go to a city. But she wants to work in a shop; it's all she can talk about. A shop or an office.'

'And you trust him for this?'

'He is a good boy. Besides, anyone who tries to boss my daughter will find themselves with serious trouble on their hands.'

Cem saw Mustafa was proud of this, proud of his unbendable daughter. He said that he understood. He said he was sorry that he had caused any trouble and that it was time for him to leave. He got up to go, but Mustafa said there was one thing more.

'There's still the matter of the debt—but we have an idea about that.'

Cem sat down again.

III

Harry was sitting on a bench outside the Honey Hut. The sweet fusty smell of geraniums was in the air as Cem sat beside him.

'I'm sorry about the meeting, Harry. Sorry that I was late, and didn't interpret as you wanted.'

'It doesn't matter. Nothing does.'

'What do you mean?'

'Nothing can be proved.' Harry looked at the pile of papers in his lap. 'I've read them all, and while it *seems* certain, there's no absolute proof.'

'You're not disappointed?'

'Not at all—I'm absolutely jubilant. It's enough for me. They laughed at me, you know, back home. This is wonderful. He was here and it is satisfying to know that. It seems there was a skull, Ned's, but it's buried somewhere, İbo said. There's so much to think about.'

Harry put both hands to his face. He was sobbing again.

'The magnitude of the thing is overwhelming.' He dabbed at his eyes and blew his nose with a loud trumpet. 'I decided long ago to only deal with the dead. To only deal with what had moved into history and people who were no longer with us. At the university, after Marlene and the children left, everyone was very sorry and gave me lots of casseroles and roasted chickens. As if someone had died.' Harry smiled. 'Which was true, but they didn't know it had been me dying. Dying in the staffroom each time I tried to convince someone about Kelly. My colleagues pitying me. Marlene had been a wonderful wife, but I ruined it.'

Cem looked into the distance. It looked as usual in the village, people moving around, men walking to the tea garden, and from it.

'Being in my wife's arms was like being buried in warm, soft soil. "Look at this face," I would say to her. "Who can love this?" She'd laugh and pull me to her and say that she did.' Harry sighed and they sat a moment in silence. 'What did they want to talk to you about?'

Cem rubbed his chin. His beard was growing in now. 'Nothing.'

'Did they talk about a marriage?'

'Nope.'

'Well, that's good. That's what you wanted.'

Cem told Harry he was going to try to leave the village the next morning, but he was sure that Harry could stay on if he liked.

'Well, İbo and I have a plan: we're going to Konya to see the dervishes. You take the Cadillac and we'll go in the taxi. After Konya, he'll take me back to Istanbul.'

Cem was stung. Harry was leaving with the taxi driver?

'But you paid for the car,' he said.

'If you sell it, which you'll have to eventually, you can give me the money back in Melbourne.'

'Alright.' Cem felt small. 'I suppose I could take Mim—'

'No need; we've organised that as well. We're going to drop her at the bus stop in Izmir. That means you're free to do what you like. Time now for Cem and his quest.'

He thought about what Mustafa and Old Mehmet had said to him after the men's meeting. He didn't have a quest. His pathetic idea of rescue, of helping Meral, it was all bullshit, embarrassing. Everyone else had a plan, even Meral and Cevap.

'You could come with me?' he offered. 'A bit of Greek sun and the islands?'

'I don't think I'm in the demographic. You don't want to look like you're hanging out with your father.'

Cem had to agree that he didn't. 'What are you going to do now that you know about Kelly?'

'I'm not sure.'

'You can choose anything you like for your next hobby.'

'Oh, it doesn't work like that. Something like this chooses you, not the other way around. You see, it's more about what I can push against. Does that make sense? Some people are not comfortable with ambiguity, but I'm not one of them. Do you understand what I'm trying to say?'

Cem considered bluffing, then answered truthfully. 'Nah. I don't get it, sorry.'

Harry looked at him. 'That's a first step. Good. Say what you mean, not what you think others want to hear.' He nodded and Cem nodded too. Maybe he would try it.

'I'll walk with you. I'm meeting İbo at the tea garden.'

Cem walked down to the village with Harry and waved to İbrahim, who was waiting at the garden. The taxi driver pretended he didn't see, so Cem kept walking up the street, past the fountain where the women sat. He didn't stop for a smoke or a drink of water, simply smiled and said, 'Hello, how are you?' Down the side of the mountain, in the distance, he could see a large coach making its way along the road down on the plain. He stopped a moment and watched. It looked like it was headed to the village.

Chapter 20

My brother wants to be among the trees for his ending. It's not the seventh day, but he feels it's time. In his mind his work is done and all the threads are tucked in and snipped off. The fringe of the carpet is plaited and complete.

'Come on, Berna,' he says. 'Walk with me.'

The great forests are filled with giants whose branches stretch towards the blue above and the leafy canopies cast long shadows so black that nothing can grow at the bases. All the villagers know that if you catch a falling leaf, you can make a wish.

Mehmet and I walk under a great Kasnak oak.

'The oak does not pray,' he says to the mighty tree, and I try not to laugh. He always had a tendency to melodrama, loving those shows on the television. He worried for me when I explained my plan to him. Mehmet doesn't believe in curses, that I can give bad dreams to someone, but he wanted to help and he did, by giving

Ahmet money to leave. I chose my way and it was the best way, a rich dark path of revenge and punishment.

I keep quiet as he embraces the trees one by one and says goodbye. He weeps, but there is no shame in crying. He hugs a poplar, the most holy of all trees. 'Look how the branches sway as they pray to God,' he says.

We sit down. It is difficult and takes time, our old bones moving slowly. We rest under the tree and Mehmet believes he is thinking about his last day on earth, and all around us we can hear the forest breathing.

Now is time to speak about Ayşe. We were friends in the way that older and younger girls can be. Ayşe was the best friend of my sister, Saliha, and she loved Mehmet. They'd spoken about marriage and he'd come to realise there was some urgency. Ahmet, Ayşe told him, was staring at her and not looking away. Then, before Mehmet could speak to anyone, something happened up with the sheep, with the bee boxes. The boys had been working and Saliha was up there as well, she'd taken them food. Ahmet had spoken badly about Ayşe, in crude terms, Saliha told us, saying he planned to marry her instead of Mehmet. Mehmet jumped up and got onto Blossom, thinking to get to Jim first to ask him to start talking to Ayşe's family. My sister called out no, for him to get off and walk, but the horse started to carry him down the hill towards the village.

Behind him, Ahmet was calling out. Mehmet turned the horse to face his cousin, who was kicking at stones. He said Ahmet could walk back, that he was sick of him, and he turned the horse down the hill again. Ayşe didn't want a poor sheepherder, Ahmet shouted, a man who was too scared to go to war. That's what she'd told him, he said. Ayşe wanted to marry a pilot or a businessman.

Mehmet kept riding down the tricky pathway. Something shot past his ear and landed in the grass tufts along the steep edge. It was a rock. Another one flew. Blossom reared and her feet slipped. She pitched forwards, leaning to the earth as if in a deep respectful bow, and Mehmet went over her shoulders and down the side of the cliff.

His hand and forearm were so damaged that the blacksmith had to cut the flesh away and cauterise the stump. Our mother covered the nubby wrist with honey and wrapped it in clean cloth, hoping it would heal well. She held him, expecting him to cry, but he didn't. He was a man of nineteen and stronger than anyone realised.

Saliha knew the truth, even though Mehmet never spoke about it. My sister tried to tell it to our mother, but she wouldn't believe it of her nephew. My father listened, sitting by the window. He drank his tea and his face was grim.

Saliha spoke to him.

'Why don't you beat my cousin? It's what his father would do. He made the horse bolt. He did this.'

'I don't believe in violence,' my father said.

'Don't you believe me?'

James said he did.

'Do you know about Alphonse? He didn't run off—that was Ahmet too.' But when my father asked what she meant, Saliha poured the tea and refused to say any more about it. All she would say was that Ahmet had done something to Alphonse and that he'd been bad since he was born. Then she said something even stranger.

'And he will be bad again. Soon.'

When Ahmet first asked for Ayşe, her parents said no. They wouldn't give her to my cousin Ahmet for several more years. I like to imagine they were trying to find someone else for her, from another village, even from Yunan, but in the end, he had the gold and Ayşe's father was a man interested in money. He didn't listen when his daughter refused. He said she had to obey her father's wishes otherwise he would beat her. Saliha and I believed Ayşe still loved our brother, and while Mehmet was recovered before Ayşe died, she couldn't marry a man with one hand. His accident had aged him, too. He was a young man made old. He avoided our cousin as best he could and grew closer still to Saliha. Our sister was still talking then.

Sometimes Ahmet would come across the three of us in a huddle in the corner or on the doorstep in the sunshine as we whispered to each other.

'You are like nanny goats,' Ahmet said. 'Are you growing breasts, Mehmet? Are you becoming a woman, something to be milked?'

Mehmet smiled at his cousin and agreed with everything he said, and Ahmet would get angry and usually went and kicked something—a chair or one of the yellow dogs.

'You're jealous,' he would shout as he walked away towards Ayşe's house to ask her mother for some tea. 'You're jealous because you've lost!'

My sister would watch him and reach for her knitting. We knew what was coming for him, but between now and that time, something else was in the way. I said she should try to stop it and she told me she couldn't stop it because meddling never worked. She said sometimes it was a simple matter of letting a thing roll out onto the surface of life, where it finds its own shape in its own time. I didn't understand her words then, but later they were clear. In the meantime we would weave motifs into the rugs, she said. That was all we could do.

The morning after the wedding, oh ha, it was terrible. I did not want to leave the house. It is a curse to know what's ahead. Even at that young age my sight was strong. I wanted to stay in my bed with the pillows across my face and ignore the dark bird thumping against the window, wiping the glass with her feathers of death.

Mehmet told us later that Ahmet had walked down the street to go to the tea garden. When the other men called out to him, teasing him for leaving his bride so soon, he said she'd run away. But after our new headman Ferhat spoke to him, Ahmet admitted she'd jumped down the well.

'Why?' Ferhat asked.

'She wasn't pure so I shouted at her.' His face went purple, Mehmet said.

At the well, they lowered one of the boys down to tie a rope around her. Mehmet wanted to do it but couldn't with one hand. A boy went in with a lantern and it kept going out. The men worried he would faint and called to him to be quick. Tie the rope, they called. Hurry back up to the sun.

I stood with the rest of them, waiting.

'There's something else here,' the boy shouted up to us. 'Caught on a ledge.'

'What's he saying? I can't hear him,' the men said to each other.

The women were howling and wailing, squatting on the ground, but I stood with my dry eyes, Saliha and I, side by side, holding hands. That was the day she stopped talking, and not even my father could persuade her to say another word.

Ayşe was brought up on the end of the rope and the young man came after, coughing and retching and carrying a piece of fabric—one of my mother's headscarves. It was wrapped around a delicate skeleton, the small monkey skull stark and white against the deep blue of the scarf.

We saw Ayşe's body and there were no more words. I put my hands on her hair, which swung wet down her back. Saliha and I kissed her cheeks. The women surrounded her and did their hollering and I looked among the crows for my bad cousin. His eyes were nervous, but his mouth was smiling. Those eyes were as black as a dead fish and they moved to mine, to my sister's, and back again. His smile got larger.

'Bring me cold water,' he said to me, and flexed his arms. 'It was thirsty work, restoring my honour.'

I went to the fountain and got him water and took it back to him. I kissed my friend for the last time. I can't remember what my words might have been and I can't remember what my sister's last words were either.

At breakfast later that morning I was unable to eat, and when I asked my mother if she needed more wood from the pile, it was because I wanted to stay busy. I do remember that, and that Saliha never spoke again.

Ayşe had been doomed. The henna and waxing party was the first hint.

'All off,' the women cried, laughing as she squirmed. 'Yes, down there as well.'

The girls who weren't married laughed too, all except me and my sister, Saliha. It was expected when it came to body hair, a clean smoothness and a path cleared of brambles. Every hair from neck to ankle must be removed with a ball made of sugar and water. At the waxing parties we drink tea and eat sweets, someone plays a small tambourine, we dance. The waxer inspects the reproductive parts of the bride to make sure all is as it should be, and that day the bride was Ayşe, pale and stubborn.

Saliha and I looked at each other even before the waxer sensed there was a problem. She tried to keep the atmosphere festive, telling comic absurdities of the strange-looking genitalia she'd sighted over the years. I've seen one who had only one lip, she said, nodding to one of the older women, who picked up her headscarf and moved to the door. One had smelled of lavender, another of wet wool, she continued. The woman slipped out of the house.

'And we all know how, when it's wet, slubbed wool reeks like Satan's breath,' the waxer said. 'Did I tell you about the time I ripped off a pleasure bud?'

The younger girls huddled, listening. I made more tea. I looked at my sister again. I had never seen Saliha so sad.

There had been so much blood on that particular day, the waxer said, but once she realised her error, she went back and searched through the rubbish, the pile of eggshells and chicken bones outside the kitchen window.

'I found a mass of hair and wax and took it and melted it in a small pot on my stove.'

Girls shrieked and clutched at each other and older women scoffed, saying it wasn't true.

'And there it was: a small bead of pink flesh. I put it on my back doorstep to dry in the winter sun while I went to find a clean cloth. I didn't know what I was going to do with it. When I got back it was gone. I looked around the garden, but there were only some small brown birds hopping on the snow.'

'Did the birds eat it, Mama?' asked a small girl who was playing in the corner with a cloth doll.

'What about you, Miss Ayşe?' one of the girls whispered, unaware of the hushed conversation going on in the corner among the older women, or that one of them had left the house on a mission. 'Do you think you'll bleed?'

We all know some girls are born with no opening-skin, they have no membrane to break. We all know this, but still, there has to be blood.

'I don't know if I will or if I won't, but it doesn't matter,' Ayşe said. 'I refuse to trick him with a piece of meat.'

'You don't know a man until you are his wife,' one of the older women said, not understanding.

'Not until you have lived together for one year and one month,' another said.

'You don't know a man until you have had your first real argument,' said a third. 'But by then it's too late if he's a bad one. He either beats you, or freezes you from his bed, telling you to sleep on the floor like a dog. You might think you love him but you don't know him.'

But Saliha and I knew this was not about love. Our friend did not want to marry Ahmet and this was her protest. I put my mouth up to Ayşe's ear and tried once more.

'I thought you still loved Mehmet,' I whispered into that doomed pink ear.

'What would I do with a husband with one hand?' She kept her face kind. 'I can't marry him, Berna.'

'But he will become rich. Good fortune is on the way, you just need to wait.'

She explained her father had insisted and she could not refuse, that Ahmet had money, he had gold, and he was buying her. Her father was a greedy man and the colour of the gold had gotten behind his eyelids. We watched as the older women begged her to take the chicken liver, but she said no. The older woman had returned and the meat was ready, wrapped in waxed paper and resting in a dish of snow, but Ayşe would not accept the liver into her body.

After the party, I stood by the window and cried. I knew that my friend Ayşe was playing a kind of gambling game, with one bullet in the gun. I wondered if she hoped for no blood, as a way of punishing her father. She knew well what Ahmet was like, we all did.

We tried to weave diamonds for protection into Ayşe's dowry pieces, the rugs she would put on the floor of her new house. When our mother didn't need us, we stopped by Ayşe's and sat a while. We would chat and gossip and she would say, 'Why do you always want to weave these particular motifs into the rug, Berna? Why all the eyes? Anyone would think you expected bad luck.' She gave me a look and it made me wonder. What was she doing? 'What about sheafs of wheat, ram horns for fertility? No, Miss Berna Efendim Hanım only wants to weave eyes. Don't knock at the universe,' she said. 'Trouble will surely come. I will be dutiful, nothing more and nothing less.'

I kept my head bent during these times as if I didn't hear her. I could feel Saliha watching me from where she sat on the other side of our mutual friend.

I couldn't say why to Ayşe. I couldn't say it. People don't want to know the truth, Saliha always told me; when you look at the beans make your lashes fuzzy, she said, then you can't see the whole of the future. I didn't weave eyes into the rug, though Ayşe let me put as many birds as I liked, so I made sure to put them all around the edges of the borders, hoping they would be enough to protect her.

The rug we'd worked so hard to make was placed on the floor of the new bedroom. My friend's sense of duty meant there needed to be something lush under her new husband's feet when he stood from the bed on that first morning as husband and wife. But instead of sweet songs in the marriage bed, Ahmet shook his finger in my sister's face at the well and screamed: 'A dead animal's liver inside of a woman? What a monstrous lie!'

I wanted to put my hands around his neck and squeeze until his soul left his body, but my twelve-year-old hands could not do that job, so I fetched water when he asked and helped my mother as usual. Saliha stopped speaking and people started to use the well again after a time. I held my tongue in place and pretended, like everyone else, that all was fine, but as I got older I gathered my herbs and practised reading the beans and I began to make my plan.

Ayşe's death made my father see Ahmet half properly, but it wasn't until long after the flying woman came that he fully confronted the truth about my cousin. For six months after the flying women left my father was different. Quiet and unhappy, as if his mind was always somewhere else. Then came a scene between my father and Ahmet and it was a terrible thing to see. Both of them shouted, even that good man I'd loved since I could remember anything about the world. I'd never heard him raise his voice before, but now he was saying openly that Ahmet was a bad man. He was saying he had killed someone called Alphonse as well as Ayşe. He swore, using words I'd never heard him use, saying that Ahmet had caused Mehmet's accident and crippled him for life. That he had lied about the old chief Haluk's death and that he was a thief too.

My mother was at the stove, unable to watch the scene. She cradled her belly with one hand as she stirred a pot of soup. Too much was breaking right now in our family and I couldn't bear any of it.

The worst moment was when Ahmet told everyone my father's secret. Ahmet said it was my *father's* family that was bad; that *his* father had died by hanging in his faraway country and it was *that* man who had been a thief and killer. That he had deserved to be strung up by the neck. He smiled as he said it, we could all see his teeth, and it was these words that made my father sit down on one of the sofas and put his hands over his face. His shoulders moved up and down and none of us could believe it. He was weeping. The only tears we had ever seen come from his eyes were those of laughter, as we climbed over him, wanting our rides on his back, on his shoulders, for him to throw us into the air and catch us or make funny faces and tickle us.

I went and stood beside him. My heart was broken because my mother was dying and it broke again now. When my father looked at me with his mouth tight around his teeth and said he was sorry, that was the moment I hated Ahmet the most. I knew how Ahmet had found out. Ferhat had learned it from Adar and he had passed it on. I hated Ferhat for it, but I couldn't hate Adar. No one could ever hate him. I knew whatever reason had made him tell, it would have been out of trying to help my father in some way. Not like Ferhat, who blamed my father for his own father's death, as Ahmet did too.

'If it wasn't your hand that did it,' Ahmet shouted at my father, 'then it was your country's. It's all the same to me.' He smiled. 'You should leave,' Ahmet told my father. 'You should leave the village now.'

My father squeezed my hand and his eyes moved to where my mother stood with her back to the room.

Ahmet went to military service and came back worse, if that was possible. Talking about how he needed a new wife. I was glad I was too young for him to even consider but already my idea was growing.

Five more years passed and still my father was unhappy, but it wasn't until my mother died that he agreed to leave the village. He wouldn't leave me, he said, I was to go with him, it's what he expected, what was right. When I told my father I was going to marry Ahmet he looked at me with such puzzlement I almost told him what I was planning. My father never understood how I could choose to do it. I'm glad he died not knowing that his daughter had been such a wicked and vengeful girl, that she had achieved her childish ambition of driving a bad man from the village and had nurtured hatred in her heart for him almost as long as she'd been alive. But I did it for him and I did it for my sister. I did it for my brother Mehmet too, but mostly, I did it for my friend Ayşe.

Chapter 21

In the tea garden, Cem sat with İbrahim and Harry. He had packed but wouldn't leave until the next day; it was getting too late now to drive down off the mountain. İbrahim was listening to Harry, nodding his head at the excited explanations of what a bushranger was. Occasionally the taxi driver would look at Cem, pursing his lips as if there was something sour in his mouth. Cem was trying not to mind that the good-natured, expansive, big-hearted taxi driver had clearly decided he was a bastard without honour, so he sat, quietly listening.

The bus he'd seen down on the plain pulled into the village square and a lanky pale man got off with a backpack.

'I'd say that would be Miriam's boyfriend.' Harry cocked a finger in the air.

'Yes, our Mr Cem too handsome for that girl,' İbrahim said. 'This man more matching. Look his skinny legs and strange head.'

Cem smiled at İbrahim, thinking the taxi driver had given him a compliment, but the driver's eyes remained cold.

The backpacker came across to the tea garden and asked if there was a hotel. He said he thought his girlfriend was there. Harry said that no, there wasn't a hotel, but yes, his friend was in the village, if his friend's name was Miriam.

İbrahim stood up, a twinkle in his eye, and introduced Cem to the backpacker with the big teeth, who quickly stepped forwards and punched Cem on the nose. There was a roar of excitement from the men in the garden. There hadn't been a fistfight in the village for thirty years. Mustafa held some of the villagers back and İbrahim grabbed Phil.

A boy was sent to bring Miriam, who stepped into the scene, took one look at Cem's bloody face and rushed into Phil's arms, talking and crying at the same time.

Cem stood blinking, hands to his nose, which was dripping blood. Someone fetched a tea towel and Cem let himself be taken to Mustafa's place, where the ice was. In the next half-hour, sitting in the headman's kitchen as he held a wet ice-filled cloth to the bridge of his nose, Cem worked out more about what type of man he wanted to be. Even though most of it consisted of ways of *not-being*, it was a start, and it made him feel happier. His nose hurt, but he was moving towards something and this pleased him.

Mustafa went to the refrigerator and opened it.

'Your grandfather was jealous of this new appliance, this famous refrigerator, this super freezer. His face was black when the old porter Long-Tooth Remzi carried it into my father's house. Someone pointed out there was no electric outlet in the kitchen and Ahmet laughed the loudest and longest of everyone who was gathered to watch the installation. "Who cares about whitegoods?" he said. He said he was leaving because the air was not good for his sleeping. He said something about dreams, Berna told Gül, who told Mehmet, who told my father, who told me.'

Mustafa bent and chose an orange from the bottom shelf. He sat in his chair, his shoulders slumped. Cem pressed the tea towel against his nose and watched him. One of the girls came in, the one with the yellow eyes. She stood at her father's side as he peeled the orange. He removed a segment of orange, made sure all the white threads were gone, and handed it to his daughter. He waved the orange at Cem, who said no thanks, he didn't want any.

Mustafa gave some more segments to his daughter and they finished the orange together while Cem sat in the kitchen with the tea towel on the bridge of his nose.

Chapter 22

Mehmet and I arrive back from the forest and there has been a commotion. We sat under the trees for a long time and were forced to leave as it started getting cool. My brother, of course, is still alive, as he will be in another month, another year.

At the tea house, the men are gathered for the five-thirty repeat of *Fathers and Sons*, but the television has not been switched on. They are roused by a fight between Cem and the girl's friend, who'd arrived by bus just now, it seems. The men calm themselves and someone turns the television on and as they wait for the show to start, they discuss the plot. Half of them bet that the fiend Ikan will get the girl and the other half believe it will be Samsun.

'Whatever happens, the two characters will battle it out in a field with yellow flowers and someone will get shot,' I say.

'Or stabbed,' someone suggests.

Sugar is tipped into tea and, as the show starts, chairs scrape across the cement floor as they are moved into better viewing positions.

Mehmet and I talk a little about the boy and the arrangement that has been made. He doesn't trust him to pay, but I know he will do the right thing. I know my grandson will make reparation to the village. My brother goes home and he will lie awake in bed all night, listening as if he might hear death coming, but it will not come yet. Just as the answers haven't come fully out of the dark for the history man. Death, truth, proof, life: it is all the same. No, the history man does not have his final proof—that is buried in the ground near the bridge—but, in the end, the question has to be: does it even matter?

Chapter 23

I

It was night and Cem stood at the window of his room. The yellow dog was there once more, a way off from the foraging howling pack, sitting hunched with its rounded back, watching him through the glass. He wasn't marrying Meral and he wasn't taking Miriam south to the beaches. He would say goodbye to them all tomorrow. Shake Phil's hand. Say farewell to Harry and promise to meet him in Melbourne. He would travel by himself and perhaps meet some backpackers in shorts and singlets. He would go to Greece, to the islands. He had a plan now. Something to do first. And then, after that, he would find something to do next.

He dreamed of dogs and amber eyes and carpets. Trees of Life and wedding combs and birds encircled by borders of yellow and cochineal with plaited end-fringes and medallions in ochre. Cornflowers along rivers and rugs underfoot or hanging on walls or scattered across green fields. Hanging from lines being beaten and turned, then washed in rivers and fried in the sun. An entire world of rugs.

II

In the morning he visited Mehmet and called him Uncle, kissed the old man's hand and pressed it to his forehead. Gül scowled at him until he kissed her hand too and then she smiled and showed him her gold tooth. She made him sit in the salon for coffee. She brought her best cups. She talked a lot and rapidly, fussing over him.

After they had their coffee, Gül flipped Cem's cup upside down on the small saucer. They waited until, finally, she turned the cup and studied it. Her eyebrows, which had been raised with anticipation, settled back to normal.

'There is nothing here,' she said.

It wasn't his fault that the coffee had nothing about him. It was a stupid superstition, but, even so, he was disappointed. He'd been sure that overnight something had started to form.

Next he went to Mustafa's house. The headman was eating oranges again.

'You have a bruise,' Mustafa said. 'Your eye.'

'You don't want me to take a girl?'

'Correct,' the headman said.

'I don't know how I misunderstood.'

'You are too full of something. I don't think you know the word in Turkish.'

'Maybe,' Cem said in English.

Mustafa peeled another orange and offered a piece to Cem, who tipped his chin back and tsked no.

'Take some,' Mustafa said. 'Eating oranges helps you think. They slow you down. Oranges make your heart wet and it's important that a heart be kept moist.'

Cem took a piece of orange. It was delicious. He told Mustafa that he'd been right, the orange was fantastic.

'You should listen to people more,' the headman said. 'Often they know something you don't. Some men think sons are important, but I love my daughters very much.' Mustafa passed Cem another piece of orange and called for his youngest girl.

'Go with him to Berna's.'

Kehri said that she would.

'Doesn't she need a chaperone?' Cem asked. He was going to try to do everything right from now on.

Mustafa lifted his chin. 'She's too young. Besides, you are family.' He stopped what he was doing with the orange and looked intently at Cem, then pulled off another segment and lifted it to his moustache.

Cem and Kehribar walked past the fountain to Berna's house.

'I like your eyes,' Cem said.

'People say they're from an animal. My grandmother says so.'

Cem frowned, but the girl skipped beside him.

'Don't worry about me,' she said. 'I'm fine.'

He looked at her as they walked. 'How is your sister?'

'Meral has love. Sometimes she has so much love inside of her she slaps her own face. She is very happy.'

They passed through the village and there was a breeze on his neck, on his cheeks where the hair was itching. He saw puppies lying next to the fountain. The car was parked over there—what a sight. He was lucky; it was a stupid thing he'd almost done.

By the time they arrived at Berna's, he was sure that there was something inside him. He could feel it beating a faint rhythm. If someone read his coffee cup, they'd see it now, maybe a minor mountain formed in the brown grounds, a tiny snaking river. No matter how small or insignificant, there had to be something inside of him now.

Berna's kettle was boiling and she made normal tea for Cem and apple tea for Kehri.

'What would you like to know?' Berna said. 'You have some questions.'

In between blowing at her hot tea, Kehribar helped Cem to understand some of Berna's words, taking some of the old vocabulary and making it simpler.

'My grandfather says he has bad dreams. I think he might be guilty about something. What did he do?'

'You don't accept it was the refrigerator then? Good. Only an idiot would believe that. The truth is easy to understand. Sometimes a person needs to start a new life.'

'Did he hurt my mother?'

'Never here. What he's done in Australia I cannot know about. You know it.'

Cem didn't, not really.

'The men want me to come back and help with the new bridge. Or send money. Or both.'

Berna sucked at her teeth. She touched Kehribar's cheek. 'Look at her.' Kehribar's cheeks went red. 'Look at the colour of her eyes. She is innocent yet in the family she was the last of seven girls and the most hated by her mother, a woman who died with her much longed for newborn son also dead between her legs.'

'Should you say this in front of her?'

'She knows,' Berna said. 'She knows better than any of us, so why hide the truth? Her mother was very disappointed that it was another girl and threw her at birth. It was lucky I was there to catch her before the cord ripped. But this girl doesn't need to pay any debt to the village because the mothers in her family are monsters. It's not her responsibility. Do you understand? Don't worry about helping other people. First you have to help yourself.'

'What did my grandfather do?'

'A girl went down the well in the old-old days and everyone knew it was because of Ahmet. They thought he was dangerous and no one wanted to give their daughter to him. My father had trouble with him and left the village.'

'What did my grandfather do to you?'

'He left me. That's all, and in the end I think it wasn't so bad. I am still here and he's not.'

III

At the cars, there was a lengthy and ritualised farewell. Cem accepted a slab of honeycomb in a plastic box, studded with tiny ants that were almost the same colour as the oozing liquid. He planned to throw it into the first bin he came across.

The square was crowded with people. Berna, and Mehmet with his gold-toothed wife. Mustafa's daughters were there, including Meral. Nearby stood Cevap, and Zeynep, the dancer with the long eyebrows, was there too.

Cem cleared his throat. 'I want to say something,' he said and everybody quietened to listen. He was sure they would have heard about his failed speech at the men's meeting. 'I'm going to come back once I have some money, to help with the bridge or anything else you need in the village. I won't send a daughter or son. I'll come back myself.' No one moved and no one spoke. Cem swallowed and was about to add that he didn't know when, and he didn't know how much money he would bring, but that he *would* be back, when someone started ululating.

It was Berna. She stepped forwards with her fingers in a line above her lip, making the loud trilling, and others started to join in. Then a drum sounded, and an oud, and people started clapping the beat. Zeynep came forwards and lifted her arms. She was dressed in something grey, and her bare feet were a smudged orange, the henna fading. She turned her back to the crowd and Cem saw some of the men's Adam's apples slide along their throats.

Zeynep's hair hung down her back and her arms were incredibly long, he realised, the tips of her fingers stained with henna. She lifted her arms to the warmth of the sun overhead with the index finger on each hand pointed straight out and the rest of the fingers and thumb forming a fan like a bird's wing, at rest in the air. She took off her headscarf and tied it around her hips. It was an ordinary scarf of nothing-much colour, but once the drum settled to its beat the scarf began its ride, and one hip rose seemingly of its own accord while the other lowered. The first traced a circle in the air, until it returned to the base point, by which time the next hip was performing the same magic on the other side. Over and over, as her hips circled, her arms were held still, the fingers splayed, hips forming figure eights, plump ladies, until the movement was fluid and without beginning or end. The oud and the drum stopped together on one strong beat and Zeynep stopped too, shifted her weight and her arms so that one stretched up above her head and the other lay low, next to her buttock, but with a kink in the elbow that was perfect. All the men shuffled to see better, including Cem.

She waited and then, at a strong beat of the drum, the hip that had been hovering in the air dropped with such clarity that the scarf looked like it was being beaten against a washing rock in the river, struck and raised, struck and raised again, over and over until all the men and women in the square were clapping and shouting *hopa!* in admiration.

Zeynep's face was transformed and Cem realised his grandfather hadn't lied. Berna had finger cymbals now and picked up the pace and she danced with Zeynep, and if the younger woman had become transformed into a beauty, the older one was a teenager, lithe and fluid, bending from the waist, her head almost touching the ground, her arms snaky and writhing, shoulders vibrating, as supple as a ballerina. Cem was pulled into the circle and he danced too. Others joined in, even Mustafa, who put his arm across Cem's shoulder for the traditional dance, and when they finished, everyone called *hopa!*, but Cem wanted to keep dancing. He wanted to tell

Harry that women didn't usually dance in public, in front of the men, that this was special. He wanted to tell Harry that he'd never danced so well in his life. He wanted to hug Harry and say that he loved him, hug Mustafa too. And his grandmother. He loved her; he loved them all.

Cem said goodbye, got in the Cadillac and checked the rear-vision mirror. He had to adjust it a little. Harry was in the taxi's passenger seat and as Cem opened his window, Harry also opened his and they said goodbye once more. Cem said they'd catch up in Melbourne. Harry patted his shirt pocket and said he'd look forward to it.

Berna came and touched his face. She smiled and gently pulled at his cheek. She shoved a rolled rug into the back and gave him a package wrapped in paper and told him it was for his grandfather. To help with his sleep.

'Love your life and love your Australian girl when she comes and if you must run, run! Give the rug to your mother or keep it for your future wife. Did you tie anything on the tree? You should wish for her now. For the girl you love.'

'No, I kept forgetting.'

'You can come and do it now, there is time. There is always more time than we think.' Berna tipped her chin at her brother and Mehmet shook his stick at her, but Cem said it wasn't important, that he didn't believe in superstition.

'Yes,' said Old Mehmet, coming forwards. 'Better not to. It can get in the way. Superstition can be wrong.' He glared at his sister.

'Well, we need something in our lives,' Berna said.

The taxi, with Mim and her backpacker boyfriend in the back, pulled out. Cem saw the yellow dog and put his hand out as he passed, but it flew at the car and he pulled his arm back in. He put his foot down on the accelerator. Behind the cars women tossed buckets of water on the road. İbrahim was leading the way—*I know the roads in Turkey better, I will go first, some bastard truck driver will be on wrong side*—and as he followed, Cem could see Miriam and Phil kissing in the back seat.

At the first stop, he threw away the honey and the package from Berna. And when the road split, the others went right while he turned left. He waved and waved at Harry until he couldn't see his face anymore.

III

Here is just the place we are for now.

ADAR ASLAN

Chapter 24

I

The summer of 1950 was extremely hot. Halide liked to drink fresh lemonade in summer, so James would walk down the street to the store with a string bag or two. He'd fill the bags and, while Ekat the shopkeeper put the cost on the tab, James stood at the front of the shop and watched for the ferries coming into the port. He walked back home up the shady street, the pastel-coloured houses on each side of the road flecked with buttery light through the plane trees. There was Füsun's with her little chair on the porch. There was the writer Bahçe and his wife, Melek; she washing the windows and he watching her while smoking an imported cigarette. Later, he would sit at his typewriter in the back room and work on some novel or other. James walked on, balancing the lemons on each side, slowly making progress up the steep hill, Halide's houseboy trotting a way behind.

Finally, here was their house. Fresh and white, the wooden slats intact now after the work done on it last summer. Even Bahçe had climbed a ladder to help, and after the working bee, they'd rested a while in the cool garden, the women sipping lemonade and the men *pastis*.

'I've got the lemons,' he called to Halide as he set them on the bench in the dark kitchen. He could hear music playing from her study, a room, like all of them, with high ceilings and rich tapestries and fine French furniture.

James found her on her couch, reading. She held up the book and he sat, inching down, his knees hadn't loosened up yet after the winter. She leaned over for a kiss.

'Thank you for the lemons, my heart. How are your legs?'

'You're welcome, my darling, and they're fine. The walking helps.'

'What's happening on the street?'

She always wanted to know what was happening on the street. It was a habit from her early years in the Istanbul suburbs, when women hung out the windows of their apartments, watching the street theatre below. Cucumber sellers, bread and sesame rolls on barrows, water transporters and occasional soldiers.

'Nothing unusual. Bahçe is taking a break, Melek's doing the windows.'

'He's smoking, of course? Watching her?'

'These people aren't ready for your women's rights.'

Halide sniffed. 'What exactly is it about progress and equality that they are not ready for?'

He touched her knee. 'Listen to this. Ekat got a new tin opener and he told me the customers all wanted to have a try at opening tins. The next thing he knew, every tin in the shop had been opened. He has them all over the benches and floor. He gave me some to give to you; I put them in the kitchen.'

'Tins of what?'

'Vine leaves and I think peppers.'

'Many?'

James nodded.

'How did you carry them?'

'I met your boy.'

'Of course, he went to the post for me—and look, we've had a letter,' Halide said, opening the envelope. 'From Linda. I haven't read it yet.' She scanned the page. 'They're coming next month.' She looked at her husband's face. 'You must be polite to him. He talks about something new from Orwell, ostensibly a fairy story but with a political truth. He wonders if allegory is the way to proceed.'

'I've been thinking about it hard and Bahçe has too. He says it has to be a novel, otherwise it's just someone telling you something, didactic. People don't listen to that, not in the same way they listen to stories.'

'But if the person telling you something is the son of a man everyone wants to know more about, and if that son is someone no one knows about, a secret son—'

James leaned over to kiss the top of her head.

'When do they arrive?'

'Middle of August.'

'Good. We'll have plenty of honey by then.'

II

When Halide and James had first arrived on Büyükada, the house had been peeling, the paint coming off the wood because of the salt in the air. The island sat in the wide blue Sea of Marmara, not far by boat from the city. James preferred the island to Istanbul. The city was too busy, with people selling things and crossing your path on the street. He had found the noise ceaseless and invasive after the calm of the mountain.

'We shall live in Büyükada then,' Halide said, seeing his face after a month in the city. 'My aunt left me a house there. It's pleasant, especially in summer when the breeze can save a person's soul. But you'll have to leave the car behind.'

As soon as he stood in front of the water, with the trees and grand white house at his back, he loved it all: the white wooden mansion with its tall windows and airy rooms, the ceilings as high as the treetops, all these things were charming—but it was the expansive garden that won his heart, and he loved to potter among the fruit trees while Halide took the ferry to Istanbul for shopping and lunches with her intellectuals.

'How were the revolutionaries?' he'd ask after she came back from a day in the city.

'They're fine. We're just little old ladies who like to wear pants and smoke French cigarillos.'

James noticed Abdul hovering by the door, peering in. It had taken her boy and James several years to get used to each other. Abdul carried in tea for Halide and bent his head when she scolded him for not making some for her husband.

'I can get my own tea,' James said.

'That's not the point. He knows better.'

After they moved, the first thing he did was start some bees. He gave honey to the neighbours and sat and smoked a cigarette with

Bahçe in the early evenings. He listened to the writer insist that the novel was the most powerful of all the art forms.

'*I'm going to rehabilitate my father's reputation*,' he wrote to Linda in America. '*Halide has persuaded me, you know how persistent she can be. She agrees with you and says my father's story deserves telling, and that the documents we have are irrefutable. Time, too, has made me see things differently. A friend here, who's a writer, suggested writing a book. His name is Bahçe, which means garden. Isn't that a delightful name?*' James sat at the window, thinking about how to continue. '*People need to know that he wasn't—how did you put it?—"a callous murderer". That there is evidence it was an endeavour for a republic. I've been in contact with a man in London who has a copy of the declaration. Imagine, in this country, the man who rebelled against the Ottomans to create a new Turkey is now the country's biggest hero but my father died for it. I know now that men can make mistakes even when they think they are avoiding them. It has taken me a long time to learn this.*'

Linda wrote back saying she was happy about all of it. And that she and George would be arriving at the usual time and to please make sure there would be those meatballs for dinner. George had been unable to talk about anything else for the past month.

III

The afternoon they were due, James took a phaeton down the hill to the ferry, telling the man to go slowly. No cars were allowed on the island and transport was by horse-drawn carts. He tried to engage the driver in a discussion about automobiles, but the man was a purist and spat through his teeth and said *otomobil* as if he couldn't even hold such a word in his mouth.

The guests were installed in one of the bedrooms at the top of the stairs. It had a good view of the water and the tops of fir trees, with a balcony where birds liked to come and sit on the railing. Before dinner, James and Halide took them down the winding tree-lined path to their private beach, where they lay on striped towels and walked carefully over the rocks.

'It's divine,' Linda called from the water.

They ate a barbecue dinner of meatballs and chops cooked by Abdul and supervised by Halide, and at nine o'clock Abdul cleared the table and they moved to Halide's salon for coffee.

'What of the book? Should we talk about that now?' George asked. He was a publisher and had a small moustache, black brilliantined hair and highly-polished shoes, which he insisted on wearing even down to the beach. George understood the nature of passion and had been happy for Linda to keep flying.

'I think it should definitely be fiction, a novel,' James said. 'Children are not the only ones who like stories, plus I couldn't bear it if people laughed.'

'Novels speak to the child in all of us,' said Halide.

'That's a lovely way of putting it,' said George. He took out a small notebook. 'May I?' he said, and Halide said he could.

'But one problem is novels aren't true,' she added. 'Write that down.'

'They can be the truest of all writing.' George turned to James, who told him that was what his friend Bahçe thought. 'Do you have anything yet?' the publisher asked.

'We're working on it.'

'You suggested there might be a parallel between Turkey's first president and your father.' George got up and went to stand at the mantelpiece. 'Something to do with a republic? Australia's not a republic, though, is it?'

'No,' said James, embarrassed, looking at Halide. It was her line, trying to make connections, always political.

'What was Atatürk's position on women's rights?' Linda was sitting, her legs crossed, smoking a cigarette and balancing a small cut-glass ashtray on her slacks. She'd rolled up the sleeves of her silk shirt and loosened her tie and the shoes she'd kicked off in the portico were solid and well-worn.

'He admired emancipation in theory, and valued women mostly for their availability. Our president reserved his true affections for trees and animals,' Halide said. 'He loved the Turkish people in general and the Turkish peasant in particular, but it was all rather theoretical.'

'How interesting,' Linda said. 'Did he ever marry?'

'He did. He inspired wild romance in women. There was a cousin, a rumoured suicide. And there was Latife. You would have liked her; she wore men's breeches. But it only lasted two years.'

'Because of the pants?'

'No, she chastised him in public too often. He was a mixed man. Hitler said Turkey was the only country he wouldn't fight and Atatürk was immensely pleased by that. "But we'd fight Germany!" he used to joke behind his hand. "In a heartbeat." He'd snap his fingers and laugh and then lecture a person for hours about the merits of Telefunken electronics.'

'You knew him?'

'My first husband did. I've never seen a man with such energy. He could be exhausting.'

'I wonder,' said James, 'if anyone suspected Hitler, when he was a child I mean.'

'What would they have done anyway?' Halide stubbed out her cigarette. 'You're thinking of Ahmet? Don't, my love. It's not helpful, his guilt doesn't belong with you—and besides, Hitler was a monster on an enormous scale, you can't compare.'

'Hitler created a legacy of guilt,' said George. 'Look at what Germany has inherited.'

'There's no such thing as a guilty nation. Children and grandchildren can't inherit national guilt,' Halide said.

'Ah, but you said "national guilt,"' James pointed out.

'Let me finish. Governments, yes, that's different.' Halide stopped speaking. 'Oh, I see what you're talking about. I still don't believe it's the case with a personal situation, like a family.'

George leaned forwards. 'What about the Armenian issue and guilt?'

'We don't talk about that,' James said, and Halide stubbed out her cigarette.

Abdul came in to refresh their drinks. James waved him away from his glass, wanting to pour his own.

'They don't like each other,' Halide said. 'Neither does his boy like mine. They're competitive. They argue about which of us'—she drew her finger between herself and James—'has the ultimate authority in the house. They can't work it out, which means they can't settle their own statuses. Abdul is much older than James's boy, so I say he is more senior, and he agrees with me, but of course James's boy says his master is the foreigner and therefore a guest. Hospitality beats age, he believes.'

'You have a boy?' Linda said to James.

'He was begging down at the port. I brought him home to Halide and she said we could look after him. I tried to tell him he wasn't a servant, that he could go to school, but he simply wants to be with us and help. I'm teaching him to bowl.'

George looked confused.

'Cricket,' Linda said.

Abdul came in again with the coffee, glowered at James, and set the tray down in front of George, who poured from the silver pot.

'Maybe Abdul wants to learn to bowl too,' George said.

'On the republic idea, have you thought about going back to Australia?' Linda said. 'Have you ever considered politics?'

'The only politics I've ever been interested in are those of the bee. Bahçe and I are writing our novel. It will be enough. And if it's not, then the intention was there.'

'You know what I think?' George was back on the sofa. 'The novel is dead, people have been saying it for years. But memoir, the truth? People are ravenous for it. You publish it under your name. The title is *My Father: Edward Kelly*, and bugger the consequences. You'd make a fortune.'

James was shaking his head. 'But the truth is ludicrous. I know it's true, but others won't believe it. It stretches credibility, don't you think? The scene where you fly into the village, Linda?' He smiled. 'People would laugh and it would degrade the story.'

Halide cleared her throat. 'It doesn't matter what people think, does it? You think your blood is tainted, but you're not him. Lots of boys have lost fathers. He was just a man, in the end. But for you to want to tell the story, isn't that enough?'

James touched his wife's hand. 'I am like him. I left my child.'

'She was seventeen,' said Halide. 'A woman intent on marrying the man of her choosing. She knows she is welcome here with us. And your father, well, there wasn't any choice in his case.'

'We think it's good to try, Jim,' said Linda. 'About your dad. Novel or not.'

'The title?' George said. He held up his small notebook.

'We already have one,' said Halide. '*The Secret Son.*'

'Marvellous,' said George, writing it down. 'That's very good. Now, who'd like some cognac? Also tomorrow can we go around the island in one of those horse and carts?'

IV

Later that night, as they held each other in bed, Halide talked about plans for a picnic and James listened. It had been necessary for him to leave the mountain, and the intersection of circumstances that drove him away had seemed particular to the time and location, but once here on the island, he had started to see the patterns of humans, common and replicated, repeated over time and across place. There were the same squabbles between neighbours, feuds and family fallings-out as back in Hayat. The local headman was as frustrated and ultimately petty as the two that James had known on the mountain. People talked big and lived small, and to him it seemed to be the way of the world. It would be the same in London, Paris, Melbourne and in Beechworth too.

By the time Meryem had died in 1938, Ahmet was grown and there was nothing more James could do. Ahmet had taken the round nugget, the one shaped like an egg. He'd taken the revolver too, and so he had stolen power from James. They'd fought and fought again, and in the end, Ahmet was the true son of the village. James had left in the lorry with Adar, Mehmet and Berna waving him off. He'd gone to Ankara and found Halide and they'd been happy, but no matter how often he had rationalised it to himself, over the years, one fact remained. He was a father who had left his child behind. He had done the very thing that his father had done. He had left his defiant daughter, a girl hellishly stubborn about doing something he couldn't understand, and he would always be sorry about that.

Chapter 25

I

At eighty-one, he wore a green turban, folded elegantly in the old style that Halide said her grandfather had affected. In the end, questions about humanity, religion, and even good and evil had ceased to exist in the place where his thoughts had calmed and become still. He'd cultivated a distant benevolence towards the living and seemed hardly conscious of anyone other than his dear Halide, the woman who had supported him with family money and love, not letting him take a ferry to Istanbul to exchange his single finger-shaped gold nugget for money in the bank.

'You keep it,' she'd said and touched his face.

It was ending and they both knew it.

The Secret Son had gone out into the world, but nothing had come of it. There'd been a small flurry of interest in London and New York, some literary types latching on to what naysayers had called 'a wild flight of fancy', but in the end the novel had been deemed just that and not worthy of further attention. The pseudonym that Bahçe and James had invented to protect his and Halide's privacy had proved effective, and George's publishing contacts meant that anyone trying to trace the author had found little helpful information about Frances Adams. The book had created barely a ripple in Australia.

James regretted leaving the things behind in Hayat, everything except for the single nugget that he'd taken with him to Ankara. There might have been a period when he could have sent for the artefacts, as he called them, but when he'd left, he'd wanted nothing to do with them or with the father who had endowed him with bad blood. His only thought had been to get to Ankara, to find the woman who wrote him letters in such impeccable English and who was the most easily-reached person he could think of seeing once Meryem was gone. In his time with Halide, as he made a life with her on the tranquil island, he began to view his father and his own past differently, the decisions he'd made and not made. Halide had told him, sternly at times, that he shouldn't blame himself for any of it but still he was glad he had buried the skull near the old bridge.

He was most often to be found in his large garden. He liked to sit in the place where the vegetables pushed through the sweet earth, where he could listen to birds and feel the breeze. In the garden he pottered with his boy from the docks, who reminded him of Adar, his dear old friend who had died after suffocating in his sleep. His neck had become more twisted as he got older and eventually the oxygen had closed off and he was gone, Berna had written.

James and his boy worked side by side, each pausing occasionally to say, 'Look at this,' holding up a vegetable or flower. Sometimes, when his eyes were bad, he sat on a wooden kitchen chair which he'd lugged down the gravel path and call out his instructions. A visitor might push through the wooden gate into the garden and stand a moment, taking in the figs, the climbing beans and cabbages. There was an ancient bony-withered donkey going round a small well, and sometimes James would pull his chair over to it to encourage the animal.

'Come along, my son,' he would say, and hold out a palm to touch the animal's dry nose as he passed on each revolution.

If he heard a visitor coming down the path, he'd step forwards in his old blue gown, bending because he was deaf but listening hard. Sometimes it was Bahçe, who had published his third novel and was now an enormous success. Bahçe liked to visit to complain about the literary elite in the city and comment on how peaceful and remote it was out here. Thank God for these moments of escape, he'd say. Thank God for this garden and this donkey and this chair. Thank God for this fig. Never had James known an atheist to mention God so often.

Other times, it was the gossipy shopkeeper Ekat who pulled up a seat next to James at the well and leaned out to pass a hand over the donkey as it turned, making jokes about donkey *döner kebaps* and how tasty they would be.

He sat in the garden and an old buzzing came into his ears. He worried that the bees were thirsty. It was a very hot August and he took especial care to make sure the water drums were filled along the side fence; that the corks or sticks were bobbing on the surface. That no slime was allowed to grow on the surface.

'On a hot day one apiary can drink—'

‘I know, my pasha, two hundred litres,’ Halide would say, looking up from her coffee, her tomatoes, her book or letter. He’d give her a curt nod and touch her cheek then shuffle back to the donkey. These days he could only walk from house to donkey and back again. There were no more trips down the hill to the store or to the ferry port. The circle of his life had drawn in close.

Halide would bring him a tray of iced lemonade, moving down the garden path, stopping at small tables placed along the way in the shade where she would put down the tray and rest a while, rotating on the grass to look at the views. She had never tired of the place. Sometimes, visitors would see cut-crystal jugs of iced lemonade left on trays in the garden, abandoned if Halide had forgotten them while turning on the spot to take in the vista, or after hearing the rattle of the old washing machine on its final spin cycle, knowing she should get the clothes out while it was such a good drying day. The shuddering sounds would call her back to the house, where she would call for her boy to come and help her hang it out or, if he was busy, the other boy.

‘Ahoy, my friend,’ the neighbour Bahçe would call out to James, walking down the path, a glass of lemonade in hand. ‘Look what I found on the way. Your wife is a marvel.’

II

Halide came to his room late one morning.

‘Put on your special green, my pasha. We’re going out.’

She held his hand as they walked to the phaeton that waited outside the front gate. When he got close, he could see that it was one of the expensive carriages, the decorations vivid and intact, the tassels fringing the roof glossy and plump. The driver and Abdul helped them in and Halide and James sat back in the rocking seat, facing forwards. As the driver clicked to the horses and the carriage pulled away, Abdul and James's boy stood at the garden gate waving, holding hands. Like their mistress, they knew he was near the end.

Halide instructed the driver to take the Long Tour. Once they got a little higher from the town, James smelled the figs and the sand, and on the breeze from Istanbul came rosewater, the spices from the Egyptian market and birds in musty cages, the fish at the docks being fried and pushed into bread. The light filtered through the trees as they jogged along, the horse making its noises, the smell of its shit coming warm and rich, until they stopped near the bottom of the Monastery Road where the donkeys called out and pulled faces.

The breeze from the sea was stronger on the other side of the island as they turned around the coast, and James closed his eyes and saw the white pathways down to the beaches. He saw Halide in her navy and white bathing suit, her strong legs and fine shoulders, that red lipstick on her mouth, always smiling and always talking, in motion, alive and wonderful. The carriage jolted and ran away down steep roads and Halide clutched at James and shrieked like she would have when she was a girl. He kissed her cheek again and again.

When they got home he kissed her once more, thanked her, and went out to the donkey to tell him about the trip around the island.

III

At night, Halide and James would sit in the back room and listen to the wireless radio and so it was they'd heard the news that the famous blonde American actress Linda and George had told them about, the 'sex bomb Marilyn' (Halide had been quite taken with the term), had died. James had gone to bed with the buzzing louder in his ears.

The last morning he'd been awake for hours. The tinnitus had gone and now in his ears was his mother's voice, talking to him about when to stick and when to leave. As he got out of bed, he had a single thought of how his time should end, with periwinkle blue, so that was the colour of the shirt he put on. Before Halide was awake, he went into the garden and pressed his hands against the tree bark and let the leaves trail through his fingers. He smelled the oily air of eucalypts and the wood smoke of camp fires. The bellbirds were singing. He sat down underneath the biggest tree and waited for the animals. Soon there were wallabies and roos, thudding in and balancing on their tails, and they stopped to wait with him. Then a wombat shuttled across the lawn and a koala climbed down from the tree and into James's lap. He'd never held a koala before, had avoided them with their piss and scratching, yet this one was as placid as a baby. He wasn't scared of death; he feared it as little as to drink a cup of tea but he had hoped to see Alphonse once more.

There was another man there too, sitting beside him. He was much younger than James and with a full, black beard and out-of-date hair. James smiled and said something in his second language.

'Get this one,' James says to the koala in Turkish. 'Guess who it is?' He laughed and his false teeth clacked together, the new porcelain ones Halide had got him from Ankara. The Turkish words were yellow on his tongue and he looked for the bull, but he couldn't see it. The other man sat at his son's side, a grin splitting his face.

James spoke to the trees and the sky, to the boxes of bees, to the tiny ants threading along the tree trunk. Finally, Alphonse came across the grass and climbed up the front of James's shirt and across to his shoulder, where he perched. He reached out a tiny monkey hand and held on to James's ear and stayed there while the brass band came and made the garden a bright glittery place. The rainbows arched and there were shelves of books and the printing press roared and then, after that, the darkness started to come. They sat and listened to Halide's voice, up the path, through the open window as she moved about in the kitchen, giving quiet instructions to Abdul with the Marmara breeze coming up the hill, scented with pine and bees in the garden doing their work. Flying out and flying back home with heavy legs and bright wings and clean hearts.

Chapter 26

I

Six years after his trip to the village, Cem had taken up jogging and was out early one morning near his office in the city when he saw a woman being punched and dragged by a man. He and another passerby went to help her and Cem was shot twice in the stomach. The hysterical woman had lost a clump of hair, which lay on the footpath next to her. She sat with Cem and held his head as he lay in the gutter. She thanked him, but all he could hear was a buzzing in his ears and all he could see was the yellow dog sitting beside him. The dog stayed until the ambulance came and took him to the hospital.

In the ambulance he thought of his family at home. Jenna, pregnant with their second child, and their girl, Venus, three years old and wanting to 'do it myself', and he tried to tell this to the man sitting next to him, about how bright his daughter's eyes were, how wide open and trusting, how she loaded up her curling hair with shiny clips, all across the crown, but he couldn't seem to make the words and realised he was gurgling wetness instead, and he heard them say he was losing a lot of blood, and then they were ignoring him and doing things with machines and instruments and pushing something down on him, and as he started to drift, scenes started playing like a movie behind his eyelids: the top deck of the ferry to Santorini, the way Jenna had rolled her eyes and turned her back when she'd seen him standing there, stunned, on the deck, Beeb and Sally running over to him, saying 'Hi!'; the six weeks of travel, the arguments about how he always left the bathroom flooded after a shower, how he never made the bed; her calling him sexist and dumb, him saying he was going to learn how to make lentil soup and use the washing machine when he got home, so how the fuck was that sexist?; him accusing her of being racist and applying stereotypes and Jenna laughing so much she had to run to the toilet saying she'd peed herself he was so fucking funny; the time in Dahab at the bottom of the Sinai when they'd smoked dope and she'd spewed and he told her he loved her and the time somewhere else, he couldn't remember where, when Jenna had been lying topless on the beach and a bunch of English guys were calling out to her and Cem had wanted to go and tell them to shut up, but she had said, 'Why would you do that? It's not your business,' and she'd marched over to the guys and stood there, towering over them, hands on hips, her nipples large and brown and accusatory, and said to them, 'What's your fucking problem?' and the guys were embarrassed and apologised, and Cem couldn't have admired her more, but it took a while for him not to be embarrassed by her too; and then after that, him arriving home after the trip and how he sat in the kitchen with his mother and held her hands and asked about her childhood, how her life had been in the village, and he asked her what she missed and she told him she'd always wanted to learn how to paint some bird pictures and maybe some flower ones too and she told him, 'There was a little blue flower that grew along the river in the village, and a bird that would come and sit on my windowsill when I was a girl. It had a smudged orange breast and a very cheeky eye. I would like to paint that bird,' she said; and then there was Harry, dear Harry, who'd written them a letter after his stroke with the return address simply marked as 'Death Bed' and he had enclosed some things that he thought Cem might find of interest, and there inside the package were a series of Kelly letters, notebooks and journals filled with all the details of the visit to Hayat, along with tiny handwritten notes about Cem, descriptions of him and what he ate and drank, down to the last detail of how many sugars he was taking in his tea and there was even a graph charting Cem's sugar consumption over the week that they knew each other and the line on the chart spiked alarmingly in the middle and Jenna said she'd assumed her husband had always had a sweet tooth.

II

They were going to Turkey, taking the children to the village. Cem had promised to go back and once he was recovered from the thing that happened in the city, once the court case was finished, he and Jenna made their plans. He couldn't imagine what the villagers would make of his wife, this wild, kinetic woman with her diaphanous kimono-style dresses, her track pants and strange hairstyles, the way she didn't care that her belly bulged over the top of her jeans; the way she sometimes went braless because she couldn't be bothered putting one on. They'd had an explosive argument over how she couldn't just sit the way she liked to—'You know,' he'd said, 'with your legs wide open even if you're in a dress.' And not in the village, that was definite. Jenna was incensed. After that, for a whole week, she'd asked, 'Is this okay? The way I brush my teeth?' 'Is this okay? The way I sit to shit? To wipe?' 'Is this okay? The way I breathe?' 'Am I walking in an acceptable, male-approved manner?'

He loved her, desperately, and his heart was squeezed with joy whenever he was with her and with their girls. It was that simple.

III

Ahmet, smoking in his room, had tried anger first, then evasion and finally weeping, but Cem was persistent. He told his grandfather he knew about Ayşe and he knew about the stolen gold.

'I only took one of them,' Ahmet said. 'How is that stealing?'

Cem said he knew that Ahmet's stepfather's father had been someone this country cared a lot about.

'Who knows what for?' said Ahmet. 'Police killer.'

'I'm taking my family to Hayat for a holiday. I know you still have the gold and I want you to give it to me.'

'I used it to come here. To bring the whole family and to buy this house.'

Ahmet smoked his cigarette. Outside the window, he looked for the cats. It was getting dark and they would come.

'You didn't. Uncle Mehmet said he gave you money to come.'

Ahmet coughed.

Cem stood up to leave.

'You can have the gold. What do I care? Stupid people. But what do you want it for? This is what I ask.' Ahmet dry spat. 'He was always a too-lucky bastard. He falls off the mountain and lives! He becomes a rich man from the lottery. He marries Gül, such a beauty.'

'I want it so the village can rebuild the bridge. They don't have the money.'

'What, the carpets not selling? No one wants them anymore? So surprising!'

'You should have warned me they would want something from me,' Cem said.

'I tried. You didn't listen.'

'You should have made me listen. You told them you would send a grandson. You should have told me the truth, about everything.'

'What even is truth?' Ahmet closed his eyes. 'What older man can make a young man listen and pay attention? We think we know everything when we are young, no one can tell us, only life can do that, and only slowly, over time.' Ahmet coughed again and waved a hand at the drawer beside his bed. He told Cem the key was on the top shelf of the wardrobe.

The gold was at the bottom, in one of the knitted knee-length village socks. It was heavy and round as if cast in a mould. Perfectly oval, like a large egg.

'Thanks, Dede,' said Cem.

'I don't want your thanks. Who can even care about it anymore?'

Cem kissed his grandfather's hand and pressed it to his forehead.

Ahmet lit another cigarette and leaned his elbow on the windowsill. If he kept watch perhaps she wouldn't come, perhaps she wouldn't bring her cats, her birds, her ghosts and memories. He would keep watching and then she wouldn't come.

In the end, the forest really is breathing. I hear it now. Seven years after the boy came from Australia and seven years after he and the university man left the village, my brother Mehmet and I go to the trees once more.

'Come, Berna,' he says, 'now is the time.'

The beans told us seven, and the bird told us seven too. In the end, these things are never wrong.

We step together into the dim and I watch as he moves slowly from trunk to trunk. He embraces them as friends, weeping and farewelling each in turn. An acorn hurtles down from a branch to land and roll against his shoe.

We look at each other. I don't tell my brother that the boy is coming back, coming right now, and will arrive this day even, with a wife and two children. I don't need to say that they are the collective heart of a family in the act of closing the circle. Yes, the son of the village is driving up the mountain, bringing funds for the bridge, to complete the expensive stone structure that stretches across the river. They will dig around and find the skull of my grandfather. There will be much discussion about whether to take it back or leave it. For some reason, I cannot see what they will decide, but whatever it is will be the right choice.

My husband who left me still writes sometimes. He thinks if he stays in touch with the village he cannot die, as if there is some eternity to be had in postcards, scratched with his pathetic letters. My next letter to him, written in Kehribar's neat script, will be to tell him that his cousin has died. I will ask him about the medicine I gave our grandson to bring to him and whether it helped his sleep. If he took it properly, it would have lifted the curse.

None of these questions are Mehmet's concern. If I tell him any of this, he will want to stay, but I know it's best that he leaves now. My grandson will be here for the burial and this thought makes me happy. He is bringing a wife and children and this makes me happy too.

Squirrels ignore us as I make a nest in a bed of fallen leaves and pull the dried piles around my brother Mehmet the Old so that they stick to his suit coat and crinkle into his neck. My brother lies in the forest and smells his final smells, the rich lime of the earth. He watches his end view and moves his eyes, gently sweeping across the vista so he misses no detail. The colour of the light, the feel of the air, all of it is important. I sit beside him and I watch. I keep my eyes open and see it all too.

The deep autumn sky is above the trees. I point out the small parts of blue to my brother and he nods and says yes, how beautiful. He lists the trees, says them aloud: Taurus fir. Cedar of Lebanon. The flowering ash. Maple. Downy oak. We are surrounded by trees so tall we have to lie on our backs to see the tops.

Our mother's voice now: *Catch a falling leaf and your dreams will come true.* Her mouth laughing and her lips kissing the necks of small children. We are there, together. An old man and his old sister together in the big Kasnak-oak forest.

My brother holds my hand and he leaves; he leaves me sitting alone with the oaks, their heathen branches fixed and still, the wind whispering around us and the light coming through to make patterns in yellow and black on the forest floor. After a time, I get up and go to tell the others. I tell them to put the kettles on because Cem is coming, winding his way up the mountain road with his new family. I tell them to come and bring my brother's body so I can wash him and wrap him and make him ready for the earth.

I tell them that all is well. That we will build our bridge and laugh our joys and that this is the way the world works. I will tell them this and then I will feel tired and will wash my hands and sit a while, and perhaps have some *dolma* and one cup of thick coffee, middle-sweet. I will listen to them talk about their silly television shows and I will have another coffee and perhaps a small piece of baklava. It's true: Bilal's sweet honeyed pastries are the best I've ever set my teeth to. Later tonight, in my bed, I will sleep the long sleep of satisfaction, with dreams of light and trees and coffee and pastry. I will sleep the long sleep of satisfaction, alone in my narrow bed, and it will be true and utterly complete, for I think I have done my job well.

Acknowledgements

Many thanks—

To my agent, Virginia Lloyd, for believing in me and my work.

To Jane Palfreyman and all at Allen & Unwin, for making it happen.

To my family and friends, for their love and encouragement, and especially to Christina Stripp, Andrea Goldsmith and Serje Jones, for their support and critical feedback.

Real people provided inspiration for some of the historical narrative and characterisations of this novel; I wish to express my debt to their existence and hope that no one objects to me honouring them in this way.